BLACK DUTCH

BLACK DUTCH

Matt and Bonnie Taylor

Walker and Company
New York

First published in the United States of America in 1991 by
Walker Publishing Company, Inc.

Published simultaneously in Canada by Thomas Allen & Son
Canada, Limited, Markham, Ontario.

Library of Congress Cataloging-in-Publication Data
Taylor, Matt.
Black Dutch / Matt and Bonnie Taylor.
p.   cm.
ISBN 0-8027-1145-6
I. Taylor, Bonnie.   II. Title.
PS3570.A946B55   1991
813'.54—dc20   90-20322
CIP

Printed in the United States of America

2   4   6   8   10   9   7   5   3   1

For
DANN
Elizabeth Heagy Taylor

Who always sees
the future in the past

THE FAITH OF OUR AGENT, TONI MENDEZ, AND THE TOUCH OF HER EDITOR, ANN MAURER, HELPED THIS MANUSCRIPT THROUGH A LONG GESTATION.

IT WAS PETER RUBIE WHO FOUND A REMARKABLE SOLUTION IN AN UNEXPECTED PLACE.

BLACK DUTCH

ONE

Sleet and driving snow stung Ben's face as he dashed, shivering in his Florida-weight flight clothes, from the weather station. All he had for warmth was an ancient army Air Corps jacket, a legacy from his long-dead father. His foot slipped on a glazed spot and the scramble to retain his balance and his dignity cost him both. He fell hard. Freezing slush bit at his hands and soaked through his thin pants.

Fascinated by this performance, the lanky young woman stood a little way off, slouching amid a pile of packs and ropes. It looked as though she and her gear had been dumped hurriedly.

Ben understood. The crew of the Lear jet was as anxious to get out of Asheville as he was, before the storm closed the airport. Under the steady stare of her amused dark eyes, Ben struggled to his feet, zipping up his leather jacket and mumbling.

"What?" she yelled against the wind.

"H'lo," he repeated gruffly. "I'm your pilot. Ben Hagen."

"Then I must be Georgia Jones—H'lo." She mimicked his deep voice and stuck out a hand for him to shake. Bundled up in a thick blue jacket, she was almost as tall as Ben, her face, tanned and animated, framed by a white hood.

They gathered up a reasonable amount of her gear, then at Ben's half-growled insistence, piled on the rest. The surging snow told him there was no time for two trips.

The woman smiled. "Not much of a talker, are you?"

He tried to think of a retort as he led her down a row of sleek corporate aircraft, but couldn't. She carried her share of the load with ease and Ben barely managed to keep ahead of her.

"How'd that antique slip in here?" she wondered aloud as they neared the last plane in line, a Douglas C-47, its rounded nose pointed high and its tail dragging.

"It belongs here more than most," Ben said over his shoulder.

"Think the old booger can still fly?" She had a gambler's arch to one eyebrow.

He dropped her gear on the icy apron beside the old plane. "It better. It's the one you're going in."

Her quick laugh annoyed him and it showed. He wrestled the cargo door against the wind and began tossing in bags. New rope was coiled on one of them.

"Don't let that line drag," she cautioned him.

Ben stepped back and looked into her dark eyes. It was like peering into a double-barreled shotgun. "You want to do it?"

"Sure," she replied and hoisted the bag lightly into a corner.

"You goin' climbing?" he asked against the gusting wind.

Interest brightened her eyes. "As soon as I can. How'd you know?"

"I was in the Army Rangers."

"Oh." The light flickered out. "Well, can you tell me anything about the face on Arnold's mountain? Will it make a good climb?"

"Don't know." He started up the boarding steps. "Never been there."

"What? Can you find it okay in this storm?" she called to him.

"I'll find the mountain, but setting us down on a grass strip in a snowstorm could be something else."

From high in the cockpit a powerful, rich voice reverberated. "And it's a skinny little slit in the mountain—pardon me, ma'am—that's just waiting to gobble us up."

"His name's Jim Garrett," Ben said. "The project's security chief."

Georgia ignored the offer of a hand up into the plane. At the top of the ladder she hesitated, then with an audible sigh levered herself in. Wondering if she was really that scared to fly with him, Ben pulled the waist hatch closed.

Garrett twisted around the bulkhead to see Georgia.

"Come on up here, missy, and I'll let you sit on my lap and play with the empennage."

Georgia leaned closer to Ben. "What's the empennage?"

"It's the tail, honey," Garrett hooted.

"Your copilot has only one string on his guitar," Georgia said loud enough for Garrett to hear.

"He's not my copilot," Ben replied. "At least not officially."

A hearty laugh sounded from the cockpit. "Hey, missy, you oughta hear that one string hum when it's stroked."

"Steady there, cowboy," Georgia called back. "You're not making a very good first impression."

An explosive "Hah!" answered her. "The hell I'm not."

"I think he sees himself as a soldier of fortune," Ben said as he lashed her gear neatly along the floor and bulkheads.

"Seems kinda strange, having a hired gun for an amusement park." Georgia's voice carried in the cavernous interior despite the gusts against the aluminum skin.

Garrett shouted back. "You'll be glad I'm there, missy, when you see what's going on."

Georgia's eyes locked on Ben's. He shrugged. "Don't ask me. I just signed on." He motioned with his head. "There's another passenger. I don't know what he does."

As they made their way up the incline to the cockpit, past a row of new all-terrain vehicles, Georgia almost missed the gray-haired man in his sixties seated midway in the baggage area. He was reading in the dim light and did not look up.

Ben patted a hinged stool behind the pilot's seat. "First class, if you want it. Or you can ride in the cargo area."

Georgia glanced back toward the tunnel of the C-47. "This'll do fine."

Absently untangling the seat belt, she focused her attention on the oblique quarter profile of the cocky copilot talking into a radio headset. He was reddish blond with the scarred, patchy complexion of a fair-skinned man who'd spent too much time in intense sunlight. And he was big. Probably six inches taller and fifty pounds heavier than the leanly muscled Ben, and twenty years older.

While Ben checked to see that his other passenger was belted in, Georgia could turn only far enough to get a glimpse of him, but she waved and he nodded.

In the pilot's seat, Ben issued a couple of orders to Garrett and adjusted the altimeter to field altitude. He threw the main switch and gauges began to dance. There was a tooth-vibrating tremble throughout the cold aluminum of the C-47 when first one and then the other of the big radial engines shuddered into rough operation. A scratchy voice squawked instructions over Ben's cheap radio, and the cargo plane, its nose high in the air, began an awkward waddle down the taxiway.

Clearance for takeoff came quickly. Wind gusts buffeted it broadside, and dry cascades of snow blew in spirals behind the propellers as the C-47 took the runway.

"Tail's up," Ben shouted, and almost at once they were airborne, plunging into the heavy head wind. Asheville, North Carolina, spread below like a city in a cup. In the fading twilight, shadows were long on the snow-swept slopes. The old Douglas creaked loudly as Ben banked to a southwesterly heading.

Farmsteads rolled under them in swollen waves of white. Now and then there was a dark splotch where a town muddied the blanket of snow. Swirling wisps of evil-looking scud filled the skies.

Ben pointed toward the mountains looming ahead, their peaks lost in clouds. "You can't see them properly now but those are more than five thousand feet." His voice had the awe of one who'd grown up in the flatlands.

"That's an anthill in Africa," Garrett bellowed.

Georgia leaned toward Ben's ear, half-covered by brown curly hair. "I'm afraid he's got you there. In Colorado these wouldn't even quality for foothills."

Ben twisted to see her. "These will seem mean enough if it's storming when we land on Arnold's mountain."

Georgia laughed. "You're a real confidence builder. Just how old is this rattletrap?"

"Don't let the noise bother you. That's the voice of experience."

"How old?" she insisted.

"Probably his age." Ben inclined his head toward Garrett, who winked as Georgia focused on his seamy jaw.

To her unspoken question he volunteered, "Call me the satisfied side of fifty."

"That sounds fine for you," Georgia said, "but I'm not so sure about this plane."

Ben's reply was unintelligible in the noisy cockpit, but Garrett's was plenty loud.

"Kick those bastards up and boost the manifold pressure. Let's get ahead of this storm before it closes in and upsets missy here."

Ben's hand protectively covered the throttles.

"Horseshit," the big man said, watching the maneuver. "Why are you babying those old Pratt and Whitneys? Use 'em up and charge Lexington Arnold for new ones."

For reply Ben put fingertip pressure on the left engine's throttle, reducing it imperceptibly to underscore who was in charge.

Garrett laughed. "Have it your way. I don't give a shit. But remember, I've seen that runway and you haven't."

"Just fly the plane, you guys," Georgia intruded. "It's bad enough being cooped up in this thing without listening to a squabble."

Both men retreated into belligerent silence. Garrett could have passed for a three-star general in the outfit he wore—a costly reproduction of a British bush jacket and khaki-colored trousers. But close inspection showed both their years of wear and careful mending. On his right hip, canted forward, was a military-style automatic pistol. On his left, giving symmetry, he wore a commando knife with a knuckle guard of serrated steel. The grip was glossy black with three oblong circles cut out of it.

"What about the runway?" Ben asked at last.

Georgia leaned forward.

"It's not a one-way field, but it's real close," Garrett said. "It'd be tricky landing there now. In a half hour you'd need to be a lot better than I think you are."

Ben checked the air-speed indicator and then read the weather notes that he'd jotted down at the Asheville airport.

"We've got a ground speed of two-twenty-five or so," he said. "We oughta be there in fourteen or fifteen minutes."

Garrett smiled, revealing a broken canine tooth that gave him a ragged look at odds with his starched and creased clothing. "No problem, then . . . if you don't mind a little wind shear."

"You seem to be enjoying this," Georgia said. "Why?"

Garrett turned to her. His eyes were a clear, cheerful green with large, dark pupils that signaled he was either a man to be trusted or a con artist. "You've put your finger right on it. I like my life dipped in salsa."

To Ben's surprise Georgia's reply was friendly. "I like a little salsa, too, but that doesn't mean I want to crash into the side of a mountain."

"Don't worry, missy. I'll help young Ben here get this bugger down."

"If I can't make a safe landing I won't make any at all."

Georgia tapped Ben on the shoulder. "If Garrett's the only one who's seen this place, maybe he should land the plane."

Ben's angry intake of air was loud enough to bring a grin to the copilot's face. He put his hand to the gun and shouted above the cabin noise, "You want me to commandeer the plane, missy?"

"My name's Georgia, not Missy or Honey." She glanced at the display of weaponry on his wide hand-tooled belt. "I thought Lexington Arnold was building an amusement park. What the hell's going on up there?"

"Bad trouble . . . We're sort of an emergency recovery crew. You. Me. Ben. Even him." A thumb aimed toward the cargo compartment.

"Trouble with whom?" Georgia asked.

"The locals would be my guess," Garrett replied. "Now that they've seen what Arnold's building they're no longer happy that he bought 'em off. Or it could be sabotage. Arnold has his enemies, and this project seems to multiply them."

Ben's brow furrowed. "Scuttlebutt says the charter outfit before me left in kind of a hurry."

"Kind of a hurry?" Garrett chuckled. "They left without their last paycheck."

[6]

Ben looked over to see if Garrett was serious. "This Arnold pays his bills, doesn't he?"

"Got full tanks, don't you?"

Ben nodded. "I checked him out and his credit's the best. Still . . ."

"Still, there's rich guys who like to fuck-over the charter pilot? Tell me about it, pal. Why do you think I've sequed into being an armed problem solver? People get a bill from me, they jump to pay it. Nobody tells Jim Garrett that the check's in the mail. They're afraid I'll handle collections the same way I handle problems."

"What kind of characters have I hooked up with?" Georgia asked. "A jolly gunslinger, a testy pilot who flies a plane that shakes like it's falling apart, and a boss who can't decide if he's building an amusement park or preparing for war."

"Or going to hold a séance," Garrett added. He had an odd look in his eye and nodded with derision at the space immediately behind Georgia.

"No séances, Miss Jones."

Georgia jumped at the mellow voice. Turning, she was startled again, although this time she tried to conceal it. The quiet passenger was standing beside her and his violet eyes were level with hers although she was seated. He was wearing silver wire-frame glasses and was less than five feet tall. From his pinched smile it was clear that her reaction was an old story. He pretended indifference.

"Mountain people are not easy for outsiders to understand. Mr. Arnold hopes I can bridge the gap."

"Dr. Hearst's a witch doctor," Garrett groused.

"A parapsychologist and professor of anthropology," the small, pale man corrected. "A specialist in the people of the Appalachians and their spirits."

Ben kept silent, his eyes glued to the snow-rimmed windshield.

"You mean . . . like ghosts?" Georgia asked.

"Shake your rattle at her, Doc," the copilot scoffed.

Dr. Hearst drew himself up as tall as he could, but still looked like an elf in a business suit. "Many find it necessary to provide synonyms for what I say. But I assure you I'm a master of English. And what I'm telling you is that the mountain's former residents believe a presence of some sort dwells there."

"A *presence?*" Georgia sounded incredulous.

"The mountain people call it a devil, but I can hardly do that, can I, Miss Jones?" he replied over Garrett's rude laugh.

"You're here because Arnold believes a devil's causing trouble at the project?"

"You haven't met Mr. Arnold, have you?" Dr. Hearst's smile was wry. "He considers such beliefs nonsense, but he's hoist on his own petard."

Ben twisted around. "Hoist on his what?"

"A medieval expression," Dr. Hearst murmured apologetically. "I should have said Mr. Arnold is the victim of his own dreams."

"How so?"

"With his money, he could have bought land for his theme park anywhere in the country. He wanted a mountain with mystery and intrigue."

"If he wanted a weird place he hit the jackpot," Garrett put in.

"That is its reputation," Dr. Hearst conceded. "It's ironic. Lexington Arnold sought a location with a history that he could exploit: someplace eerie. He found it and paid off all the mountaineers, but he couldn't run off their spirits. Some of the local people say his dream now haunts him."

"That's why he called me." Garrett winked at Georgia. "He thinks those ghosts will stop sneaking around his property when I unload a 9-mm slug in their direction."

Dr. Hearst's thin face tightened. "Shouting in an airplane is no way to conduct a discussion of the profundities of the human spirit," he said and returned to his place.

For a while there was no sound except the rolling engines and the squeaking, popping aluminum frame. Mesmerizing snow flashed toward them from a gray sky. Ben watched the omni-range needles line up and then reduced power and eased back on the yoke. The plane descended in a wide arc.

"There's the face." Georgia pointed to a sheer stone wall that rose like old teeth on the side of a gnarled, densely wooded mountain.

"Ho-leey Christ, look at that!" Ben exclaimed.

In the gray twilight a huge charred pit gaped black and dead against the encroaching snow below. A fire of demonic intensity had engulfed the leading edge of a road construction project winding up the mountain from the valley. Several pieces of road equipment were reduced to dull black melted shapes, their fuel tanks burst like bombs. The charred pit was roughly circular. Smoke still rose from it, and the smell of burned fuel and molten metal reached even into the cockpit of the old Douglas.

"That happened last week," Garrett told them. "Arnold called me the same day. I'll catch me the baggy-pants fucker that did it, too."

"Look down the mountain—there's another burned area— even bigger," Georgia said. "My God, this looks like a war zone."

"Not quite, missy," Garrett replied. "That's controlled burning. A quick way to clear land for the golf course and condos. They did that a month ago."

"Field's dead ahead," Ben announced as the altimeter unwound. "Cinch those seat belts tight."

Crosscurrents and eddies tugged at the wings and rudder, giving the C-47 the feel of a freight train running downhill on rough track. Darkness closed around them as the horizon of endless mountains rose.

"Gear down and latched, green lights on, pressure up . . . I've got a wheel," Garrett said.

Ben checked through his side window. "I've got a wheel. Hold off on the flaps . . . the wind's dicey . . ."

A fast river fell toward the valley from a notch in the snowy peaks. Georgia's gaze riveted on the thin patchy white runway chiseled into the side of the mountain. Tiny lights marched in ragged lines into the blackness.

"Landing lights on . . . ," Ben said. "She sure wants to weathercock right."

"That could change suddenly."

"You guys better be good at this."

Ben's right hand eased the throttles forward.

The cones of light from each wing magnified the surrounding twilight.

"Ought to have plenty of runway in this headwind," Garrett yelled to Ben.

"If I can find the end of it . . . Christ!"

A strong gust from the left swept the nose in a wide yaw only thirty feet above the ground. Ben fought it back to center and chopped the power. The C-47 hit with a thump. Boulders and trees flashed past on either side of the wide-winged plane. Up ahead, through the falling snow, a man with orange guide lights wig-wagged it to a sheltered spot.

After they rolled to a stop Georgia nudged Ben's shoulder. "You knew what you were doing, despite all my bellyaching."

Ben's grunted reply betrayed his lingering irritation.

"I want to catch the field manager before he runs for cover," Garrett said, and pushed by Georgia. Hurriedly he unsnapped the tie-downs in the freight compartment and shoved open the plane's door against the almost horizontal snowfall. "Hey, Hansen, give me a hand."

The bearded man stuck his head in the door and hollered a welcome up to Ben. "Mr. Arnold's hired a chopper to lift these four ATVs to the bald. Is it okay to let 'em sit in here till then?"

"Sure, but I want to be here when they're unloaded," Ben called back. He watched out his side window as Garrett and Hansen, lugging a heavy locker between them, headed toward the field office. A round-faced young woman in a bulky coat appeared out of the mists. She fell in step beside Garrett.

The sound of the gyros' decaying spin soothed Ben. It was the song of another successful flight. He reached for the log. When his preoccupation with his paperwork was complete he turned to find Georgia still perched on the jump seat, observing him.

"You're pretty thorough, aren't you?" she asked.

"I am about flying."

"Everybody should be particular about something."

Ben could only stare into those dark eyes.

"What I'm trying to say is I'm sorry I made the crack about wanting Garrett to land your airplane. I'm a stickler myself about equipment." She rose energetically to her feet. "Speaking of which . . ."

"I'll help you." Ben followed her into the cargo area. There was no sign of his elderly passenger. Evidently he'd also started off for the lodge.

At the open hatch Georgia stopped abruptly. "Where'd you and that drawl come from?"

"Florida."

"Today?"

"Yeah."

Shaking her head, she gathered up a light load. "Wait here. I'll run down to the lodge with this stuff and borrow a coat for you. Thin pants and that old flight jacket aren't enough in this weather."

"Don't bother. I've got what I need right here," Ben said, peering out. Snow was already accumulating into soft sheets on the wing. "But I'll need to secure the plane before giving you a hand."

Georgia jumped out. "Okay. I'll just make a quick trip and come back for more."

Ben pulled the door closed and rooted through one of his duffel bags. Shivering and dancing on first one foot and then the other, he slipped off his slacks, shoes, and shirt and tugged on the new thermal underwear he'd bought at the last minute. Then he redressed. A borrowed red wool jacket turned out to be a couple of sizes too big and smelled of mothballs. Griping about it under his breath, Ben gathered the gust locks from their storage slots, reopened the door, and dropped onto the glistening snow. Beyond the whitened fuselage there was a sharp gasp.

"Who is it?" Ben called in the whistling wind.

"Hush," came a soft voice.

Ben plodded through the snow toward the sound. Dr. Hearst was standing immobile, his face turned toward the dark gloomy forest that mounted the slope of the mountain. A tiny, gloveless hand was raised to command silence. Ben tried to peer into the screen of trees. Finally Dr. Hearst looked up at him appraisingly.

"I don't see a thing," Ben whispered.

"What do you feel?"

Ben struggled with the question. "Cold."

The small professor reached between the lapels of his own

custom-tailored suit jacket and placed a hand against his starched white shirt.

"My heart is pounding," he said in little more than a whisper. "I hesitated to come here, to take part in this enormous commercial venture. But I know now I did the right thing. There is something mysterious and magnificent on this mountain."

Ben, surprised and put off by his words, again scanned the woods. "What do you think's out there?"

"Can't you feel the power? More than machines and money are at work in this isolated place. An elusive force, something I have sought all my life. Doesn't it touch you?"

Uncomfortable with the question, Ben stared into the dark depths of the white-laced firs and tall pines. "Sorry," he said after a moment. "I'm only a practical guy with no imagination and not much interest in anything beyond flying. I'll have to leave the forces to you."

The intense eyes behind the round glasses filled with disappointment but the voice was friendly. "I understand. I was not prepared for my own immediate recognition of a presence here. But unlike the mountain folks, I sense it's good, not evil."

To change the subject, Ben said, "You're shivering."

Dr. Hearst did not answer, nor did he stir as his companion ran to the plane door. Ben grabbed the flight jacket but turned back, deciding if it wasn't heavy enough for him, it wouldn't do for his elderly passenger either. He tossed the jacket on the tail of the Douglas and at the hatch grabbed a packing blanket on the run. Wrapping it roughly around Dr. Hearst, Ben said, "Let's get out of this storm."

Ben picked up the discarded luggage and they slowly started downhill, walking in tracks smeared by the snow. Through the bare trees the lodge's lights came in view. Faint sounds wafted toward them in the freezing wind—the rapid percussion of a diesel engine, a whistling in the tall pines. On one side the trail fell away into a vast deep valley that tonight was a pool of indigo swirling with white diamonds.

Georgia met them halfway to the lodge. She radiated confidence. Her delight at being outdoors, even in the rising wind and snow, was evident. "I was wondering why I didn't catch up to you," she said to Dr. Hearst.

He smiled. "I was detained. You seem to be over your anxiety.'

"I'm glad to be on the ground."

"But it isn't airplanes that bother you, is it?"

"I never said it was." There was a touch of resentment in her voice.

"That's right, you didn't." Dr. Hearst took his bags from Ben. "You go back with Miss Jones. I can manage now."

They watched him trudge off, the blanket billowing like a cape behind him.

"Where's he been?" Georgia asked.

"Staring into the woods. He thinks he saw something."

"Did he? It's funny but when I walked down I kinda had the feeling someone was watching me. . . ."

Back at the plane Ben put the gust locks in place while Georgia unloaded the rest of her bags. Remembering his leather jacket, he ducked under to the tail.

It wasn't where he'd left it.

"You got my jacket?" he yelled.

"That leather one?" she called back from the other side of the wing. "Where is it? I'll grab it."

"You don't have it mixed in with your gear?"

"Nope."

Ben felt a surge of apprehension. He reentered the plane, tossed things around, then poked around in the snow under the tail. Gloomily, and with unfocused suspicion, he went to help Georgia gather her gear.

TWO

When they broke out of the dark woods a sprawling lodge of weathered gray logs loomed before them. A monstrous silhouette against the night sky, it was perched on the edge of a ridge amid gargantuan bare oaks and evergreens. Spotlights under the eaves of its angular shake roof cast surrealistic images on the snow.

"Some digs, huh?" Georgia said.

Ben glanced up. His mind had been on his missing jacket. "I suppose it's as close to roughing it as rich men like to get."

"Not anymore. Workers at this end of the project stay here now. And will, I understand, until the road's paved."

They tramped up the steps and across a wide porch. Georgia nudged open the thick double doors, and Ben followed her inside. Rustic chandeliers illuminated a great common room, dominated by rows of desks and video display terminals. Even at this late hour a half dozen computer operators were clicking away, peering intently at flickering green screens. A few rockers and loungers sat empty before a big stone fireplace filled with a dancing blaze that sent sparks in a whirlwind up the chimney. The air was aromatic with the scent of burning cedar.

Georgia drifted toward a stuffed, upright, seedy brown bear raging at an archway. The dining room beyond was packed. She motioned Ben over.

"Let's eat before we check in. Road gangs don't leave leftovers."

"You'll never get away with it," a voice with a friendly, mocking quality said behind them.

They turned, and a middle-aged man in a tweed jacket, polished wing tips, and a hand-tied bow tie of subdued tone extended a thin hand to them. "I'm Spaulding, the lodge manager."

Georgia introduced herself and Ben. "We're starved. Can't we grab a sandwich?"

"You'll both need to check in first."

Ben felt irritation steal over him. "Why?"

"I'm afraid Mr. Arnold is very insistent on form, even under siege." In a more soothing voice the lodge manager added, "Sign in at the appropriate desks—you'll see the signs—and I'll have your bags taken upstairs. Then you can have a good hot meal with Dr. Hearst."

Ben went to the transportation desk grudgingly. A pasty-faced clerk whistled through his teeth and attacked the computer keyboard each time Ben uttered a word. Grating and grinding, a printer produced a green-inked manifest.

"Here's your assignment for tomorrow," the man said without looking up. "Where's the one for tonight's load?"

Ben reminded him that he had just arrived on the mountain.

"You're supposed to have a printout. Don't fly without one again, but when you do get one, don't fool around. We're in a hurry here."

"What if the weather's bad?"

The clerk stopped whistling. "What about it?"

Ben laughed contemptuously and walked toward Georgia at another desk. "Damn computers," he growled.

She turned amused eyes on him. "Personally, I can't live without them. I'm getting one sent to my room tonight."

Ben tilted his head toward the transportation clerk. "Why don't you take his?"

Georgia briefly observed the whistling man. "Can't. I think he's attached to it."

While she finished checking in, Ben glanced down the nearest row of monitors. Most were filled with text, but on one he saw a three-dimensinal projection of the mountain itself. He watched as the intense operator, working from drawings on his desk, manipulated the image, changing the contour of the land, clearing the wooded slopes with a swoop and adding roads and formal landscaping, buildings, and even lakes.

Only a few of the workers drifting out of the dining room nodded Ben's way. Most seemed preoccupied, even worried. When Spaulding caught his eye, Ben whispered for Georgia to hurry.

At a corner table laid with fresh linen and gleaming silver they sat across from Dr. Hearst. A second table nearby was set for one. When Georgia realized the lodgekeeper was going to eat alone she called for him to join them.

At first he seemed confused, then, coming over, smiled ruefully. "With all the changes I assume it's acceptable."

A jittery, heavyset waiter served them English roast and vegetables. Dr. Hearst poked at his peas, but both Ben and Georgia went to work on their dinners with enthusiasm.

Spaulding's brown eyes glanced back and forth at them. "Not bad for a field hand's meal, is it?"

"Field hand's meal?" Georgia repeated. "I take it you're used to serving fancier stuff to fancier folks."

"Ahh . . . I must admit it's hard to see such an elegant place turned into a bunkhouse. When he was the president of Columbia University, Dwight Eisenhower had his breakfast by this window." He picked up a spoon and held it before her. "Solid silver . . . Look how flexible it is. For dinner it was washed at least three times and rubbed by hand. Those who came here in the past expected such service, and appreciated it. Those who come now don't even notice it."

"So wash the silver once and let it go," Ben said.

Spaulding's back stiffened. "Mr. Arnold bought this place with all its traditions, and that's what he'll get until I'm ordered otherwise. True, he's changed the menu and had me store away many valuable pieces, but on the service he's been silent."

"Could you be a man out of his time?" Georgia asked, a sparkle in her dark eyes.

"Perhaps," he conceded. "These days I do feel more at home with the antiques in the attic."

Dr. Hearst, who had moved on to his roast and was carving it into precise pieces, looked up with curiosity. "You don't like Mr. Arnold's plans for the mountain?"

Spaulding touched his mouth with a napkin. "It's not my place to judge what men do with their property."

"But?"

The jowly waiter, silver coffeepot in hand, returned to the table and began pouring as Spaulding answered. "Now that the mountain folk are gone there's nothing but wilderness for miles in any direction. This is a true retreat—a place of serene beauty unsurpassed by any spot on earth. Yet"—his eyes slid from one to the other, settling at last on Dr. Hearst—"on this mountain there is something strange, something that doesn't want change." He seemed to regret his words instantly, as he reached for the sugar bowl and passed it around the table.

"Please," Dr. Hearst whispered, touching the innkeeper's sleeve, "go on."

Spaulding's brows narrowed. "I've talked too much already. It's not a topic that Mr. Arnold encourages." Looking about, he leaned forward conspiratorially. "I will say this much. When the site for the lodge was cleared decades ago the local high-landers warned the builder that a wicked creature—a beast they called Black Dutch—dwelled up here."

Although Dr. Hearst's eyes brightened at the name, the waiter's hand began to shake and he nodded toward the window beyond their table. "Night fog. He'll be about in that for sure."

"Come now, Mr. O'Sullivan," Spaulding chided him delicately, "our guests are tired from a difficult day. We should say no more."

"Be blessed they don't have a difficult night," the waiter whispered with an Irishman's bitter scorn. "I tell you he's getting worse."

Spaulding tried to relieve him of the coffeepot, but the waiter didn't seem to notice. "And Daisy's out in this terrible mist . . . I don't like it."

"Your daughter's gone out again tonight?" Spaulding betrayed a touch of anxiety himself.

"All my life I've lived in fear of that demon, and now a braggart in a soldier suit lures her into night fog like it didn't matter—like he knows better than us what prowls the mountain."

"I'm sure if she's with him there's no need to be worried

about . . . anything happening." Spaulding's reassuring words lacked conviction.

"You weren't so optimistic when she was a tyke and we combed the mountainside. In a fair panic you were."

Dr. Hearst was rapt. "What happened?"

Spaulding replied quickly, as if to be sure it was his version that prevailed. "She turned up—unharmed—at the lodge door while we poked and prodded in the thicket for . . ."

"Ah, yes," the Irish waiter interrupted passionately, "naught was wrong with her body except a sprained ankle, but she was out of her head repeatin' tales of a rock candy room and a teddy bear who carried her home."

Laughter at the lodge entrance, far away at the west end of the building, drew Spaulding's attention. He nodded silently toward the doors for the waiter's benefit.

Ben turned, too, and saw Garrett entering, bundled against the cold and accompanied by the young woman who'd met him at the landing strip. When she slipped out of her coat, Ben saw she was plump and that her straight brown hair was very long, reaching below her waist.

The waiter stalked away toward the kitchen, oblivious of Spaulding's call for him to leave the coffeepot.

"He's a long-time employee and usually very efficient," the innkeeper apologized.

"I found Mr. O'Sullivan interesting in the extreme," Dr. Hearst said. "He truly seems to fear this Black Dutch. I can't help but wonder why. If he'll sometime give me a more detailed account of his daughter's experiences when she was lost I'll be most grateful."

Spaulding pressed his delicate fingers together. "I doubt if either he or Daisy can recall much more. She was only three. But I can tell you that whoever or whatever Dutch is, he's a figure of the shadows, always sliding out of sight. I guess that's where the name came from, and the fear. He's considered by many an omen of bad luck. When anything goes wrong, someone always claims to have glimpsed Black Dutch or his shadow."

Ben's face grew dark with skepticism. "Like when?"

Obviously forgetting his own admonition about talking, Spaulding settled back. "When the fog rolls in. And at night.

[19]

From the earliest years any guest who ventured outside after sunset returned in a hurry." He paused for effect. "It's hard to explain the unsettling feelings that occur in the dark. When the sun goes down this lodge becomes a fortress against the mountain itself."

Georgia's hearty laugh surprised him. "Sorry, Spaulding, but I was born in West Virginia. I know cabin tales when I hear them. The doors weren't locked tonight."

"As long as the desks are manned," he replied stiffly, "Mr. Arnold wants at least the front entrance open, but I can assure you I check it every night before I retire. It's an old habit. And now, with the renewed dangers . . ."

"What renewed dangers?" she demanded.

"Fires, and avalanches, and even acts of violence. On a rainy night a few weeks ago, before Garrett came, a subcontractor walked up to the site bulldozed for the alpine village. I was told he was worried about erosion. Anyway, the next day we found him, unconscious, at the bottom of a washout."

"What happened?" Ben and Dr. Hearst asked at the same time.

Spaulding looked baleful. "He could have slipped. It was a treacherous area. All he could remember was the sound of falling rocks and the lights on the trail going out. We do know the electric line was ripped from a relay box by brute force."

"That doesn't sound very demonic to me," Georgia said. "Is that it?"

"Well," Spaulding replied, "there was also Mr. Tartaglia's disembowelment."

Ben's fork hung poised before his mouth. Dr. Hearst lowered his.

"This better be for real," Georgia said.

"Oh, it is," the innkeeper responded. "When the electrical cord was repaired—and broken again—the men began to talk of leaving, especially the locals. So a portable generator was flown in and Tartaglia was ordered to guard the site. Things were quiet until the first foggy night. That's when Tartaglia, armed with a shotgun, glimpsed a form wrestling the two-hundred-pound generator over the embankment. It fell against a road grader, ruptured the fuel tank, and whoosh"—he motioned dramatically—"an explosion. Flying fragments ignited other pieces of equipment, and before dawn the head end of the road project was in flames."

"We'd wondered at the charred landscape when we flew in," Dr. Hearst said grimly. "What happened to Tartaglia?"

"He fired at the intruder, stumbled, and fell down the edge of a ravine toward the inferno. We in the lodge heard the shots and the explosions and rushed out to find him clutching his intestines. A jagged pine stump had caught him in the lower stomach. We didn't get him out of there a moment too soon. The fire swept up the ravine. In fact the heat was so intense several men were overcome fighting it. The pilot before you, Mr. Hagen, made his final flight taking them and Tartaglia out. He feared losing his planes, I believe."

"And just what did this 'form' with the generator look like?" Georgia asked.

Spaulding slowly let out his breath. "Tartaglia said it appeared to be part of the fog itself—'a horror with a single eye like a locomotive.' "

Georgia glanced sideways to see how the others were taking all this. Dr. Hearst sat enthralled, his small hands gripping the edge of the table. Ben was frowning. "Tartaglia was juiced," he said.

"How can I argue with you?" Spaulding gestured, palms up. "If you stay here very long you will decide for yourself if these are only tales." He turned to Dr. Hearst. "You may find out more about Black Dutch from the old-timers. They love to talk about him but I warn you they won't be specific. They turn evasive at direct questions, perhaps because no one can prove he really exists."

"Well . . . ," Dr. Hearst said. "Esoteric folklore is what Mr. Arnold wants me to research for his park. It is fascinating to me that this entity bears the name Black Dutch, a term known well in other parts of the Appalachians. It's from a European strain of immigrants who settled hundreds of years ago on land that is now part of the Smoky Mountains park."

"You mean they were Dutch?" Georgia asked.

"I assume so. However, nobody truly knows. They were an unusually secretive and mischievous clan. Other settlers were ever wary of them."

"I've found most highlanders are suspicious," Spaulding said. "It seems to go with the mountains."

"I'm sure you're right," Dr. Hearst agreed. "But considering the attitudes of the outside world toward them, perhaps those suspicions are justified."

Georgia pushed herself away from the table. "Since I'm backwoods-born I can tell you something else about hill people. There's nothing they like better than razzing outsiders. Until you've seen this notorious Black Dutch for yourselves I wouldn't put too much stock in him. Now, good night, gentlemen, I'm going to bed."

Later, the men all walked out together, passing under the bear and through the long common room to the stairs. Climbing first, Dr. Hearst slowed to listen as Ben mentioned his missing jacket to Spaulding.

"Hopefully it'll turn up," the lodgekeeper said. "But permit me to repeat that things do have a way of vanishing up here. I maintain a small fund to replace items."

"That jacket can't be replaced," Ben rumbled. "Maybe you ought to get a watchdog, if things vanish so regularly."

"The previous owner once had a ferocious Doberman trained for that very purpose. A fine animal. It caught rabbits all one summer. I tell you that dog's teeth were like a saw. Too bad it ran into trouble on a hunting trip. Some around here miss it still."

"Bear get it?"

"I can't say. Whatever it was, it killed the dog and dragged it up to the bald."

"Sounds like a bear to me," Ben insisted.

"Perhaps, but before it ate the dog, it did something quite unusual. It built a fire and roasted it. Medium rare, as I recall. Well, I'm for the kitchen. Good night."

Ben climbed the dark, carpeted stairway to the second floor after Dr. Hearst, then ambled down a long hallway with several boars' heads adorning the walls. His room was at the end. The door squeaked comfortingly.

Inside was a bed big enough for a family, a desk, chairs, and a sofa. There were windows on two sides and a fireplace in which three cedar logs crackled. On the mantel Ben spotted a cobwebby bottle of brandy with a card signed by Spaulding.

Ben checked his watch. Although he could have a drink and be legal to fly again by morning, he let the brandy pass. What he wanted was a shower to ease the aches of his fall at Asheville's airport.

But that, he soon learned, was impossible. The old-fashioned bathroom was outfitted with a freestanding tub on fat, ornamental legs. A steamy bath would have to do.

Murky firelight filtered into the dimly lit room as he stretched out in the water. Ben thought about the landing on the side of the mountain. It had been rough. A lot rougher than he'd let on to Georgia. He could have damaged the C-47. Maybe he hadn't done the right thing rushing up here in December to fly for Arnold. If the project was shaky over a couple of simple accidents it could go belly-up. And his own situation was shakier still. He could still lose his airplane, caught up here, living from payday to payday on credit cards already over the limit. And then there was his father's flight jacket.

"I wonder where it got to," he said aloud.

The wind whipped naked twigs across the snow-dusted windowpanes, leaving scratchy lines like a mad stylus and making an eerie noise. Ben glanced up and then settled back in the warm bath.

Black Dutch. He laughed. Most likely a mountaineer in baggy overalls sneaking around. Making trouble. Or whiskey.

THREE

Ben awoke at the first flash of a pink radiant dawn. From the kitchen below he heard pots clanging on cast-iron stoves. Outside his windows the morning was a dazzling sight. Ice sparkled on every twig and tree branch, and the white ground glittered under a clear blue sky purged of its burden.

Figuring he'd be one of the first to the dining room, Ben shaved and dressed in a hurry. When he stepped out in the hall he found himself not ahead but in the middle of the second floor's dash downstairs. The aroma of percolating coffee sharpened his hunger as he joined the clamoring numbers pushing toward a steam table buffet set up beyond the bear.

Georgia, wearing blue slacks and a white shirt, was already eating. She was sitting with Dr. Hearst and another man at a table by one of the large bay windows. Ben tried not to keep glancing their way as he neared the end of the line. A thickset young man with an overflowing plate was headed for the empty chair next to Georgia.

"Hey," Ben called.

The man stopped.

"There's a seat." Ben gestured to a place at another table and slid into the one by Georgia.

"Good morning," she said brightly.

The man seated on her left seemed amused as he stuck a rough paw across the table toward Ben. "I don't suppose I'm the reason you were so eager to sit here, but welcome. My name's Cal Lorthor." He had a head of thick white hair, cropped short, and deep crinkles around his eyes that looked as though they'd come from a lifetime of outdoor work.

Ben introduced himself and then, avoiding Georgia's eyes, exchanged nods with Dr. Hearst. Behind him, an expanse of glass created the illusion that the dining room was cantilevered into space over the valley. Wispy clouds raced past.

"It's a beautiful day," Georgia said. "I can't wait to get outside."

"It's not my place to tell you—the boys with the computers will do it quick enough—but you may as well stick around this morning," Cal informed her. "You and Ben are first up for the indoctrination talk—from the Man himself."

Ben shook his head. "Not me. I'm a charter pilot, not an employee."

Humor pulled at Cal's mouth. "Lex Arnold hired you, didn't he?"

"He contracted my plane."

"Whatever—but I suggest you check with the desk before you go flying."

"Will you and I be working together?" Georgia asked Cal.

"You bet! And I'm looking forward to it. Building one of those things will be a first for me."

Ben stopped peppering his eggs and the volcano of grits. "What thing, Georgia?"

Cal's brows arched in surprise. "You haven't told him?"

"Why should I? He'd only laugh."

Ben was puzzled and didn't like the smile on the big man's face. "Why should I laugh?"

"She's a closed-track, steep-grade, gravity-driven light rail transit specialist," Cal said.

Ben looked to Georgia for a translation.

"I design roller coasters."

"Roller coasters?"

"I'd rather you go ahead and laugh than look so stunned," Georgia said. "You think they just throw those things up by chance—like tinkertoys?"

"Georgia Jones is an honors graduate of the Colorado School of Mines," Cal interjected. "She could design a streamliner track to the top of Everest."

"Well, I, ah . . ." Ben cleared his throat. "That's really something."

Even Dr. Hearst laughed.

"We're all engineers of one sort or another up here," Cal said, "except our doctor of the occult here, and you."

"And Garrett," Georgia added.

"Ah, yes," Cal agreed, "Garrett too. Right now he may be valued more by Lex than the rest of us put together. These work stoppages are costing him thousands of dollars a day."

"I wonder if the problems here stem from his taking away the mountaineers' heritage as well as their land," Dr. Hearst speculated.

Cal's eyes hardened instantly. "That's a bad choice of words, friend. Lex didn't take anything. He paid top dollar for every inch of this mountain."

"I know he paid for the land, Mr. Lorthor," Dr. Hearst replied in his usual mellow voice. "That doesn't mean the people who lived here for generations no longer matter. There was talk in the breakfast line about an old lady bundled off the mountain. That a son sold the family farm out from under her. Is that true?"

Cal's scowl deepened. "What's true is that Mrs. Grandy's senile and doesn't know what's in her own best interest. All Lex did was move her from a cold shack down to a first-class nursing home in the county seat."

"But she didn't want to go."

"You expect Arnold to wait for her to die? I told you she's senile. If I get that way I hope my Lilly locks me up and throws away the key."

"That's where you differ from the people of Appalachia. They revere their old." Dr. Hearst raised his hand to keep Cal from protesting. "Give me a chance to make my point. There is constant trouble on the mountain, is there not? You spoke of work stoppages."

"Too goddamn many of 'em," Cal rumbled, banging his fine china cup into its saucer.

"Then permit me to suggest that Mr. Arnold's project would be better accepted if he made it a reflection of these proud people rather than excluding them."

Cal threw back his head and laughed. "That's absurd. The mountaineers were eager enough to sell their land and slide down to the valley. They weren't worrying then about *heritage* or a confused old woman."

"How can you be so sure?" Dr. Hearst asked evenly.

"Simple. A good many of them are back up here asking for jobs, although God knows there's not a lot they can do besides common labor. And they want to do that at their own pace, and whenever they please. Arnold's not going to put up with much more."

Georgia, who'd followed all this very closely as she ate, leveled worried eyes on Cal. "My office in Denver is antsy that Mr. Arnold also doesn't like our roller coaster design, even though the thing's already so tall they'll have to pipe in oxygen for the riders."

"If Lex has so much as looked wistful over those plans, Denver might as well X-take 'em," Cal said, "and start over."

"That's what I'm afraid of," Georgia groaned. "Something tells me that if I'm on call to see Arnold today, I'd better take a closer look at that design."

"And I," Dr. Hearst said, rising with her, "have much reading to do."

Ben watched them cross the room. Georgia, leading the way, held herself tall and walked with a swinging stride—as though she were more interested in getting somewhere than how she looked doing it.

"So now you're stuck eating with me," Cal joked.

Ben glanced down at his barely touched breakfast. "I ought to check at the desk about this business with Arnold." He started to get up, but Cal motioned him back.

"You've got time to eat. Enjoy it. Anyway, it's part of the program that you and I chat a while. Lex's gonna ask me about you. What should I tell him?"

Ben scraped jam onto a piece of toast and chased it with coffee. "You tell me," he said at last.

Cal took a moment, studying the long line of Ben's jaw. "For starters I'll tell him you have a quick eye for the female form. Then I'll tell him you're not much of a talker. And you don't like barbers. What else?"

Ben raised his blue eyes. "Tell him I fly when I say it's okay, not when the computer does. Tell him I'm going to pick up a small plane locally to make kitchen runs and that it'll take eight hundred dollars a day to keep me and two planes on this mountain."

[28]

"That it?"

"Well, I don't know what 'X-take' means . . . and that story about the old lady gripes my ass."

Cal stabbed at the air with his fork. "Take my word for it. Mrs. Grandy's better off than she's been in her whole life. She's got electricity, and porcelain plumbing, and lives in a controlled environment, warm in winter, cool in summer."

"Does the bus take her to a mall once a week?"

"Sarcasm! By God, Ben, I didn't think you had it in you." Cal smiled broadly, showing even white teeth. "X-take's a computer term. It means killing out whatever you're working on."

"I don't like computers."

"I'll also let Lex know there's no bullshit about you when you do decide to talk. It'll take some doing, but he might even end up liking you."

Ben grunted a reply and finished eating as quickly as possible.

Back in his room, he stared a long time out the window at the endless stretches of rolling mountains. In his hip pocket was a proposal for a passenger air taxi to the project from the Asheville airport. It could make a big difference to him, even if it meant going further in debt for a couple of commuter planes. But if Ben had to bet, he'd bet he'd blown it with Cal. He reached for the crumpled envelope and, rechecking his figures, took a razor-thin slice off one. Eliminated another. When the time came to go to Arnold's office, Ben refolded the paper into the envelope and took it with him.

Georgia was in the great room talking to a female computer operator who also turned out to be the doorkeeper to Arnold's sanctuary. Cracking his door, she timidly announced them, and stood aside for Ben and Georgia to enter. A man of ordinary height, a little overweight, greeted them enthusiastically. He was wearing a sky blue pullover sweater, faded jeans, and thick-soled work boots. His soft brown eyes and bushy brows, under a high forehead and thinning gray hair combed straight back, gave him an almost cherubic look, like an old-fashioned shoemaker. But Ben instantly picked up on the pinpoints of diamond-hard light deep in those eyes.

For his office Arnold had claimed the lodge's gun room,

paneled in the dark, redolent wood of an old English estate. The somber space was cluttered with stuffed game animals, some standing on the floor like sturdy rocking horses, a stag's head over the fireplace. A large library table, sitting square in the middle, served as his desk.

"You each have a talent that recommends you for this project," Arnold began. There was a practiced quality to his voice. "Mr. Hagen, your record in the Army Rangers suggests courage, something your predecessor lacked. And your reputation as a pilot is excellent . . ."

His gaze went to a sheaf of papers on his desk.

". . . if not your reputation as a businessman."

He waited, but Ben, clutching the envelope, said nothing.

"Miss Jones . . . you are here because the owner of your firm and his tired sages of the past—the mining railroaders and the cogwheelers—can't come up with something juicier than that." He gestured to a graphic display on a computer terminal beside his desk. "I'm close to calling in another outfit, and if I do—"

Georgia sat stiffly, taking it without a flinch.

"—I'll also rethink who gets the passenger-moving systems from the parking lots to the various levels of the mountain." Arnold ticked them off on his fingers. "That's the steam train, monorail, chiar lifts, the funicular, and the sit-down escalator."

"I'm sure my boss wants to see you satisfied with the roller coaster, Mr. Arnold."

"Of course! That's what's wrong with the old son of a bitch," Arnold bellowed. "He wants me satisified and I want to be tickled shitless."

Georgia laughed, lightly at first and them with enjoyment.

Arnold, arms crossed, sat back on the corner of his desk. "Good for you. Maybe I've found someone from that firm whose body temperature is still in double digits."

"It's not that bad, Mr. Arnold."

"Maybe, but your boss knows I'm not happy. That's why you're here, to resolve the differences between my expectations and your firm's presentation."

Georgia's brow furrowed. "Mr. Arnold, I never—"

"—worked on anything bigger than an eighty-foot

coaster?" He smiled. "I didn't ask Avery to send his most experienced. I wanted an engineer with the touch of an artist, someone who could grow with the project. He picked you."

Arnold took two leather portfolios from his desk and handed one to each of them. Ben peeked inside at the pastel renderings on linen paper and the sheaf of slick brochures. Hastily he returned his own crumpled envelope to his pocket and glanced up as Arnold clicked a remote control. A white square of light, turning to the spectrum at the edges, flashed on the wall and then filled a screen descending silently from the ceiling.

A map of the eastern United States appeared with a red circle in the mountains of North Carolina. Arnold approached the screen as the picture changed.

"We own this entire mountain, base to summit," he began, walking in front of the image. Patterns of green foliage rolled across his face and clothes. "Most of it was in a hunting preserve that came with this lodge. The rest, owned by a few dozen homesteaders, was rather easy to acquire." He shook his head. "That's why I can't understand all the trouble up here since we started construction. In all my life I've never seen such brooding, superstitious people. Now it's looking like some of them are vicious criminals. But that's Garrett's problem, not yours."

He clicked to an autumn view. "Most Americans can drive here in less than a day. For three seasons the weather's perfect. And there are marvelous plans for winter. In two years, if we meet our goals, this mountain will be a wonderland."

"A theme park like Disney's?" Georgia asked.

Arnold tapped a finger on the great mountain. "Look at this, Miss Jones! The vastness of the landscape overpowers that term. If you must call it anything, call it a recreational utopia."

The next slide was an aerial shot of a foamy river slapping the walls of a gorge.

"This is a remote section upstream that's perfect for rafting, but it's presently inaccessible. We will fix that."

Another click.

"These are the existing gemstone mines—buckets of earth and a sluiceway. We'll punch a hole in the mountain. Give people a ride deep inside. This project's more in keeping with your own training, Miss Jones, but I was told why you didn't want to work on it. I understand."

Another click.

"Ah. Here we are. The face. What a dramatic opportunity for staging. Imagine an elevator the size of a gym climbing that height. It's marvelous."

Georgia leaned forward and Arnold gave her a long time to study it before he went through the rest of the slides. When he flicked the lights back on, he began pacing and his voice took on a more melancholy tone.

"I don't tell everyone this. But you, Miss Jones, must understand my thinking if the roller coaster design's ever to be right." As he moved about the room he glanced down at his feet and back up at the ceiling like a dedicated method actor getting into his part.

"I grew up poor," he began. "The Christmas I was seven— the year my father died—my mother was determined to bring some cheer into our home even though she was only working in a dime store."

He hesitated at the mantel but seemed to be looking at nothing. "We went to the woods outside town several times and finally found what she said was to be the key to our Christmas treasure—a spiked, dead thornbush. Taking that brittle, leafless thing on the bus earned us a lot of stares and a rude remark from a man whose arm I accidentally scratched, but we got it home in one piece. The next day my mother planted it in a stoneware crock." Arnold glanced down at his hands. "Painting it I pricked my fingers until I cried, but when it was finished that bush was gorgeous. Silver. I can still see it."

His head came up, as if he'd just remembered they were in the room.

"What magic my mother created with a thornbush, a dime bottle of silver paint, and a nickel bag of gumdrops. One went on every thorn. Mint green, cherry, orange, licorice, lemon, and pure white. What was that white? Cinnamon?" His gaze strayed to the stag's head.

" 'You're always going to remember this tree,' she told me, 'and do you know why?'

"I said, 'No, Mama.' "

Squirming in his chair, Ben checked Georgia out of the corner of his eye. She was totally absorbed in the story.

" 'Because it shows we can create wonders out of trifles, if we but try. This tree's for you to dream on.'

"Every Christmas until the year I left for the Marines, we made one . . . She died while I was on Iwo Jima." He hurried on as if the rest of it barely mattered. "After the war I got into construction, took a few risks, and by forty was a millionaire. Over the years I piled up money. Even when the government ordered that divestment two years ago I came out ahead, to the gall of the tax people. And suddenly I realized that was about my only pleasure in life—making an IRS lawyer angry."

Arnold pivoted back to the screen and clicked a new slide into place. It was a springtime shot of the broad tabletop of the mountain stretching out beneath a triangular peak.

"My little story represents your field of challenge, Miss Jones, one that your employer's top designers couldn't adjust to. Having anything higher than a roller coaster upset their sense of proportion and stifled their enthusiasm. The idea of a thing being both spectacular and secondary baffled them. So you've been sent with the hope that an artistic mind can grasp what is to them so alien."

Georgia nodded uncertainly.

"On the very top of this mountain I'm putting something of my own. A great—I mean huge—tree with soft sparkling lights. My mother's little dream is going to be turned into a monument."

Before Georgia could react, he turned to his terminal, punched a few keys, muttered "No, wait," punched a few more, and a new graphic representation appeared on his screen with lines of data under it.

"I'm considering molded lucite over a stainless steel framework, but there's a problem with cantilevered stress on the limbs." He sat rapt at his terminal for a moment or two. Then, with a couple of practiced strokes, he turned the screen blank.

"You tackle the roller coaster," he said to Georgia, who'd been watching in fascination. "I'll take care of the tree."

FOUR

Spaulding was waiting for them when they emerged from Arnold's regal sanctum an hour later. Ben's face showed the numbness that overcame him when Arnold and Georgia began interminable discussions about beams and stress and spans. But there was a light in Georgia's eyes and it was to this that Spaulding responded.

"Eager to start work?"

"I sure am. But first I need to get a look at the mountain." She turned to Ben. "Want to come?"

"Now?"

"Why not? The snow didn't amount to much and I'm only going as far as the bald."

Ben's thick, dark brows raised. "The bald?"

"That's what we country folks call a tableland. It's at the base of the face. We can make it in two or three hours."

"I'll go," Ben said, "if I don't have to fly."

After checking with the transportation desk, he gave a thumb's-up sign. Spaulding promised to pack them a cold lunch and hurried away.

Within ten minutes Ben and Georgia were bundled up, provisioned, and outdoors. Frozen leaves and snow crunched under their boots as they strode up the misty trail. At the airstrip, Ben paused to check the C-47 and then hurried to catch Georgia, mounting the steep northern woods at a point where there was a faint suggestion of a break in the underbrush. As she ducked under the drooping branches of a snowy pine several small birds flitted away. Over her shoulder Georgia flashed Ben a smile.

"This is more like it, right? You looked sort of battened down in Arnold's office. Don't like dark-paneled rooms filled with stuffed animals, do you?"

Ben shrugged and stuck his hands deeper in his pockets.

Mocking him, Georgia jammed closed fists into her own pockets and hunched her shoulders. Frowning, Ben followed. From far ahead came the faint sound of falling water. They climbed diagonally toward it, skirting a stand of rhododendron so thick the hard ground under the dark foliage was bare of snow. At last the ridge's rocky backbone came in sight. Stepping out of the woods behind Georgia, Ben realized why the air had become a damp weight upon him. At the bottom of a steep incline, misty sprays shot skyward from a narrow stream, tumbling between dark lichen-covered boulders.

"Awful gloomy spot for an amusement park," Ben said as they worked their way along the water's edge, deep in shade.

Georgia glanced back at him. "If the tourists don't like gloom they can wait. The weather changes all day. Besides, if you'd listened to Arnold you'd know parts of the park are supposed to be gloomy."

"I heard."

"But you didn't like it. Right?"

"It's his mountain."

"Ha! You didn't even like his story of the tree."

Ben started across the rocks after her. "Sometimes a man can tell too much about himself."

Georgia let his words lie between them. When she spoke there was no teasing, no challenge. "If you weren't such a harsh judge, Ben Hagen, it'd be a lot easier to like you."

"Bull. I'm no judge."

"Bull yourself! You just admitted you judged Arnold."

"I didn't like his story. I wasn't judging him."

"Oh, Ben, you judge everybody. You may do it quietly, with your mouth shut. But guess what? Your verdict's right there—on your face."

Ben tried to stare at her blankly, but his angular jaw tightened in anger. "I haven't judged you, have I?"

She peered at him speculatively. "You're trying. Only you're a far tougher judge of men than women—men don't have what you want."

With a wink she started up the mountain again, following the creek for a while before crossing it. Ben, red-faced, worked on a rejoinder, but the fit of her jeans a few steps ahead distracted him.

It wasn't as though he were staring, he said to himself. Where was he supposed to look? She trekked on at a steady pace, and his eyes kept straying to where she'd worn her denim seat to near white.

After pushing on for a half mile, they broke out of the mist near a terraced overlook. Behind a log shelter a ledge formed a vertical barrier to the top stretches of the mountain for all but the most agile hikers.

Without hesitation Georgia began to scale it. Pebbles spilled down as Ben climbed after her. Atop the ledge, cedars clutched the steep hillside with snarled roots. Georgia weaved a path through them, mostly moving west, straight up the mountain. When they broke out of the woods it was only a short, hard haul to the edge of the bald.

Georgia arched her back and peered over a stark field, possessed of a silence broken intermittently by ghostly whistling winds. Naked rocks in the snowy turf gave it the appearance of a boneyard. Only a few myrtle bushes struggled to survive amid the ice pools trapped in stone. Ben noted without comment that Georgia's gaze didn't linger on the bald but went quickly to the far side where the great rock face jutted toward the sky.

Seamed and gnarled in places, it was essentially sheer, like a curtain in a theater—but one so vast that only an epic tragedy could play behind it. Imitating Georgia, Ben craned his neck, searching for a break in the severity of the wall. He found none.

"Who'd have thought there was any such climb in this part of the country?" Georgia marveled.

"How long would it take, do you think?" Ben asked.

She studied it. "Most of a morning. Less with somebody strong on belay. 'Course, the Rangers would drive bolts and climb it in an hour."

Ben eyed her sideways but said nothing.

They started across the tableland. Halfway Georgia stopped and unslung her knapsack.

"I'm hungry," she said. Kneeling, she began to pull out

their lunch. "I don't believe it! Spaulding packed a linen table-cloth and napkins. What's this? Wafers and caviar. And a tin of French candies. What's in your pack?"

Ben dropped down beside her. "Martenelli's apple juice . . . and roast beef sandwiches."

Tendrils of vapor drifted across the face as they ate. After finishing her sandwich, Georgia began working on the caviar and crackers. Ben watched her until she looked up with those dark eyes and stared back. He self-consciously turned his attention to the face.

"How will tourists get up that thing?" he asked.

"Ummm . . ." Georgia swallowed a cracker. "That'll be no problem. Arnold will put the mine there"—she pointed toward the east—"the railroad tunnel will go nearby, and right about there, in the middle, he'll build a sky lift—a pair of counterbal-ancing elevators as long as a subway train."

Ben followed the line of her extended arm up the brooding cliff. For a brief moment his mouth drooped in an arc of sorrow before the mask of indifference returned.

Georgia kept on talking, but she had seen his look, and understood.

"Once the road is cut from the interstate and a better access is opened to the lodge, this will be the next target. It will be like Crusaders attacking a citadel. Cal will raise at least one hoist for construction up here as soon as possible."

Ben nodded and turned his attention toward the horizon, where billowing clouds and mist obscured the valley below. A melancholy wind wailed across the bald.

"Bother you?" Georgia asked.

"Why should it?" he muttered. "I don't live here."

Her laugh was instantaneous, and by the look in Ben's eyes, insulting.

"I'm a pilot," he proclaimed with fervor. "All I care about is keeping the C-47 in the air."

"Could you be as hard as you sound?" She gave him a pinch on the waist.

"Hey!" he protested.

She laughed again. "That's what I thought—soft as a baby's belly. You can't fool me. I've seen others try your trick."

"I don't play tricks."

"Only on yourself. What you're doing is dealing with change by pretending you don't give a damn."

"Why did Arnold say you wouldn't be working on the mine?" Ben parried.

Georgia stiffened, then slowly shook her head. "Forget it, Ben. I'm not going to let you get away with that. We're talking about you right now. So tell me what was in that scuzzy envelope."

"What envelope?"

"You know. The one you were fumbling with in Arnold's office."

"That was nothin'."

"Nothin'," she mimicked in a deep voice. "I'm not gonna tell you nothin'."

He glared at her. "You think you've got me pinned to a butterfly board, don't you?"

"Not me. You've pinned yourself. But I could help you get free . . . maybe."

A shy smile started at one corner of Ben's mouth. "I'm ready."

Georgia smiled back, then folded the tablecloth and stuck it in her backpack. "Let's have a closer look at that face."

They ranged all the way to the tableland's northern terminus. The face continued beyond, bending backward into a laurel-covered ridge. Georgia had eyes only for the ridge, but Ben's attention wandered lower to the gentle slope at its base. Bare, the hillside was rippled like a corduroy road. Leaving Georgia, Ben hiked down onto it and knelt. Clots of snow-crusted soil crumbled through his fingers.

"It's an old tilled field," he called.

Joining him, Georgia toed a rotting stalk. "Corn, at least a year old."

Ben straightened and scanned the area. "There's an overgrown path on the far side." His voice rose with curiosity. "Maybe it leads to a homestead."

"Let's save it," she responded quickly. "I need to check out the rest of the face today."

By the time they doubled back to their starting point an hour had passed. As they walked on, following the wall, Ben stopped twice to show Georgia where great circles of grass had been blown flat by a helicopter. Georgia nodded absently, her attention still focused on the great gloomy curtain.

A background sound of cascading water changed to a mind-riveting roar at the southern edge of the bald. Georgia offered no protest when Ben pushed on to the river slicing through a shoulder of the mountain. Upstream fifty yards, amid tangled groves, torrents churned through gnawed rock in a mad, wild descent. The deafening sound caused Ben's pulse to pound as he and Georgia picked their way along the slippery rocks. In seconds their hair and clothes glistened with freezing droplets.

"This must be a section of the rapids in Arnold's aerial shot," Georgia yelled above the roar. "It looks like an easy place to drown."

Ben pointed toward an outcropping on the other side, half hidden by drooping branches. "Look there."

Georgia strained to see the series of reddish colorations near the waterline. "God, you've got good eyes. Those markings look like part of the rock to me. What are they?"

Ben leaned forward on his knees. "Maybe hand prints. Or primitive drawings of animals. They look Indian."

"Guess we ought to tell Arnold about them—just in case they're for real."

"And Dr. Hearst."

They retraced their way to the bald.

"I'm glad we got up here before the ATVs," Georgia said, still shouting, then, with a laugh, lowering her voice. "Once those fat tires start digging in the meadow it'll be changed forever. But I forgot, you don't care about that."

The blue-tinged mist thickened into fog as they started down the main trail. Georgia plunged into it. Ben tried to keep her in sight but couldn't, stumbling on roots and rocks that the athletic woman ahead of him seemed to skirt by instinct. When she finally realized he was no longer close, Georgia turned back and found him muttering darkly as he worked to free the thick wool jacket from a bare blackberry vine.

"Did it attack you?" she teased and began to untangle him.

"This damn coat's big enough for a horse," he complained. "I need to find my—"

They both froze, listening. A singsong howling rode toward them on the wind. They looked at each other. It came again. Ben tugged himself free, and they moved through the trees toward the caterwauling below.

"Sounds like a tomcat wailing," Ben said.

"To have lungs like that a cat would have to weigh three hundred pounds," Georgia replied. "It's singing . . . I think."

Finally they could make out the deep-throated words.

"Waltzing Matilda, waltzing Matil-l-lda . . ."

A subdued giggling reverberated in accompaniment.

"In the shelter," Ben said.

"Maybe it's O'Sullivan's devil . . . Hal-lo," Georgia called loudly. "We're coming down."

The song still drifted up.

". . . and waited till his billy boiled . . ."

"Hal-lo there . . ."

"Oh, come on down." It was the sarcastic voice of Jim Garrett. "You really think you're capable of sneaking up on me, the great swagman?"

Again there was an undercurrent of giggling.

Georgia scrambled down the small cliff above the shelter, dropping the last ten feet. Ben was right behind her.

Garrett's arm was around the waist of the waiter's wandering daughter. Up close Ben could see she had a wide, guileless face with deep blue eyes. Her silky long hair stirred in the wind.

"Hi," Georgia said to her. "I met your father last night. I'm Georgia Jones. This is Ben."

"I'm Daisy," the answer came with a giggle. "We're on guard duty."

"Guard duty!" Georgia eyed Garrett. "Just what or who are you trying to scare off with your singing?"

"Oh, that's for show. Just like these are." He patted his holsters.

"I don't think Arnold hired you for show."

"That's where you're wrong, missy. Show 'em power. That's his style. Arnold figures if these yokels see my arsenal and I knock a few heads, trouble will stop in a hurry."

"Not too many heads up here to knock, except mine and Ben's," Georgia said.

Garrett grinned. "Gotta start rounds somewhere. I'll hike down to the construction sites later."

"Not singing that song, I hope." Georgia turned to Daisy. "Weather's closing in. You want to go back with us?"

"It *is* a long way to the camps," Daisy said slowly.

Garrett slipped one hand under her and swept the laughing woman up in his arms. "I carried you halfway up this mountain, I guess I can carry you down."

"It's gonna get cold, and foggy," Georgia warned.

"Well-l-l . . . ," Daisy started.

"Do as you like," Garrett told her. "I may be out another two hours."

Daisy's arm stole inside his fleecy jacket. "I'll rest a while longer and come down with Jim. The cold doesn't bother me."

Garrett gave one of his explosive, one-syllable laughs.

Georgia and Ben slipped on down the trail. After a minute or two Garrett resumed his strange love song.

"*. . . camped beside a billabong . . .*"

FIVE

As they dashed downward through the misty woodlands, the fog lost its wispiness and began to gel until it was white as cream sauce and almost as thick. It stole through the underbrush, blocking out the ground only a few feet ahead. Once more Ben fell behind, moving as hesitantly down the rugged slope as a soldier in a mine field.

Georgia was waiting for him at the trail near the airstrip. "Do you sense anything, Ben?" she asked, setting her pace to his.

"Like what?"

"Like someone watching you?"

"In this stuff? How could they?"

She laughed uneasily. "You're right. This fog just gives me the creeps, I guess."

"Or Spaulding's tales are getting to you."

The lodge appeared suddenly like a liner in a storm, its yellow lights coalesced into an occluded glow. Inside, the great room was packed with idle workers. Many stood before the huge windows. But there was nothing to see but drifting white seas.

"Coffee?" Ben tried on Georgia.

"Un-unh," she said. "I'm gonna hit the terminal. In my room."

"How about dinner tonight?"

She smiled ruefully. "You may as well know, Ben. I'll be on this roller coaster design until I come up with one that works."

"You mean through *dinner?*"

"I mean through Christmas, if necessary."

Ben's last view of her was a pair of jeans hurrying up the stairs. After checking in, he headed for the airstrip. At the C-47 he popped the cargo door and climbed inside. The ATVs were still tied in place. As he started up the incline toward the cockpit he almost stumbled over a pair of combat boots, attached to legs that stretched out of the darkness.

Ben stooped to peer at the prone intruder. At first, in the weak light, he couldn't tell if the long-faced man was alive or dead. There was not a flicker of an eyelash. Rubber bands held scraggly hair behind two big ears. Ben nudged a rib with the toe of his shoe. No movement. He nudged harder. There was a moan and then one eye opened.

"Who are you?" a sleep-filled voice rasped.

"That's what I'm asking you, buddy. Why are you snoozing in my plane?"

"It's warmer than the ground."

When the man sat up Ben saw beside him an empty bottle of the Rolling Rock beer he stocked in one of the C-47 lockers.

"You believe in making yourself at home, don't you?" Ben grumbled.

The man grinned. "Guess I do. Name's Mac Powell. I fly a chopper. You're welcome to take a snooze in it anytime."

"You signing on?"

"At the project? Hell, no. I hire out by the hour. That's as long as I'm willing to commit myself. Hansen radioed me to come move some machines."

Ben continued his climb to the cockpit. At the door he turned back. "In all your nosing around my plane you didn't see a leather jacket, did you?"

"If I did I'd have it on." Mac lay back down. "Let me know when you're ready and I'll get those ATVs off your hands."

"You going flying with beer in you?"

"In this fog? Relax, pal. Once these things are moved to the chopper, I'm through for the day."

Ben nodded toward the locker. "Why don't you get us both a beer and I'll radio for Hansen to come help."

It was mid-afternoon before the ATVs were strapped for the cargo helicopter's sling. Afterward Ben walked with the pilot down to the lodge and ate dinner with him in the staff's alcove off the kitchen. At Powell's request, Daisy, dressed in her maid's uniform, sat with them briefly, laughing and trading stories, but she left when Garrett beckoned to her from the door.

The next morning the sky cleared just long enough for Powell to airlift the ATVs to the bald and return to the valley. Despite his orders Ben decided not to fly a scheduled run to Asheville. He knew he wouldn't get back that day if he did. A stagnant cold front was drifting toward the mountain. By noon, leaving the lodge meant plunging blindly into a misty white world.

The weather stayed that way the rest of the week. Garrett, his pistol and commando knife at his waist, strutted in and out of the lodge under gloomy stares from the confined project workers. Since no one drew pay for sitting around the fire, they were an ill-tempered and restless bunch. Only one crew was working, on the ramp at the overlook. Up there the fog was thinner, a speck of blue sky showing through now and then.

Ben wandered up the mountain to watch, as much to keep away from the whistler at the transportation desk as from boredom. He'd knocked on Georgia's door once, but only once. When she'd opened it he'd glimpsed a spidery design on her computer screen. Paper and drawings were scattered around the floor. She rejected abruptly his suggestion of a walk and the door closed. It reopened, only as wide as one of her dark eyes. "I can't get a handle on it. Don't take it personally." The door closed again.

It was Saturday before the fog lifted enough that Ben could see one end of the runway from the other. Exuberantly, he hurried back to the lodge and told Spaulding his plan to lease a small plane at the airfield in the valley. The innkeeper jotted down supplies badly needed by his kitchen staff. "You want a ride?" he asked, handing the list to Ben.

"Over those chuckholes? No thanks. Isn't there a foot-path? I could use a little exercise."

Spaulding nodded. "Head for the lake. Once you pass the cleared area along the southern shore there's a huge weeping willow tree. The trail starts there and cuts straight to town. I wish I could go with you. It's a lovely walk."

Ben found the trail easily enough, but it wasn't straight, not like the highways slicing through the pancake landscape in Florida. This one weaved back and forth and up and down, through glens and around ravines and rocky outcroppings covered with fern. From time to time crackling noises, or a faint rustling, intruded among the pines and tall skeletons of denuded dead trees, always off to the right, as though an animal was pacing him.

The woods changed, growing more lush and green with ferns and trillium on the lower slopes. Ben stopped when he glimpsed what appeared to be a cascading, oval mass of Spanish moss draped amid leathery laurel leaves curled under by the cold. Spots of red, berries that had lingered on small mountain ash, decorated the surrounding scene. It was a dazzling sight. His gaze shifted toward a hint of movement in the laurel. Not far from the tangle of moss a young deer was nibbling on the tender bark of a sapling. Transfixed, Ben watched. The deer flicked its ears and grazed deeper into the underbrush. It was a scene of tranquility on which Ben was hesitant to encroach. Ever so slowly he was backing away when a bullet sang like a bee in the foliage above him. Both he and the deer started. There was a second report, and another bullet punched its way through leaves and bark. Ben hit the ground.

"Cease fire!" he yelled through a mouthful of snow and wet leaves.

A startled murmuring from below reached his ears. Ben cautiously raised his head and scanned the area. He wasn't surprised the deer had bolted, but something nagged at him. The moss. He couldn't spot it either, anywhere, and realized it'd been white, more like angel hair than the gray stringy air plant so prolific in Florida woods.

He called aloud. "I'm coming down."

They stood in the base of a small hollow, waiting for him—an elderly stooped mountaineer, a younger man with an ax, and a boy holding an old Savage bolt-action .22 with a mended stock. All three were dressed in overalls and denim jackets. By their feet was a large spray of mistletoe and behind them two evergreens lay on the ground.

"We're sorry, mister," the oldest said, taking the gun from the boy. "We had no idee ya was about. Are ya okay?"

"I'm fine," Ben replied. "Your shots weren't that close. I just didn't want them getting any closer."

"Ya've got leaves on your mouth," the dark-eyed boy gulped.

Ben used his sleeve. "Whatcha up to?" he asked, letting his Cracker accent thicken.

"No use deny'n, we're collectin' for Christmas," the younger man said. "When we heard they was goin' to pave over this piece we sort of figured we'd do like always . . ." His outsized hand indicated the greenery at his feet. The thick stem of the plant had been neatly parted by a bullet. "It's your'n now if ya want it."

"Hey, no. I'm walking to the village, that's all."

"Ain't you from the prah-ject?" the boy asked.

"I'm a pilot, but, yeah, I'm staying at the lodge. You say this is going to be cleared?"

The old man nodded. "The hardwood's done sold off. My eldest boy's on the crew that's gonna start cuttin' this area next week." He bent toward Ben and spoke barely above a whisper. "Don't suppose there's been anymore'n them disasters up there."

Ben was not sure, through the thickness of the accent and indirect manner of speech, whether the man had made a statement or asked a question. He shrugged.

"Don't get Dad started on his Black Dutch tales," the young man put in, as though Ben were somehow encouraging him.

"Tales," the old man huffed. " 'Tain't no tales. 'Tis the truth. If you'd a-been thar when I was a-gettin' baptized and that black devil appeared, you'd a-been a-hollerin' till now."

Ben tried not to smile. "Devil?"

"I was but a tad when that black monster fell out of a tree and sloshed right thar in the river amongst the saved. The preacher lit out after him with a stick, but the devil got away."

"Sounds like you had a run-in with a bear," Ben said.

The old mountaineer stared off into the woods with watery eyes. " 'Twern't no bear. 'Twas a devil. Jest you beware walking by yerself through these hollars."

"Come on, Dad. We got to git back."

"Look," Ben said, "if you're heading down the mountain, I can give you a hand with the trees."

The men looked at each other and then back at Ben. The one with the antique rifle pulled the bolt, checked the chamber, and handing it back to the boy, said, "We'd be mighty grateful. Our place is on the river, a good walk with these trees."

One of the firs was at least ten feet tall. Ben lifted the trunk and the old man moved to the top. "This har tree's for the church. If you git tired, holler, and I'll switch with ya."

The other two, carrying the mistletoe and the smaller tree, started out first and were soon out of sight. Long before the river came into view Ben's fingers were numb with pain, but there was no way he was going to trade places with the old mountaineer. When at last they approached a narrow log bridge the boy ran out of a white frame house on the opposite bank. With a grin, he greeted them and took a place on the tree to share Ben's load.

"Ma's heatin' cider and cuttin' her fruitcake," he said. "I ain't never knowed her to cut her cake 'fore Christmas."

Ben spent longer with the family than he'd intended and didn't argue when the father offered to take him the rest of the way to town in his pickup. At the airstrip Ben jumped out and, after a quick check of his watch, hurried across the damp grass to a small aluminum trailer that he guessed was the office. There was no answer to his knock and no sign of activity except for the wind rattling through the tin siding of two open hangars. Ben started toward them. The first one held a Cessna 150 trainer and the old helicopter that had lifted the ATVs to the bald. Its detached crop-dusting gear was stacked in one corner. Ben wondered if its intractable pilot could be around somewhere. The rest of the hangar was filled with farming equipment and car relics.

In the other, Ben passed a Piper Cub and a second Cessna before he saw what he wanted. A For Sale sign was taped on the window of a fabric-covered Maule, about twelve years old. He walked around it a half dozen times, then renewed his efforts to locate the airport manager. He was on the far side of the hangar, working on an Air Coupe with a bent prop and buckled wing.

"I thought those things couldn't be wrecked," Ben said behind him.

A shot of tobacco juice flew out and the ruddy-faced man twisted around to glare at Ben. "Can't," he said, "unless ya try to land one in a cornfield. What can I do fer ya?"

Ben asked if whoever was selling the Maule would be willing to lease it out for a while instead. The man shrugged and, without uttering a word, began walking toward the trailer. Ben was left to decide for himself if he should follow. He did. Stepping inside, he heard the man talking on the phone.

"Come on over directly, Doc," he said and hung up.

"Can I use your phone?" Ben asked.

"I reckon. It's not hard."

The door slammed behind the man.

Ben called the number Spaulding had written on his note, and the local grocer agreed to deliver the supplies.

Back at the hangar the airport manager gave him the keys to the Maule with a warning. "Doc Standish don't want you startin' it or nothin'. He never smoked in it, neither. Picky man, the doc."

Ben sat in the little plane for almost an hour, poring over the Maule's engine and airframe logs. Finally a car pulled up by the trailer and two men got out. One, thin and balding, wore a white smock and the other, tall and hawkish, was in a brown suit with a shiny badge on his lapel. Ben climbed out of the Maule. The tall one reached him first and stuck out a bony hand.

"I'm the sheriff, Jack Rice. This here's Doc Standish."

Ben nodded.

"Hear you're needin' a plane. How 'bout showin' us some ID?"

Without a word Ben pulled out his wallet and found his pilot's license, crammed with endorsements. He deliberately handed it to the doctor.

His eyes darted over it. Nodding, he passed it on to the sheriff, who took the time to read both sides. "I didn't think a flatlander could be pried out of Florida in the winter," he said, giving it back to Ben. "What're you doin' way up here, son?"

"Totin' groceries."

Rice looked at him. "I'd say you need to tote less and eat

more if you hope to fill out that red coat anytime in the next ten years."

In spite of his best efforts, color rose in Ben's cheeks.

"I wish the preacher didn't talk no more'n you," the sheriff said, chuckling. "Maybe we could get to Sunday dinner before two."

"I didn't think leasing a plane was a police matter."

"It isn't, normally," the sheriff responded. "But these aren't normal times. There haven't been this many strangers wandering about Larkspur since the Civil War. There's dope and stuff showing up in town. A lot of folks are gettin' snake bit, if you know what I mean."

The resentment in Ben's eyes fell away. "Sorry. I've been bit a few times myself." He aimed his next words at the doctor. "I spent the last hour reading your maintenance logs, and I like your plane a lot. I'd be using it mainly for local hops and around the state. I'll keep it in top condition and I carry full insurance. What else can I tell you? Oh, yeah, I don't smoke. Never have."

Ben was in the air within an hour. The return to the mountain strip was complicated by fog, and it took several passes before he could land.

Later, when he picked his way through the mist to the lodge, he was surprised to find Georgia on the porch, sitting in one of the rough-planked rockers. He settled into one beside her.

"Does this mean you're finished?"

She sighed. "No such luck. I needed a break, that's all. My head was stuck at the computer so long rigor mortis set in." She eyed him sideways. "Been flying?"

"Just to the valley. I rented a Maule. It's a great little plane. Fast and gutsy."

The squeak of the big door caused them both to turn. Dr. Hearst greeted them, crossed the porch, and leaned against the rail. A thin wind rustled his hair, and he hunched down in his thin suit.

"Don't you have an overcoat?" Georgia asked. "I'm getting cold just looking at you."

"Don't worry about me. This is my kind of day."

"Why? Because the howling wind and fog are good for you Duke professors to chase ghosts?"

"I'm sure ghost chasing's exciting work, but it's not mine," Dr. Hearst replied. "My work's historical, not hysterical."

Georgia laughed. "I like that. I never heard of a parapsychologist with a sense of humor. You're a first."

"Ah-h-h. I'm afraid we are a thin-skinned, stuffy bunch. But I find it difficult to be too reticent around someone as disarming as you."

He rested his chin in his hands, his elbows propped on the banister, and stared into the mists, thickening where the mountain ran in a great V to the valley.

"Actually you weren't far off target, Miss Jones, teasing me about the fog. I do find it . . . alluring. And this mountain touches me in a way I cannot yet explain. Maybe it's the classic tragedy."

Georgia glanced sideways at Ben. "Do you know what he's talking about?"

Ben shook his head.

"Then permit me to tell you," Dr. Hearst said. "In 1838 the Cherokees were forced from their homeland, which included this mountain."

"The Removal," Georgia pronounced.

Dr. Hearst grimaced. "You must have gone to a very conservative school to call it that."

Georgia's shotgun eyes opened wide in surprise.

"To the Indians it was 'The Trail Of Tears,' but it doesn't really matter what you call it," the small professor intoned sadly. "No name can reflect the horror for the Cherokees."

"Why were they driven away?" Ben asked.

"Rumors of gold on their land. It was winter, but the whites didn't want to wait for spring to stake their claims. The soldiers marched the Cherokees to Oklahoma like cattle—poked by bayonets and lashed by bullwhips. More than four thousand perished, including the Indian family who once lived on the tableland above the lodge." He hesitated, then shook his head. "I'm sorry. I find this very difficult to tell. A Cherokee mother and her children were alone in their cabin when the soldiers came. The children ran into the woods and were never seen again. Some say a bear killed them. Others say they

[51]

fell from the face. Their mother died outside Cape Girardeau, Missouri, of a broken heart, the story goes. Their father was killed, along with others, in a ferocious attack on the military garrison located near where the valley town is now."

Ben, his lips in a tight line, gazed down into the valley. Georgia rocked back and thought out loud. "So when you peer out into the fog it's the Cherokees you're . . . remembering."

"Yes, remembering . . . or perhaps sensing is a better word," Dr. Hearst suggested. "After all, Cherokees are the most spirit-conscious people on earth. They communicate with their dead, with their progeny, with the animals, with the birds, with the very earth itself in ways too subtle for most whites to understand."

Ben looked at him. "I admit I don't understand."

"It's simple, Ben," Georgia said. "He's just told us a ghost story. Well, this is sure the day for it. It's getting foggy enough for the witches' scene in *Macbeth*."

"It does have elements of that, Miss Jones. Long after the Cherokees were driven off this mountain—sacred to them, by the way—settlers saw ghost fires that disappeared without a trace and heard strange howls at night." Dr. Hearst struck an unconscious pose of a scholar in his lecture hall, head down, pondering whether to share some fine point of knowledge that might be beyond his class. "I am considering the possibility that this is still sacred ground and that we are to receive a message here from a people who faced extermination."

"Extermination?" Georgia repeated. "Isn't that a little strong?"

"No. Sad as it is, there's no evidence the American government cared at all if the Cherokees died. That enough survived to maintain their traditions is remarkable. There are dozens of North American Indian tribes that exist no more, anywhere."

Dr. Hearst held out his hands toward the descending fog. "On a day like today, if you care enough and are sensitive enough, it's possible to feel the Indians pass. Long lines of hopeless families. You cannot see their ragged clothes or hollow eyes, but you can feel their despair as they go to die in the sunlight."

Almost mournful, his voice sank to a murmur. "For them the marching is fixed in time . . . forever caught in this fog."

His silver-framed eyes fixed on Ben. "As a pilot, you know that life-threatening experiences are the ones never forgotten. They're always with us." He inclined his head in the direction of the unseen creek rippling over rocks in the ravine below. "And if you walk a creek in the fog you'll find it's not the same as on a sunny day."

Ben was moved by this in a way that made him uncomfortable. He realized he had to ask a question. "If they died in the sunshine why do they march in the fog?"

A smile tugged at Dr. Hearst's mouth. "I will try to explain. Many of my colleagues talk of 'plasma' or the 'medium,' as though the fog's weight allows it to carry more. To me it's foolish to use carpenters' tools to measure a vision. It's like knowing that a rose is more beautiful in subdued light, not in the glaring sun where it grows. The reality is that fog pulls us back into a smaller sphere, restricting both our vision and our emotions. It demands we deal with *this* place, *this* happening, and *this* moment in eternity."

"Only thing I know about fog is that it kills pilots," Ben said. "The inner ear sends messages to the brain that are wrong, and with no horizon a pilot can get so confused he'll even put his plane in a dive."

"Perhaps the role of fog in your sphere is the same as on this mountain—it cancels out the normal world. As Spaulding says, there are unexplained things here that touch even the most stoic of visitors sooner or . . ."

His voice trailed off as echoes of running footsteps, and then sobs, came out of the fog. The three on the porch tensed. In the next instant a man, his face and chest smeared with blood, appeared around the edge of the lodge. He faltered at the steps when he saw their startled expressions.

"I've been attacked," he gasped. His trembling fingers released their hold on a rifle, and he fell sideways to the ground.

The first to reach him, Ben recognized the young man he'd steered away from Georgia's table their first morning on the mountain. A bloody piece of tooth clung to the corner of his split lip and a deep gash ran down one cheek.

"Get Spaulding," Ben said, and Dr. Hearst, shouting for the innkeeper, rushed indoors.

A crowd quickly gathered on the porch. Garrett shouldered

through and thrust his face next to the injured man's. "What happened to you?"

The shaking of the man's body became almost a spasm. "Rocks. An avalanche."

"Where?"

"On the bald . . . I was target shooting."

"Target shooting?" Garrett snorted. "In this fog?"

"It's clear up there," the man moaned, blood seeping from his mouth.

Garrett's usually sardonic eyes had a glint of steel in them. "Where on the bald?"

When he had his answer Garrett went into the lodge, returned in moments with a big game rifle, and started up the trail.

As Spaulding applied a cold compress to the injured man, Georgia leaned over to Ben. "This man needs a hospital. Do you think you can get him to Asheville?"

He glanced over her head at the swirling mist.

"Get a couple of these guys to carry him to the field."

Ben took off running and was ready with the Maule when the cortege appeared at the head of the trail.

He took off into the light fog with his scared passenger at first groaning loudly and then becoming very quiet as they were enveloped in white. Snatches of the conversation with Dr. Hearst ran through Ben's mind as he flew the needles, deliberately not staring out into the shifting clouds. As he anticipated, the fog gradually dissipated and a hazy sun popped into view.

"Relax. It'll be clear the rest of the way to Asheville," he shouted over the engine noise.

The man beside him opened his clinched eyes.

Ben set the course and radioed ahead for a weather report. When he again glanced over, his passenger was staring over the side. The shaking was less.

"What were you shooting at up there?"

"Birds," came the muted reply.

"Birds?"

The man, annoyed, pulled the ice pack from his mouth. "Yeah. Birds. I heard a bunch of them chirping in the myrtle."

"You're not supposed to shoot birds," Ben said with disgust.

"Why not?" the grunt came back.

Ben glared over at him. "If you really don't know, ask whoever let loose the rocks."

"I hope Garrett blows his head off," the man mumbled, returning the bag to his jaw.

Ben lapsed into silence. After a while he radioed Asheville Control and requested that an ambulance meet them.

SIX

Grounded in Asheville, Ben fretted through negative weather reports with nothing to do but nap and pace. Lifting off from the mountain strip in fog had been far easier than getting back was turning out to be. Not until noon the second day did the sky clear enough for a takeoff. At the project the bald was visible, but the runway and lodge were still lost in a white sea. He circled for an hour, watching the gas gauges closely and keeping in radio contact with Hansen. The time to give up and return to Asheville or make a try at the valley strip was fast approaching.

Finally he heard the news he'd been hoping for—increasing winds were lifting the layer of mist from the runway. Dropping a wing, Ben circled lower beside the gray seamy face rearing ominously above the clouds. Minutes and fuel slipped away.

Only a few hundred feet above the runway a dime-sized view of ground popped open. Ben turned the little plane sharply and threaded his way through the mists. In another two minutes he was taxiing to the tie-downs. As the Maule rolled by the radio shack, he got a glimpse of Georgia, hands on hips, dressed in jeans and a wool plaid shirt. She ran over to the plane and pounded him on the back as he dropped to the ground.

"Hansen said you've got a pair of balls, Ben Hagen, landing in this stuff. Personally I think you're crazy."

He flashed a one-sided smile. "It's clear on top. Fog should be burned off by this afternoon."

"Terrific!" she exclaimed. "I was hoping for that."

"Why? You going climbing?" Ben stooped under the wing to block the Maule's wheels.

"Not today."

"Anything happening up here?"

"Oh, Garrett's on the bald, Dr. Hearst is poring over his books trying to find a benign spirit that drops rocks on people, Spaulding's saying 'I told you so,' and Cal's wondering aloud about sabotage. He's ordered security checks on all the new men hired from the valley."

"What's Arnold say?"

"At first he was furious, yelling at Garrett to find who's doing this or he'll get someone who can. Now he's locked away with his engineers. How's your passenger?"

"He's all right. A couple of capped teeth and a few dozen stitches in his face and he'll be as good as new."

"Coming back to the project?"

"I'd guess not."

Ben finished his tie-down, and they walked together off the field.

"How's your work going?" he asked.

"Not at all well. That's partly why I've been eager for the return of a flyer I know who's not too tall, or dark, or handsome, and frankly needs a shave."

"You don't have to look like Clint Eastwood to fly a plane."

"Clint Eastwood's your idea of handsome?" She laughed. "Okay, mine too. Sort of horse-faced, but he's not the only one." Her eyes danced as she viewed his frowning visage. "You say it's clear on top?"

"Clear enough."

"After lunch how about taking me up in the little plane? I want to see what it's like to take a roller coaster ride without rails."

The weariness of two days' boredom fell from Ben like chain mail. "You really want to go flying?"

"Sure." She grinned at the change in him. "What've I gotta do?"

"Get dressed in something warmer. If you're not wearing 'em already it won't hurt to put on long johns."

Georgia peered over her shoulder, trying to see her backside. "I better stay away from the kitchen if I look like I've got long johns on when I don't."

"There's nothing wrong with your . . . ah . . ." Ben saw she was laughing at him.

"I know," she said. "I've caught you sneaking a look once or twice."

A half hour later Georgia, snuggled into thick pants and her heavy blue jacket, jogged back to the airstrip. Ben was already there, walking around the freshly fueled Maule. Chalky mist lay on the mountainside below like a down comforter.

"What are you doing?" she asked.

"Checklist."

"Are we going to be able to go? There's still lots of fog around."

Ben motioned straight up with his thumb to the blue-speckled sky. "That's what counts. Let's go."

Georgia climbed into the tight cabin beside him. The engine turned easily. When all the instrument needles were up, Ben moved the throttle forward. He could tell from the way Georgia's gaze bounced around the cockpit that she was entering into the spirit of the thing. This wasn't a trip; she was going for a ride.

The sun cast a faint shadow from the taxiing plane on the patchy snow. At the southern end Ben turned into the light wind, gave power, and the Maule practically jumped into the air. Quickly he banked to distance them from the mountain shoulder that nearly made the field a one-way strip.

"That's weird," Georgia said loudly. "I can't see the lodge, but there's the smoke coming from its chimneys."

Ben peered over the side. "Look closer. You'll catch a glimpse of Garrett stalking around the grounds."

Georgia strained to see, then realized Ben was teasing her. "Okay, you got me. Before you put on this aerobatics show, how about flying over the bald? I want to see the face from as many angles as possible."

Ben nodded and put the plane into a steady climbing turn that brought them to the level of the bald. A few hundred feet higher he cranked it back into slow flight, hanging near the stall, one wing held high so Georgia's view was unobstructed.

She tapped on the window. "Look! There's more smoke. . . . Isn't that near the deserted cornfield we found?"

"Could be," Ben replied absently, adjusting the fuel control to full rich.

They cruised the face. While Georgia sketched and made notations Ben studied the landscape. Below the bald the intertwining slopes were steep and rocky, a rough wedge coming to a craggy point toward the south. A fresh-cut ATV trail snaked across cleared and burned areas and into the higher wooded stretches. Through the umbrella of bare trees Ben spotted the broad river surging from the back side of the mountain. Halfway to the valley it was joined by the small stream that ran close to the lodge. The lake he'd hiked around looked a lot smaller from nearly a mile up, its banks dotted with partially finished buildings, construction barracks, and stacks of lumber. A long line of yellow road equipment stood beside the new six-lane road weaving up the mountain toward the lodge.

Georgia flipped her notebook closed, and Ben set course for the gently rolling farm country in East Tennessee. Black fence rails zigzagged across the white landscape under them.

"You ever think about taking up flying?" he asked.

"Off and on. Or sky diving. But rock climbing suits me best. I get it all—outdoors, risk, excitement, and a minimum of gear to fool with."

Ben nodded. "Just you and the climb. Not like the Rangers with a bolt driven into the rock every eighteen inches."

She cut her eyes sideways at him. "Well, maybe every two feet."

"The Rangers don't climb like that, except on an assault." He didn't try to hide his irritation as he made clearing turns over a vast field. "How scary do you want this?"

"Thrill me."

"Lazy eight's the closest thing I know to a roller coaster ride."

"Go for it." She gripped the seat with one hand and wrapped the other around the handhold.

Ben took the Maule into a full-speed shallow dive until he was approaching redline airspeed. He knew Georgia's stomach was fluttery from the relatively minor G forces exerted upon her but she made not a sound. At the bottom of the dive he pulled back on the controls. The forces intensified, pushing their heads backward. Ben kicked in rudder and ailerons. The Maule fell off on its right wing, nose down, building up speed rapidly as it plunged toward the crossover point. The air frame hummed from dynamic stress, and the sense of speed, usually lost in an airplane, became acute.

Georgia hung on with white knuckles. When the speed was at its peak Ben horsed back on the yoke, sending her southward. He came back up and, rolling onto the left wing, dove back toward their starting point.

Three times he made the complete circuit. Georgia's face was ashen after the first climb, but the color steadily returned. She was actually whooping like a Colorado rodeo rider during the final swooping turns.

"Ready for the finale?" he asked.

"Do it!" she exulted.

Ben again let the Maule build to the redline, then pulled it up sharply into a climb steeper and more pulse-pounding than any yet, almost vertical.

Georgia could feel they were about to fall. "Uh-ohhh," she groaned, then, "Wooo!" as the nose-high plane hung on the edge of the stall. Cross-controlled, the Maule twisted backward, pivoted on its down wing, and fell from the sky. The earth was a swirl of green and brown and white as the spin developed and the airspeed indicator rocketed toward two hundred miles an hour. Georgia gaped, her eyes struggling to find something fixed in a world gone dizzyingly awry.

Ben waited longer than he should have to hear her say "Enough." But it didn't come. Even though sweat beaded on her forehead, the glitter in her eyes showed she'd hang on without protest. Ben kicked in the opposite rudder until the plane was corrected to a straight dive. Then, with the air frame humming and crackling under the increased stresses, he hauled back on the stick and forced the plane toward level flight. As their weight doubled the two flyers sank into their seats.

When there was once again a horizon in the front windows Georgia explosively expelled her pent-up breath.

"Marvelous!'" she exclaimed. "I'll never make a roller coaster ride that scary."

"It wouldn't be possible if you tried," Ben said offhandedly.

He was only trying to be agreeable, but her glance revealed she'd taken it as a challenge. As they headed back for the mountain Ben wished he'd made himself clearer. Georgia wasn't one to take a dare casually, and he feared that meant she was going back to solitary confinement in her room for God knew how long.

SEVEN

Ben cut the power, put the little Maule into a gentle glide, and approached the mountain strip as an eagle might, silently into the wind. It was one of his favorite moments in flying.

"Look out!" Georgia exclaimed as the wheels touched the ground. Dr. Hearst, unaware of the landing craft, was limping across the grass runway in front of them. Ben swerved instinctively, almost ground-looping the Maule.

As they whizzed by, Georgia wrenched around in her seat and saw the look of alarm on Dr. Hearst's face. She also saw what kind of condition he was in.

"He's hurt!" she gasped, unfastening her seat belt.

As soon as the plane slowed at its tie-downs she jumped out. Within seconds Ben was racing after her toward the small figure, stumbling along, a torn backpack swinging from one strap, the other broken. All the way down one side, from his hunter's cap to his tan wool pants, he was muddied.

Georgia took his arm. "Dr. Hearst! What happened?"

He looked embarrassed. "Nothing . . . really. I slipped on a mossy rock at the river."

"Trying to reach the painted markings?" Ben asked. "I told you I'd take you when I could."

"I know, but you were away and it seemed so near. I'm all right. Really I am." He resumed his tortured walk.

"So you found the spot?" Georgia asked, supporting him.

"Yes, but I couldn't get close enough to say what their origin was." He patted the dangling pack. "I did get photos."

Despite his protests Ben and Georgia were practically carrying him by the time the lodge was in sight. As they passed the majestic red spruce on the side lawn a large dark form caused them to hesitate. Mac Powell's helicopter, its rotor barely moving in the light air, was nestled in the snow. Beside it to be loaded were haphazardly gathered piles of supplies. Garrett, dressed in faded, but sharply creased khakis, was leaning in the open hatch, gesturing.

The boxes of flares, plastic explosives, camping gear, and No Trespassing signs were inspected with foreboding by Dr. Hearst. "Surely you're not going to use explosives on the mountain," he called toward Garrett's back.

The mercenary swung around. "You bet your little ass, I am." His green eyes sparkled devilishly. "I've been chewed out for the last time because of some damn hillbillies. When I get through there won't be an acre of this project that isn't posted. Anyone who fools around on this mountain now's gonna be carried off."

"This isn't Cambodia," Ben said. "You can't act like a thug here. If you hurt anybody you're gonna end up in prison."

Garrett laughed. "Just stay out of my way, fly boy."

He began to toss boxes into the helicopter. Powell, dressed in sloppy army fatigues, jumped out to help. He nodded Ben's way.

"I'm surprised you're taking part in any such thing as this," Ben said.

The tall pilot gave him a blank look. "What's it to me? If he thinks he can get Black Dutch, more power to 'im."

"Come on, Dr. Hearst," Georgia said. "You need to get inside. You're getting a chill."

Spaudling spotted them as they entered and led the way to the second floor, where he fumbled with his passkey at Dr. Hearst's door. He finally opened it, providing Ben and Georgia their first view of the parapsychologist's quarters.

Islands of books dotted the hardwood floor. Ben tried to read the title on a gnawed tome lying on a desk, but the gold leaf was nearly worn away. He made out the word "Goetia" and on the books below, "Kabbalah" and "Grimoire."

While they waited for Dr. Hearst to rinse off the mud and stretch out on the bed, Ben poked the embers in the grate and added a few logs. At the sound of the helicopter lifting off, the silver-framed eyes glanced woefully toward the window.

"You know, Doctor," Spaulding said, his voice edged with sympathy, "you can learn a lot about the mountain's lore right here in this building. There's no need to expose yourself to the winter cold."

"I can't stay in the lodge and find an answer to all the contradictions."

"What contradictions?" Georgia asked.

Dr. Hearst's chin trembled. "If the presence is a benevolent spirit, as I believe it is, how could it be involved in violence? Rock throwing's too petty . . . too much the hot response . . . unless . . ." He stared at the nearest pile of books, lost in pursuit of some elusive thought. "Indians await the appearance of a great shaman, referred to only as The Hairy One You Are Speaking About. It is said he comes to the earth at times of despair for the Real People. Maybe what's on this mountain is from the native culture."

"Whatever it is," Ben said, "Garrett's declared war on it."

"All my instincts tell me this hard line he's taking is wrong. I must talk to Mr. Arnold."

Georgia settled into a chair by his bed. "Don't expect Lex Arnold to trust your instincts. He's furious at what's happening up here."

"Yes, but Mr. Arnold knows this is no ordinary mountain," Dr. Hearst replied, shifting his sore body to face her. "That's why I'm here. To unravel its mysteries."

Spaulding looked up from the fire. "Of course, the mystery that's most intriguing is the one about the gold."

"Gold? What gold? I don't know anything about gold on this mountain," Dr. Hearst said. "Not from my books, nor from Arnold. And I think I'd be among the first let in on such a thing."

Spaulding looked at the three puzzled faces, and then stood. "I'll only be a moment."

When he returned, a rough, oblong crystal was in his outstretched palm. "You see what it is?"

Dr. Hearst took the crystal and held it before him with the forefinger and thumb of each hand, like a spindle in a lathe, so both Ben and Georgia could view it. "Clear quartz . . . a little milky. With clusters of what looks almost like dental work. Why, it's crystallized gold! That's very rare."

"Exactly. And it was found here."

Dr. Hearst weighed the stone in one hand. "You seem awfully certain."

"I am." Spaudling drew a chair up beside the bed. "Two hundred years ago settlers, following Daniel Boone's trail, camped on the river that cuts across the back of the mountain. A young boy named Joshua Hauser picked this up there, but it wasn't until Missouri that his grandfather caught sight of it. With high hopes of making a big strike he brought his family back. It wasn't hard for them to locate the original campsite, but no more gold was ever found. They stayed anyway, farming and trading with the Cherokees before the Indians were driven away. When the lodge was built, in large measure by descendants of Joshua, the stone was sold to the first manager, who paid far more than its intrinsic value to preserve it as a historical artifact."

"That story has the ring of truth," Dr. Hearst said. "Are there records?"

"Joshua's original map is in the lodge safe, along with a diary his mother kept during the prospecting years. Perhaps you'd like to see them."

"Very much."

"I've always considered this crystal one of the most fascinating aspects of the mountain, but with all Mr. Arnold's changes . . ."

From overhead the thump of the returning helicopter vibrated through the room. Spaulding spoke louder. ". . . it no longer matters if there's gold here." The noise died as the craft settled on the lawn.

"Doesn't matter?" Ben exclaimed. "It'd matter to me if I found it."

The innkeeper shook his head. "No, it wouldn't because it would be Arnold's gold."

"It'd matter to him then," Ben insisted.

"Maybe. But not the way you mean. Only a very rich vein would make this worth mining. Gold's more valuable to him now as a lure for tourists."

"It'd lure me," Georgia said with a laugh.

Spaulding's eyebrows shot up as voices in the hall grew loud, and angry.

"Excuse me," he said, rising.

Ben and Georgia followed him out.

At the head of the stairs Daisy, carrying a small drawstring bag, was trying to calm her father. Mac Powell stood at the lodge entrance below.

'I'm gonna stay out of this. I hate family fusses," Georgia whispered to Ben. "Anyway, I've got an idea I want to work on."

Wondering how long it'd be before he'd see her again, Ben watched as she headed for her room.

"I'll be okay, Papa," Daisy was saying when he turned back.

"You have no business up there," her father argued. "It's not safe."

"I'm safe with Jim Garrett anywhere. No one's going to mess with him."

The waiter clutched her arm. "How can you go so eagerly when he sends for you? And *there*. After what happened when you were a child? I don't want you out on the mountain at night."

Pouting, Daisy brushed his hand aside. "Papa, you always told me to forget what happened when I was little. There's no reason to bring it up now. I'm twenty and these aren't the old days. I can take care of myself."

"It's none of my business, Daisy," Powell called up, "but why camp on that miserable cold mountain? If its a good time you're lookin' for you can do better than freezing up there with an old fella like Garrett."

"Just because I've known you forever, Mac, that's no reason for you to get into this. Anyway, I thought you worked for him."

"Nope. I work for myself. I do as I please."

"Well, so do I, and it pleases me to go to Jim."

With a flip of her long hair, she hurried down the stairs and out the door Powell was holding. He shrugged his thin shoulders and went after her, letting the door slam. Soon the thumping noise started up again.

EIGHT

"It was only Daisy, squabbling with her father," Ben said, reentering Dr. Hearst's room. "If you're all right, I'll be going."

"Wait a minute, Ben." The voice was trembly with emotion. Dr. Hearst still held the chunk of crystalline mineral in his diminutive hand. Obviously he had been studying it the whole time Ben was gone.

"What can you tell about this?"

Ben took the quartz. "It's as cool as a river rock."

"Look into its depths. What's there?"

Ben turned it in his hands slowly, resignedly, unwilling to offend the professor but reluctant to be drawn into his world of spirits, either. "It's got a crack running into the center. And, of course, there's the gold."

"Turn it to the fire."

Ben did and the question came again. "What's there?"

"Flames—but the color's changed—it's sort of yellowish."

"You're seeing those flames through six hundred million years. It's like peering into the heavens, not at stars shining now but at those that were bright eons ago."

Ben looked toward Dr. Hearst. In the firelight his hair was soft and billowy, the light catching it like the sun behind white clouds.

"You're saying it's the same as going backward in time."

"Right. And now I want you to consider that if it's possible to look back in time, which we do every night, there might be people who can sense what's happening at this very moment in the next room, or even anticipate the future."

Ben laughed uneasily. "You're not expecting me to believe in crystal balls, are you?"

"Don't mock me, Ben. I'm not a fortune teller. I just don't want you to be like so many and doom man to live his life looking backward."

"I don't doom anyone, Dr. Hearst."

Tired eyes met Ben's. "I know you don't. That's why I want you to take my next words seriously. I feel that your destiny, along with Miss Jones's, is inexplicably intertwined with whatever's on this mountain." His hands dropped to the bed.

Confused, and not knowing what to say, Ben set the stone on the covers and was nearly across the room when the sad, mellow voice intoned, "Go carefully. It will leave as much of a mark on you as you will on it."

In the hall Ben debated with himself about bothering Georgia. Logic lost. At her door he took a deep breath and knocked.

The door opened the barest slit. "I'm serious, Ben. I'm going to work." It closed with a click.

That night he ate dinner alone. When it was over he went to his room. Thinking about Dr. Hearst's strange pronouncement, he stared through the ice-coated window, then grabbed his jacket and went out into the cold night. He saw a light in the small airfield office as he walked toward the tie-down area. There was nothing for him to do at the Maule. It had been secured and locked. When he stuck his head in the door to thank Hansen, Ben saw that he was playing cards with Mac Powell and a couple of others. There was a stoneware jug by Powell's elbow. He signaled for Ben to come in.

"How about a drink? You look a little frostbit."

"I think Ben must've already had a drink or two when he bought that red coat," Hansen chuckled in his beard.

"This damned coat's not mine," Ben grumbled, walking over to the cast iron stove to warm his backside. "My jacket was swiped, and if I ever get my hands on the S.O.B.—"

Powell kicked a chair toward him. "Why don't you sit down? Play a hand or two. Maybe you'll win a few bucks and get the rock out of your gizzard."

[70]

"Where'd you take Garrett and Daisy?" Ben asked, ignoring the chair.

Powell's long face sagged into a frown. "They're camping on the bald." He picked up the deck and began to deal. "You in?"

"Come on, Ben," Hansen coaxed. "Try some of this corn whiskey and give us a chance at that Florida money."

Ben dragged the chair in place and sat down. Swinging the jug over his bent arm, he gulped down a mouthful and coughed violently. "My God, where'd this stuff come from?"

"Friends of mine," Powell said. "They've got a still not too far away. I dropped in there on my way back."

"I hope they're not operating on this mountain," Ben said.

"You mean because of Garrett? That old dogface is mostly bark and brag."

"Those explosives were real enough," Ben said.

"Yeah, well, their whiskey still ain't up there, so it don't matter," he said, passing the jug to Hansen. "No one climbs that far anymore since the huntin' went to hell."

"Ah, that's good stuff," Hansen said between gulps. "It ain't been no fun workin' in a dry county. I'm all for Arnold's changin' that."

"What'a you mean?" the younger of the two workers asked.

"The man's not going to open up a big fancy resort with no liquor, you can believe that."

"Over my pa's dead body," the worker said. "Him and the other deacons in the Larkspur Disciples Church. T'aint never been no public drinkin' round here."

Hansen laughed. "Then you better start planning their funerals 'cause what Arnold wants Arnold gets."

Ben shook his head at the offer of another pull. "Poker I can handle. That stuff, no. Give me a minute." He went into the back room and fished a beer out of an ancient metal cooler. As he straightened, his gaze went to Hansen's wall of nude calendars. There must have been a dozen. Where he came by all of them, Ben couldn't even guess.

Back at the table he was dealt two queens, opened, drew a pair of deuces, won, and started thinking about gathering all the chips on the table. The second hand Ben anted and folded without a pair. The third hand he drew a pair of sevens but didn't improve it.

Next he drew a two, three, five, six, and a nine. He took a long time before deciding not to call. The next deal wasn't much better, a pair of fours, but he drew to them.

"That Daisy's as round and ready as a jelly doughnut," Hansen said, staring at his cards. "I'd much rather be up on the mountain with that plump little thing myself than playing this hand."

"Lay off the fat jokes," Powell grumbled.

Hansen scratched his beard. "You sound like you might wanta go camping with her yourself."

"I know Daisy. That's all."

"I'll take three," Ben said.

Hansen picked up the deck. "Come on, Powell, you ever take her out?"

"Gimme two," he replied. "I told ya. I've known Daisy since she was a kid, and she's always been teased about her weight. It gets old . . . Still, she's never sat home much."

"Good for her," Ben said. "Let's play." He drew a six, a nine, and a four, looked around the table, and saw Powell looking back.

"You opened, didn't you?" Ben asked him.

Powell checked his cards. "I'll go for another five."

The price of poker escalated abruptly until it was only Ben and Powell and a pot with nearly a hundred dollars in it. Powell's pot. He had three eights.

Ben went to the box for another beer.

"That roller coaster gal's all business, ain't she?" Hansen asked just loud enough so Ben could both hear and ignore it if he wanted to.

"She could warm my toes anytime," the second worker said.

Ben sat back down and picked up his cards. Four hearts and the ace of spades. "If one of you birds gets close to her she'll hand you her luggage and tip you a dollar," he said without looking up. "I'm in."

Hansen slumped over his hand. He drew two and bet the limit. Ben shuffled his fifth card into the others, flat on the table, watching the calls come around to him. He spread his cards tightly in front of his face. All red. All hearts. He raised.

There were a lot of good cards around the table. Everybody hung on as Ben and Hansen took it to the table's limit. The others had two pairs each. Hansen had a straight. Ben pulled in the pot.

The walls in the radio shack creaked and moaned.

"Getting cold out there," somebody said. "I'd better throw a few sticks in the stove."

"Colder up there on that mountaintop," Powell mumbled. "Whose deal?"

"Look at a few of the magazines in my desk," Hansen said. "That'll warm you right up."

The cards fell indifferently to Ben after that. He managed to stay ahead of the game by folding most of the bad hands and bluffing a couple.

Finally Hansen threw down his cards. "I'm going to the lodge for a sandwich before it gets any colder."

"Bring us all one," Powell said.

"Wonder how thick the fog's gotten," Hansen mumbled, putting on his jacket.

Ben's eyes raised from his cards to the window. "Jesus," he whispered.

The worker beside him gaped, too. "What the hell's that?" he exclaimed.

The other men swiveled toward the window.

In the frost on the glass was an eerie image—a face, but not like any face Ben had ever seen. Fine wiry lines radiated from the eye hollows, creating bristly halos. It was as though the visage on the Shroud of Turin had been etched in Swedish crystal.

Powell's voice was full of awe. "That's gotta be Black Dutch."

As if on signal all five men made for the door. An icy blast struck them as they burst outside. They looked wildly about for whoever belonged to the face, then stopped abruptly. Lying in a nest dug out in the sparse snow under the embossed windowpane was a perfect circle. In it were dead birds, plump little Carolina chickadees and tufted titmice, already frozen by the peppering of ice falling from the skies. The men stood dumbfounded.

Ben picked up one of the birds. In the light filtering through the open door he saw traces of blood on its breast.

"We'd better have a look around," he said.

Hansen backed up. "Hell, no. I'm not scouting around for some loony. Not without a gun."

"Garrett draws the big bucks," Powell said. "I could fly to the bald and get him."

"Yeah," Hansen agreed, "and I guess Arnold oughta be told about this."

The others liked the sound of that and started down the trail as Powell dashed for his helicopter.

"You coming?" Hansen called to Ben.

"Go ahead." Ben motioned, then returned to the office for a flashlight.

Back outside, the bright beam starkly isolated the pathetic little birds dabbled with blood. Ben moved the light to the window. A chill of doubt danced up his spine. The crystallized ice patterns were turned to prisms by the incandescent bulbs inside the shack. Except for the clear circles of glass where the eyes had peered in at them, the compelling face glittered and gleamed. Ben grew uneasy as he stared at it.

He averted his eyes. A set of bare footprints led off into the woods. He followed them past the rear of the office to a little knoll of evergreens. There the indentations disappeared on hard bare ground. Shivering, fingers pained with the cold, Ben stood almost mesmerized, peering into the foggy woods. In the wisps of vapor it was easy to imagine he could still see the rimed face of the windowpane, hanging in the air. Finally he gave up and walked back to the office to wait for Garrett and the onslaught he knew would come from the lodge.

By midnight the windswept airfield was dotted with swathed, huddled figures, looking much like Napoleon's troops freezing outside Moscow. And Lexington Arnold was the cocky general, standing with his legs spread, hands on hips, staring at the image in ice illuminated by the light inside the office.

"So that's the face of my enemy." His voice was condescending.

Up the trail Dr. Hearst, in a robe and slippers, came hobbling with Georgia at his side.

"What a marvel," he cried when he was close enough to glimpse the ice portrait.

"Marvel," Arnold boomed. "That's the face of a goddamn saboteur." The irate entrepreneur picked up the small wooden stepladder Hansen used to fuel the planes and smashed the window.

Dr. Hearst shrieked with despair.

Throwing the ladder to the ground, Arnold turned to Garrett. "He can't be too far away. Get him," he commanded. "Cal, where are you? I want a steel-wire fence ten feet tall with spotlights every fifty yards erected around this mountain, and I want it in a hurry."

As Arnold stalked away, Dr. Hearst, aghast, eyes wide, limped over to the scattered shards and sank to one knee. He made a feeble, futile effort to put two large pieces together. Blood from his fingertips spread like velvet into the melting frost.

Georgia slipped down beside him. "Oh, Dr. Hearst, I'm so sorry."

Ben recovered from his own shock and whipped out his handkerchief to wrap the trembling hand.

"I can't believe it's gone," Dr. Hearst lamented. "A vision was here and I saw it for only an instant."

Angry, and keenly aware that he shared Dr. Hearst's sense of loss although he didn't understand why, Ben reached to coax him out of the cold.

NINE

With nothing else to do, Ben took a tall ladder, climbed up, and peeled back the cowling on the Douglas's No. 1 engine. A loose fitting was leeching oil. Tightening it was as good a way as any to pass the morning and stay away from Georgia's door.

He'd gone there early, hoping she'd come out for breakfast, but she wouldn't budge.

"Don't give up on me," she'd said behind the cracked door, "but don't come back either. I'm almost there and I don't need any more distractions."

As he worked, snow drifted on the wind like dandelion seeds in spring. The knuckles of his cold hands were soon raw from slips with a wrench in the brittle innards of the old radial engine.

"Damn!" he said as the wrench again came loose against a sharp-edged fitting.

"Trouble?" The kindly inquiry came so unexpectedly that Ben found himself rocking precariously on his high perch.

"Careful there! I didn't mean to startle you. I should have cleared my throat or something."

Ben managed a steadying grip on a propeller blade and glowered over his shoulder at Dr. Hearst, dressed in a deep purple jacket, rugged trousers, and new, expensive boots. There were Band-Aids on several fingertips.

"Mr. Spaulding told me you weren't flying today and might be looking for something to occupy your time since Miss Jones is so busy."

So that's what it's come to, Ben thought. *I'm kitchen conversation.* "I'm plenty occupied," he said gruffly.

"Oh, well, I don't mean to bother you."

The softness of the older man's voice was too much. Ben buttoned up the engine and descended the ladder.

"What can I do for you?"

"First, tell me, did you examine the birds?"

Ben nodded. "Most were shot clean through. But I found a .22 short in a little chickadee's wing root. You were right. That's what the man I flew to Asheville was shooting on the bald."

"I knew it! That was not a fresh kill. We were being sent a message from the presence."

"Then your presence is human," Ben said. "That strange icy face on the window, even if it was unsettling, was formed by the dew point. Spirits don't influence the dew point."

"But human breath can? I know. Sometime you and I will have to talk about the human spirit . . . but not now. Ben, Mr. Spaulding became quite agitated when I mentioned the smoke you and Georgia saw on the bald."

"Why?"

"He said Mrs. Grandy must be back."

"Mrs. Grandy?"

"The old woman who was carried off by the sheriff. Her homestead is in the high woods, where you saw the smoke."

Ben waited for what he knew was coming.

"I want to talk to her before she's removed again," Dr. Hearst said. "Spaulding's allowed me only a day before he tells Arnold. So I'm on my way up to her cabin now. . . . I'd like a guide, and a companion."

Ben began tugging off the grease-stained jumpsuit he wore over his jeans. "Start on up the trail. I'll catch you."

Dr. Hearst beamed and did as he was told. After folding the ladder Ben returned it to the storage shed. Then he ducked into the radio shack, washed his hands, and grabbed his coat from a peg.

It didn't take him long to close the distance to the elderly hiker. Conscious of the shorter legs and stiff joints beside him, Ben set a moderate pace up the mountain. Dr. Hearst moved along goatlike, every step flat and sure and steady. There was neither the ebullience nor the feline springiness that Georgia brought to the mountain trail. He talked little. It was as if all his energy went into putting each foot in front of the other. Eventually his hand went to his hip and stayed there.

At the bald the sky was speckled with clouds, the air chill. Ben led the way across the furrowed ground to the break in the lower trees. Following it, they pushed through thick garlands of rhododendron, dark green and waxy in the gloomy light. The smell of smoke reached their nostrils long before they entered the clearing.

The house, squat and mossy gray, sat back toward the edge of a wooded ravine. Dark smoke curled from a stone chimney at one side of its tin roof.

Ben knocked on the ill-fitting door. After a long wait it squeaked open, and a tiny old woman, her head and neck hanging forward turtlelike, squinted into the light. She was so stooped, her back a perfect curve at the shoulders, that she was shorter than even Dr. Hearst. Between them Ben felt as huge as Gulliver. As soon as she saw him, her arms spread wide and her bony fingers sank talonlike around the door frame.

"I ain't going, an' that's it," she declared in a shaky voice. There was defiance in the watery blue eyes. She was thinly clad for the weather. Her chin was set like a cornerstone above a long muslin dress with a ragged hem.

Ben reddened. "Ma'am, please! Don't be afraid of us."

"Git away!" She stared beyond him as if to see how many others he'd brought along to fetch her. When she saw the small elderly professor the expression on her face softened. He stepped forward.

"My name's Peter Hearst and I've come with Ben to—"

"Ben! Whar's Ben?" She began to rock rhythmically back and forth from the anchor points of her hands on the door.

"That's me, ma'am."

Through strands of thin, white hair she took a second look at him. "My first baby was named Ben. The Lord took him back 'cause I loved him too much." Tears glazed the sad old eyes. "I must have loved my home too much, too."

She drew herself up the best she could.

"But ya can't force me to leave. Not this time. I ain't a goin' an' that's hit."

Dr. Hearst cleared his constricted throat. "We're not here

to take you off the mountain . . . We only want to talk . . . and sit with you."

A clucking came from her thin, grayish lips. "You tellin' me you came a-callin'? You didn't come to carry me off?"

"Not us. We just want to visit."

She started to rock again, her eyes on the small man as if she were trying to decide who he was. The skin on her knotty blue knuckles was shiny and seamed.

"Mrs. Grandy," Dr. Hearst tried again, "aren't you going to invite us in out of the cold?"

She thought about it a long time. "I reckon I could—if you ain't from the sheriff."

Her left hand broke loose from its stiff hold on the door. When she released the right she tipped toward Ben, and he took her by the arms. The tiny woman, alarmingly cold and incredibly light, lifted her feet in an imitation of walking as he half-carried her inside.

The dark room was only a little warmer than outdoors, and bare except for a corner cupboard and a bed frame built onto the back wall. Empty wasp hives dotted the rafters. A small fire in the stone fireplace emitted the only light, but an iron kettle on the hearth blocked out most of that.

"Thar's cherry bark for tea, but I got no bread to offer ya," Mrs. Grandy said as she sank stiffly to the thin bedding. Ben took off his coat and tucked it around her.

"That's a mighty purty coat. Color of holly, ain't it? Warm too." Her voice was high-pitched but weak, like the whistle on a steam locomotive whose fire was going out.

"She's desperately cold, Dr. Hearst."

"I know." He began to rub her hands vigorously. "This doesn't look good. Not at all."

"I'll get some real heat in here," Ben said.

The back door was secured with a wooden bar. Ben thought briefly of tossing it on the fire, but realized that such disregard for her home, even in its sad state, would be unforgivable.

"How did you get all the way up here, Mrs. Grandy?" he asked, leaning the bar against the wall.

He heard a whisper pass to Dr. Hearst.

"She says she walked." There was awe in the professor's voice.

Ben hurried to his chore. Underbrush crowded the slope behind the house. After checking inside a derelict shed he ran down an overgrown path. A crackling sound caused him to check over his shoulder, but whatever animal it was had already disappeared into the woods. Fifty yards from the house he broke into a glen. On the far side, between two dead trees, there was a wood pile. Closer, a cluster of large rocks stood more or less in two rows. Primitive carvings on the monuments were mottled and worn. Ivy covered one small flat piece of polished granite. *F. Grandy, 1982* was chiseled on it. Ben stepped around the perimeter and gathered an armful of wood.

Inside the gloomy cabin Mrs. Grandy was still talking in low tones to Dr. Hearst. Ben stopped at the hearth to blow life into the embers. Carefully he fed the driest fragments until the fire blazed up.

"How is she?" he asked, crossing to the bed.

"Shh . . ." Dr. Hearst gestured, his countenance akin to an old-time general practitioner's.

". . . It were 1925 when I come here as a bride," the words came low. "Thar weren't no one else but only Grandys and me a Hauser from the valley."

When she saw Ben the frail woman made a faint effort to rise. "I'll fix the tea. I wuz lucky to have a bit o' the bark left."

Dr. Hearst soothed her back and with a glance sent Ben scurrying again. On the mantel he found a container of what looked like cinnamon sticks. A sniff told him it was cherry bark.

"Thar's water outside," Mrs. Grandy called feebly as Ben stood with the kettle in hand.

Back in the cold he saw that the sky was darkening, and the wind was increasing. A cast-iron hand pump, coated with rust, stood close to one corner of the house. Beneath it was a quart can full of water. Ben pumped the kettle three-quarters full and refilled the primer can. In the warming cabin he plopped a few pieces of bark in the hanging kettle and pushed its metal arm over the fire.

Across the room Mrs. Grandy's weak voice wavered. "Old Black Dutch don't abide no foolishness on this mountain. He's got his ways a doin'."

"Was he here when you came?" Dr. Hearst asked.

"Black Dutch come acrost the ocean, oh, hunnerts a years ago, hunnerts an' hunnerts."

"He came from across the ocean?"

"Some did. That's why we called 'em Black Dutch. They had a poisonous kinda deviltry. Settled over in the gap and hardly ever came out." Her voice faded away. "Nobody's ever knowed for sure if he's one of 'em."

The fresh aroma of brewing tea filled the cabin. Ben rummaged through the cupboard and found a chipped blue enameled cup and several Mason jars. "There's not a bite to eat," he whispered to Dr. Hearst.

"But she's been up here for days."

"There's no food."

"Ben, I have a terrible premonition . . . Her pulse is thready. And she's still cold." He bent forward to see the old woman's face better. Her eyes held a gleam of pride and victory.

"Oh, ah'm a-dyin'," she said straight out. "The Lord's a-hitchin' up a chariot for me."

"I'm going for food," Ben said. "And the doctor."

"It's the only thing to do," Dr. Hearst agreed, but his tone was doubtful.

Mrs. Grandy raised her head. "Don't want no food, but ef it don't discomfit ya none I'd relish a drop of that 'ere tea."

Ben filled the metal cup with the steaming drink and rushed outside to add a dash of cold water. As he primed the pump his gaze went to the woods. Deep in the shadows, he saw a single eye glittering. It could have been an animal or an owl or even a man. Whatever it was, it was fixed on him, and then with the suddenness of a blink it was gone.

He pumped a little water in the cup and mounted the back steps. Jolting to a stop, he splashed the tea. On the stoop was an object that made his heart surge. He picked it up. A perfect likeness of Mrs. Grandy was carved in an aromatic piece of white pine. Angles and ratios and mechanics were the driving forces in Ben's mind, but he knew instinctively that this was a wonderful work.

The head was the size of a crab apple. She was recumbent, arms crossed on her chest. Even at rest her hands retained the sinewy tension that Ben had seen in the doorway as she braced herself against their intrusion. But the most amazing thing about the carving was that from the jawline to the hairline her face was stained a vivid red. The effect was eerie, troublesome.

Ben swung around and scanned the desolate landscape. Who, or what, was out there?

TEN

A cup of tea in one hand and the carving in the other, Ben walked slowly toward the bed. When she saw the piece of wood Mrs. Grady's eyes grew large.

"Why, hit's a sperit doll—oh Lord! He's a-done one of me dyin'." Trembling fingers reached to take it. The expression on her lined face changed, fear followed by resignation, and finally acceptance. "He's done me a-hoein' and a-choppin' and a-hullin' beans. Might jest as well come fer the end."

"You know who carved this?" Ben asked, offering her the cup.

Thin pale lips, with perpendicular creases, puckered over the rim. She sipped, staring up at Ben. "Like I said. Sperit of the mountain. Brung me carvings fer longer'n I can remember." She tried to sit up and Dr. Hearst supported her. "That ain't true. I do know it. Started when my maw brung me a bag of peaches and I left 'em down by the edge of the field. Went to fetch 'em the next morn and they's gone, but a whittlin' was thar, lying purty as you please, the grass tugged out in a perfect little circle. It was me, a-nursin' my first babe, Ben."

She closed her eyes. About the time the two men decided she was asleep her lids raised and she went on, in a whisper. "After that I'd leave things on purpose and there'd always be a whittled stick left behind. 'Twas a thankee, I reckon . . . I hid 'em, down in the food cellar by the crik. Way in the back under the taters. Paw woulda called 'em the devil's work. He had the old-timey religion and wouldn't have took to me giving stuff to an idol carver." She cackled. "But oncet Frank was over by the bald and seen him—black and glossy as a skunk. But a

man, not a devil, naked as the day he was born, a-hunchin' up
that clift steady as a prayin' mantis on a tater vine. Frank he
give a holler fer his gun an' I come a-runnin', but 'fore he cud
as much as take aim that strange 'un vanished to smoke."

"He disappeared before your ĕyes?" Dr. Hearst asked.

Mrs. Grandy waved her hand weakly. "Puff, but I seen
enough to leave him a pair of Frank's old overalls down by the
leavin' place. He put them on, too."

"You saw him after that?" Dr. Hearst asked. "This Black
Dutch?"

"Pokin' around these foggy woods ya can see a thang, or
not see it, as ya choose. But they's thar . . . b'ars an' snakes an'
varmits an' Black Dutch. It's thar home, ain't it?"

She took another drink of tea.

"Many's the time I've heard a rustlin' in the brush. But I
weren't skeered though it war like a spook creepin' about."

Dr. Hearst touched her arm. "Can you tell me how to find
him? Where he comes from?"

"No, I rightly cain't. Still, I knew when he was watchin'
me. Folks say he's got the evil eye, but I ain't no ways shore he
uses it. Leastwise he never used it on me."

Ben held out the carving. "Are they all like this? It's very
. . . very . . . wonderful."

"You fancy it?"

"I do like it."

Her head settled back. "Then you kin have that cuttin' of
me, and if you ain't a-skeered of a devil's curse you can have
'em all. I give 'em to ya, Ben."

A cough made her thin chest jump. Dr. Hearst pressed
more tea upon her, but she held up a restraining hand. "I'm a-
goin' soon." Her voice had a faint gurgling quality, deep in the
throat. "Frank's a-waitin' fer me."

Ben knelt beside her pallet. "Is your husband buried out
back?"

The old eyes were losing their mobility and their luster.

"Mrs. Grandy?"

"Thar he be," she moaned. "An' Grandpa Tom and Jesse
an' Nora. And baby Ben. They's all a-waitin' fer Judgment Day
right here." Tears began to stream down her face. "And I won't

be with them. They'll carry me down the mountain like a kilt b'ar."

Dr. Hearst tugged on Ben's arm. At a distance from the bed he asked with urgency, "There's a family cemetery out back?"

Ben nodded.

The professor looked over at Mrs. Grandy, then back at Ben. "The law says a graveyard, even a small family one, must not be disturbed or access to it denied. Do you understand what I'm saying?"

Ben returned to the bed and knelt.

"Mrs. Grandy," he said sharply and the eyes flickered open in irritation.

"I shoulda knowed ya was too loud to be Gabriel. Let me be." Her eyes closed.

Ben touched her shoulder. "Mrs. Grandy, listen to me." The eyes opened again. "You'll be with your husband. I promise you. If you die here, I'll bury you here."

A tremor went through the old body. "It's been sold off by my boy Roy. Don't you know? 'Tain't mine no more."

"That doesn't matter," Ben said more gently. "The law will let you be buried here."

"You mean that?" she croaked.

"You'll never leave this mountain."

"It's the Lord's blessing on an old woman." She placed a thin hand on his wrist. "I'll be a-countin' on you, Ben."

Dr. Hearst came over and gently brushed the gray hair from her brow.

"I ain't leavin' an' that's hit." Her taloned hand gave Ben a squeeze. "My boy Ben's done promised hit."

She went from life to death quietly, with no sound in the old cabin save the pop of wood as the fire faded to embers.

Dr. Hearst spoke at last. "She's crossed over."

Ben's answer was a nod. He was having trouble finding his voice.

"And now you and I know it's all true. We have it on the authority of a deathbed statement."

"What's true?" Ben managed.

"There is a presence of the mountain. It's Black Dutch."

Ben looked from the small wooden image to Mrs. Grandy.

Their expressions were the same: one of peace. "She said he's just a man."

"Just a man," Dr. Hearst reiterated. "Someone who's lived without close human contact for more than half a century. A man with the hands of a master artist. I tell you, Ben, I would consider it the greatest honor of my life to meet such a man." He sighed. "I suppose it's time to tell Arnold about Mrs. Grandy. He'll need to notify the authorities."

"You go," Ben said. "I'm going to dig her grave."

Dr. Hearst's brows narrowed. "Regardless of what I said, things can get beyond our control. There's no telling how Arnold's going to react to all this. He could make trouble."

Ben eased the clutching hand from his wrist and placed it, and the carving, on her chest.

"All I need is a few hours. By the time you get down to the lodge it will be pitch dark. Just wait until morning to tell Arnold."

As his taped fingertips fiddled with the buttons on his jacket, Dr. Hearst peered down at the serene face. "I'll be back with them—tomorrow." The cabin door creaked shut behind him.

Ben arranged the red jacket over Mrs. Grandy's chest and arms and went outside. He found a dull ax and a shovel with a cracked blade in the shed. At the family plot he cleared an area and hacked away at the frozen reddish earth, turning it bit by bit. An hour passed and the hole was not even a foot below the surface. Without a jacket Ben was bitterly cold, and discouraged, but something told him to keep at it, make it deep, and square the corners. He shoveled steadily. The shadows grew long and the air gave up what heat it possessed. Trembling, Ben at last hefted himself out of the ground. At the day's last light he carried a load of wood into the cabin and went for more. After several trips he set out to find the creek.

He heard it first, below the barn and back in the woods. Stumbling down the steep slope, he came to the water's edge. It was almost full dark now. A bank of icy leaves lay against the low door to the food cellar. With cold, blistered fingers Ben brushed the wood clean. When the latch wouldn't budge he picked up a rock from the creek bed and forced the swollen rod.

Inside was totally black. Images of snakes and spiders fueled Ben's imagination. He scrambled up the hillside in the dark until his hands closed on a sturdy limb. Back at the cellar he stabbed noisily into the cavelike interior and then waited for scurrying sounds. None came. He ventured in. The air was saturated with the musty smell of old potatoes, mixed with the sweeter one of apples. Ben poked around in the black space with his stick until he thumped against cloth. Grabbing a handful of soggy burlap, he flung it out the cellar door. There were small, knotty apples in the bottom.

In the other corner he found a bag of potatoes, and under it the wooden carvings. As if he were gathering kindling, Ben stacked them in one arm, counting as he did. There were twenty-eight.

Outside, he grabbed up the apples too, and with his heavy load slowly climbed to the cabin.

Inside it was darker than the woods. Ben rebuilt the fire and settled down by the hearth to inspect the carvings. A few were birds, but most were sculptures of Mrs. Grandy at various stages of her life. When he found the one of her with a baby, he held it before the leaping flames. There was a proud lift to her chin and a smile on her lips. The baby's face was indistinct, tucked against her breast. A thin little fist held a strand of her hair.

Ben emptied the apples into a cupboard drawer, placed all the carvings in the burlap bag, tied it shut, and set it by the front door. Once several of the firmer potatoes were washed and roasting in the embers he lay down on the floor close to the heat. Instantly his eyes closed.

A howling wind woke him with a start. He sat up in a cold room, the fire very low. After stoking it he took out his pocketknife to test a potato. It was crusty on the outside but soft in the middle. He edged all of them out onto the hearth to cool. Getting to his feet, Ben glanced toward the back of the cabin. In the weak firelight Mrs. Grandy's face, half in shadow, was soft, her thin lips together with no tension in them.

He opened the front door and looked out at the night sky. It was cloudy and a trace of snow was falling. The trees were bending and groaning with the wind. It seemed a lonely place to spend a lifetime. Back at the fireplace Ben speared one of the potatoes with his knife and brushed off the ashes. He ate them all and drank a cup of the cherry bark tea. After poking up the fire he lay down again but sleep wouldn't come. Thoughts of the men who would come up the mountain tomorrow filled his mind.

Rolling to his feet, he made a torch out of a stick of wood and went outside for the ax and shovel and to recheck the shed for any other tools.

Long before first light one corner of the cabin floor was taken up, and the bottom and two sides of a casket were joined together. Ben's eyes were red and heavy but he worked on. He'd never been good at carpentry, but that didn't seem to matter. Somehow he knew what to do, where to find the length of flooring that would fit next. When he ran out of firewood, he tossed discarded planks on the blaze so he'd have enough light to work by.

At dawn he stood at the front door once more, this time with a Mason jar of cherry bark tea, and watched the sky turn to gold. It was going to be one of those rare mountain mornings, the air clear, with no mists and no wind. He went back into the cabin and approached Mrs. Grandy. He raised her gently, coat and all, and carried her to the center of the room where he lowered her into the box he'd fashioned from her cabin. Then he picked up the shovel and set about finishing the grave.

ELEVEN

When the helicopter landed in the clearing near the cabin Ben was still digging. His head was below ground level. Only the spray of dirt over the edge of the grave testified to his presence. He heard the shouts but he didn't stop. With the back of the shovel he began tamping the bottom of the grave flat.

Dr. Hearst, ashen-faced, appeared at the edge and peered down at him. "Ben, the sheriff's here. And the town doctor . . . They don't understand what you've done."

Ben boosted himself out and brushed off his pants. It was a useless gesture.

"They better leave her as they found her," he said and started for the cabin.

Dr. Hearst hurried after him. "Are you all right?" he asked. "I understand the aspects of symbolism better than most"—he caught his breath—"but you've really astonished me."

Before Ben could reply, Jack Rice called him from the back stoop. "Hey, you responsible for Miz Grandy's body in here?"

"I am."

The sheriff nervously brushed straight jet black hair off his high forehead as Ben approached. "You wanta tell me about it, son? I'd give a lot to know what was goin' on in your head."

"It was her deathbed wish," Ben said, taking the steps two at a time.

"Sounds to me like maybe it wasn't such a good idea for you to spend the night up here alone."

Ben looked at him, then jerked open the door. Inside he stopped short. The casket he'd fashioned out of the floor had been moved onto the bed frame. Dr. Standish, a stethoscope swinging from his neck, was leaning over it. In his hand he held a thin blue-veined arm.

"What'd you find, Doc?" the sheriff asked as Dr. Hearst appeared behind him at the door.

"Arteries were as brittle as pencil lead. It's a wonder she lived this long. There's no need for an autopsy."

Rolling down his sleeves, the doctor turned and saw Ben. "What in the devil possessed you?"

"Mrs. Grandy wanted to be buried here," Ben responded irritably. "And she will be."

"What's that got to do with this?" The doctor stepped away from the casket.

All Ben could do was stare. His shock was total, and evident to everyone in the room. The peaceful, small face was not as he'd last seen it. Thick red paint stained her cheeks, nose, and closed eyes as if she were wearing a crimson mask.

"You weren't the one who did this?" the sheriff asked, but it was more a statement.

Ben shook his head.

"Well, I'm gonna be the one who takes it off," Dr. Standish murmured and reached for his bag.

The sheriff pulled Ben toward the front porch. "Who else has been up here, son?"

"Nobody. Just me."

"How long you been out back digging?"

"Since before daylight."

Rice rubbed the back of his hand against his bony chin. "If you didn't do this, an' I'm of a mind to think you didn't, folks are gonna say it's the devil's work."

"No, no. That's not right." Dr. Hearst stepped out beside them. "Face painting was a burial ritual among Appalachian Indians a century ago. It's not satanic."

The sheriff looked doubtful. "There aren't any Indians this far from Cherokee."

"There are no devils up here either," Dr. Hearst persisted. "Ben, you better get the carving."

Ben went inside. When he returned he handed the piece of wood to the sheriff.

The sheriff's gaze drifted across the clearing, beyond the helicopter where Powell was perched inside talking on the radio, and out over the horizon. "If there is a renegade Indian on this mountain I suppose Mr. Arnold will want me to round him up. That man sure expects a lot of jumpin'. Ordered me to get her body out today because a work crew's on the way up."

"For what?" Ben asked.

"A razing. 'Pears he doesn't want any other hill folk gettin' the idea to come up here."

"I tried to change his mind," Dr. Hearst said, "but Arnold insists this old cabin isn't *quaint* enough to preserve."

Ben aimed angry words at the sheriff. "I don't care what happens to the cabin, but Mrs. Gandy will be buried out back. Family cemeteries are protected by law. Dr. Hearst said so."

Rice half smiled. "It may surprise you, Ben, but I know what the law is. But other people who used to live on this mountain, including her son, are on their way to get her."

"That old woman wanted to be buried here, with her family," Ben said stubbornly. "Why do you think she made that climb in the middle of winter?"

The sheriff's expression turned grim. "I 'spect you're right about that."

"The grave's ready. Right beside her husband. Go check."

"Won't hurt, I reckon."

"Hold on a minute, Sheriff," Dr. Standish said, coming out on the porch. He was holding his bag. "I can't stay. The Jenkins baby isn't gonna wait for me much longer."

Rice motioned toward the helicopter. "Go on. Tell Mac I said to set you down on their stoop. If he doesn't get back we'll walk down."

As the helicopter lifted off, Rice returned the carving to Ben and shouted over the din. "Okay, show me."

He led the way around the side of the house and down the slope. At the head of the grave the sheriff stopped and shook his head. "You ever wanta give up flying, Ben, I can get you a job at the town cemetery. That casket in the cabin, and this here grave you've cut, tell me you mighta missed your calling."

"It's what she wanted," Ben repeated.

"I hear ya, son." The sheriff raised his eyes to the woods. "Guess we may as well look around a bit while we're here."

Trailing, Dr. Hearst spoke in a low tone to Ben. "Georgia

wanted to come with us, but Arnold insisted she meet with him."

"You mean her work's finished?"

"I assume. In any case she's eager to talk to you."

As they wandered along the creek, Ben's tired mind turned to thoughts of Georgia. He was now eager to get back. They came out behind the barn without seeing anyone and headed for the cabin.

"It's gonna be a tough day for the folks from these parts," Rice said, perched on the edge of the porch in the warming sun. "Mrs. Grandy begged more'n her son to sell off, but the dollars they were all gettin' seemed mighty big. Today there's more'n a few that wished they'd listened to her."

Dr. Hearst encouraged the sheriff to talk about the old days on the mountain as they waited for the funeral party to make the long walk from the valley. His head propped against the cabin wall, Ben dozed. He woke when Dr. Hearst shook his shoulder.

"Listen, Ben."

He sat up. The sound of singing drifted to him on the shifting morning breeze.

"They're comin' up the old wagon trail," Rice said. "Sounds like quite a few."

Gradually the voices grew louder, the low ones crackling, almost moaning, and the high ones trembling with sorrow. *". . . In the sweet . . . by-and-by . . . we shall meet on that beautiful shore . . . In the sweet . . ."*

Along the narrow pathway from the bald they came single file, mountain people in heavy shoes and severe clothes. A man in black, holding a tattered Bible at his side, led the procession up the cabin steps. Ben recognized the family he'd helped with the Christmas trees. Nodding, they followed the others inside.

At the casket the man in black raised a hand, and the others lowered their heads while he prayed.

When the singing began again the sheriff stepped to one side with a thin white-haired man about fifty and the preacher. Ben, standing behind Dr. Hearst at the door, felt their eyes upon him. When the preacher moved back into the midst of the singers his deep voice came in over the hymn.

"Caroline Grandy, weak and failing, climbed this moun-

[94]

tain alone. She was a-comin' home to be with the Lord. Comin' home to be near her loved ones. Comin' home where she belonged . . ." The thin man by the sheriff moaned.

"And since there was no one else to care for her, the Lord sent a stranger. A kind man, he wrapped her in his coat and built a fire so she'd be warm. And then he held her hand while she died. The last words she heard were his promise she'd stay on this mountain. And in the cold of night he prepared a place for her."

The preacher picked up the lid Ben had fashioned and began to lower it into place on the planked box.

"Now it's our privilege to join him in laying our sister to rest on the mountain she loved."

A number of the men pressed forward, gently took up the box holding Mrs. Grandy, and carried her down the slope to the family plot.

Afterward, each of the mourners came to Ben, shook his hand, and blessed him. As the last one started homeward the sheriff squeezed Ben's shoulder.

"Come on, son, you've kept your word. It's time to go."

At the cabin Ben left the solemn march and went inside. When he reappeared he was carrying the old burlap bag full of carvings.

TWELVE

Ben was barely in his room before Georgia knocked. Like everyone else in the lodge, she'd already heard some of what had happened on the mountain, and eagerly listened to his halting story about Mrs. Grandy's burial.

"I wish I had been there with you, Ben. It must have been hard on you to face that long night alone in the cabin," she said as he laid the carvings out on the bed for her to see.

Ben hesitated, and raised his tired eyes to hers. "It's funny, but I never really felt alone." A smile tugged at one corner of his mouth. "Maybe that's because Black Dutch was hanging around somewhere outside."

Georgia picked up one of the carvings. "These make quite a treasure. A connoisseur might say you've got a fortune in primitive art here. You better tuck them away in a safe place."

"I'll put them in the C-47 later. What's up? Dr. Hearst said you were looking for me."

Her face brightened instantly. "Can you come downstairs?"

"What for?"

"Arnold and I have something to show you."

Ben did not like the sound of that. Whatever had brought him trotting down the mountain to Georgia was not for him alone.

"Don't make such a face," she said, measuring his mood.

He looked down at his soiled clothes. "I need to take a bath first."

"You're right," she said, rising. "But come to Arnold's office as soon as you can."

Ben almost fell asleep in the tub, came awake with a start, and wearily climbed out. In a melancholy mood he dressed and went down to Arnold's office.

Georgia was perched on a stuffed goat in one corner of the dark-walled stronghold. Arnold's blue eyes flashed Ben's way when he came in.

"It will be a true beast, this ride." There was a certain wickedness to his voice. As Arnold leaned over the drawings, spread fanlike on his desk, his short fingers supported the weight of his upper body like columns. "By God, girl, I knew you'd be original, but this . . . why, it's downright hellish. A nightmare!"

"I don't think there's anything like it anywhere," Georgia enthused.

"Nowhere on earth! As a focal point for the park it's priceless. How far does this spiral drop?"

"About four hundred feet. Actually I think of it as a helix with the cars on the outer edge. The riders will feel like they're plunging straight down around a point, although the true angle will be nowhere near that steep."

"But the illusion!" Arnold gloated.

Georgia dismounted from the goat and crossed to the desk. With a finger she traced the line of her drawing. The pride of a creator was on her face.

"The angle of descent and the back-front cant of the car will give the illusion that it's in free-fall. Through about two hundred seventy degrees of rotation the riders will not even see the track below them."

A rich, soul-deep laugh rumbled up from Arnold like lava from a volcano. "I have had fears that I would spend a hundred million dollars for a mediocre collection of half-assed thrills. No more."

He almost began to dance in place.

"I don't foresee any unusual engineering problems beyond anchoring it in the mountainside," Georgia assured him. "It'll be strong and safe."

"I don't care if not one person gets up enough nerve to ride the thing. People will flock here just to see it. I'll ride alone if need be. Who in God's name ever heard of a roller coaster with a four-hundred-foot drop?"

He glanced at Ben through bushy eyebrows. "Dr. Hearst was just in here telling me what happened on the mountain. Sounds like you had a trying time of it."

This friendly banter was not what Ben had been expecting. He glanced at Georgia. She winked.

"I would have liked it better if that old woman had been taken off the mountain, but since she died up there, and has already been buried . . ." Arnold shrugged. "When the fencing is finished this kind of thing won't happen."

Ben didn't see the need to respond.

"Anyway, the important thing today is this." Arnold tapped his knuckles on the roller coaster plans. "Georgia tells me you gave her the idea for this marvel."

"All I did was take her for a plane ride."

"That seems to have been enough. What do you think of it?"

"It sounds great." Ben knew his words were flat beside Arnold's enthusiasm. For Georgia's sake he wished he could do better, but he was simply not up to it.

"It will need a name," Arnold was saying. "What do pilots call such a dropping turn . . . Ben?"

"Ah . . . a graveyard spin, or spiral."

"Spiral . . . Death Spiral. That might do. We'll work on it." He abruptly turned his attention back to Georgia. "I expect you'll wish to consult with your colleagues on the engineering details."

"Yes," she replied. "I thought I'd fly back to Denver after the holidays. It won't do any good to show up there now. I probably shouldn't admit it, but most of the staff will be off skiing."

"Go now if you like and stay through the holidays. We're closing down here anyway, except for the road work and maintenance. Tomorrow the corporate helicopter will come for me, Cal, and a few others. You, Ben, will fly any other workers who want to go to Asheville so they can make connections."

"I won't be one of them," Georgia said, her eyes on Ben. "My folks were so disappointed that I was going to be working out of state this winter, I made some holiday plans for them—Hawaii. I'll see them in January."

"It may be lonely up here, although I'm sure Spaulding

will put up a tree and plan some festivities for those who stay." Arnold glanced at Ben. "I suppose you'll be heading for Florida."

"I think I'll stay around. Maybe it'll snow."

"Fine, fine, do as you wish. But remember, both of you, this roller coaster design is our secret. I don't want anyone to know about it unless it's absolutely necessary. My God! Four hundred feet! It'll put me on the cover of *Time*!"

THIRTEEN

Georgia and Ben stood before a roaring fire in the common room. Across from them, in a bay window overlooking the valley, Spaulding was directing the decoration of a dark green spruce whose crown brushed the fourteen-foot ceiling. Pipes popped and clicked in the walls. Ben was glad to be back on the ground. For three days he'd been flying steady, taking workers out when all he wanted was a chance to be with Georgia. And now she was standing beside him, with no indication she was going to run off and work on her roller coaster.

"You through for the day?" she asked, appraising his attire. He was wearing a flight suit under a new thermal jacket.

"I sure hope so."

She touched his sleeve. "Where'd you get this?"

"Asheville Airport."

"The other jacket never turned up?"

"No."

"Too bad. But this one looks warm enough."

Something about the way she said that caused Ben to eye her suspiciously. "Warm enough for what?"

"Climbing." There was a soft, sardonic glow in her eyes.

"Where?"

"The face. Nobody's ever connected a roller coaster into rock like this before. I really want to put my feet on it before I present this scheme to my boss."

"Now? On Christmas Eve? We can't scale that wall and get back by dark."

"Then we'll camp on top and come down tomorrow."

Trying not to show just how much this appealed to him, Ben managed an expression of concern. "What about provisions? It could be awful cold up there."

"I have all the gear we'll need. And a quick raid on Spaulding's pantry will take care of the food. Come on, Ben. Do you know any better way to spend Christmas?"

He shook his head.

"Good. Get in your climbing duds and I'll see to the packing."

Ben took off for the stairs.

When he appeared at Georgia's room she was tying sleeping bags into a couple of bulky packs.

"Spaulding wanted to take the time to put together one of those gourmet meals, but I just grabbed some cans and ran." A big smile decorated her face. "Ready."

When they passed the airfield, Ben caught sight of Hansen and Mac Powell in the office window peeking at them. "They think we're out of our minds," he told Georgia.

"We are, and isn't it great?" she responded gleefully.

Georgia led the way rapidly up the winding pathway into the forest. Ben was nearly jogging to keep her in sight on the once pristine trail, turned muddy by the bulldozers moving back and forth to the higher reaches. The sun, low in the dull winter sky, was a hazy orange. Once they were past the slippery ramp Cal's men had erected behind the log shelter it was a straight shot to the bald.

There, Georgia at last paused and cocked her head to listen. "What's that noise?"

It was a background buzz before, but against the vast and silent tapestry of the mountain meadow the pitch was modulated.

"ATVs," Ben suggested.

"Sure," Georgia agreed. "I've been told Garrett and Daisy go racing all over the mountain on those things."

"Security work's rough, isn't it?"

Georgia laughed and started across the flat expanse. Specks of snow began to drift by as they approached the rock face, which seemed in the afternoon shadows to lean into its own precipice. Hundreds of feet up, grass and vines hung over the edge. To the north, balsam firs swayed in the wind.

Scrambling over scree, Georgia found the place where she wanted to climb. The first leg up was not more than a few degrees off the perpendicular, but the jagged rock, the color of old bone, provided plenty of holds.

"We'll take an easy route," she said. "I'll showboat for you another time. If the weather closes in, it won't matter a lot going this way."

"Whatever you say."

Georgia linked them by rope. "This isn't much of a challenge. We could do it free, but I'm not sure you're in condition."

"I could scale this with you on my back," Ben growled.

She looked at him speculatively. "If you get mad enough I bet you could. I'm sorry. What I should have said, and what I meant, is that I got you out here on a less than ideal day and I don't want anything to go wrong."

Her face full of energy, she turned back to the wall.

"We can jam-crack it after the first twenty feet. Then slip to the right on that ledge." She pointed. "You can belay there."

Ben nodded.

Georgia started the climb at a deliberate pace, testing each move, using her hands for balance, keeping the load on her legs. Within a hundred feet she was wedging her boots into a narrow crack and moving easily upward at a sharp angle. Ben waited until she reached the ledge before he started his climb. It took him longer, his larger feet uncomfortably pinched in the fracture line, and he knew he lacked something in grace.

In an hour they were above the bald. Big flakes of snow blew past, peppering their clothes. At a narrow traverse Georgia paused, signaling Ben up. When he scrambled to her side he saw puzzlement in her dark brown eyes.

"Look at that." She indicated a hand-size cavity in the rock face.

"It's what the Rangers call a bucket."

"Everybody calls a natural handhold a bucket—or a 'Thank God' hold," she said. "Look again."

This time Ben's eyes fixed on chipped marks around the weathered rim. "I never saw a climber—military or sport—do anything like that."

"There's another to the right and lower. In fact, I can spot enough 'Thank God' holds for an evangelist's tent show."

Ben craned his neck. "I guess you're gonna blame them on the Rangers."

"You guys would have driven bolts, not cut so carefully into the wall."

They resumed the climb. From time to time Georgia tapped a spot as she passed, indicating still another place where the rock was chipped away. The angle of the climb moderated, and Ben narrowed the gap between them. Three hours after first putting foot to the face, Georiga grasped an outcropping and without exertion levered herself over the lip of the summit. She gathered rope as Ben hoisted himself up.

Spots of ice dotted the pitted rock under their feet.

"No way are tourists coming up here," Ben declared breathlessly, "at least not in winter."

Not replying, Georgia moved southward across the snow-dusted expanse. At the jutting rocks that formed the pinnacle she waited for him. To the east the great valley was lost in mist. To the north the mountain dropped sharply and disappeared in a tangle of untouched wilderness.

"No one who comes up here will be cold," she whispered when Ben came up beside her. "Arnold isn't going to let tourists wander around in an uncontrolled environment." Her hands sketched lines in the sky. "From here on down he'll erect a vast rectangle of glass and vinyl. And though I haven't seen the plans for it, there'll certainly be a restaurant."

"Up here?"

"Sure." She turned toward him. "Like the rest of us you've got to start thinking of this mountain as a platform for a commercial enterprise. When the road's finished to the bald, buildings will spring up like weeds."

Their eyes met briefly before Ben stared off into space.

"You're a hard one to figure," Georgia said. "You don't have the same kind of involvement with this mountain that I do. You climbed the face, but I had a climb. You see stone and space and the end of a runway, and I see the movement of continents and whispers of buried ore. And yet . . . I don't know whether Dr. Hearst has affected you, or if it was that old

[104]

woman, or whether you've always been like this . . . you seem to be almost grieving for this rugged old mountain."

Ben lapsed into silence momentarily as he stared into her dark eyes. "I'm just a hired taxi driver, except I do it in an airplane."

"I see . . . You have no feelings for the mountain? Or the people?"

It was a critical moment between them, Ben knew. Georgia was prodding him to share part of himself with her.

"Well, I do know something about what's happening here," he said.

"Which is?"

"My life as a boy was spent in flatlands and sand dunes and wild stretches of lonely beaches. . . . You ever been to Florida?"

"Sure. Last year."

"Did you see any lonely beaches?"

"I didn't see anything lonely in Florida. Not where I was. Just signs, and mile after mile of gaudy hotels and high-rise condos with their foundations in the surf."

"That's Florida," he said. "Men exactly like Arnold bought it and I hate them for it. Now it's happening to this mountain. And here I stand. This time part of it."

Her eyes searched his face in profile as he peered off into the valley. His jaw was angular, the nose straight except for a small hump where he'd broken it when he was a kid and never had it set. She watched his breath spiraling in a white mist over the void.

"I understand," she said softly. "Even though you're the second or third poor dumb pilot Arnold's had up here, you hate yourself for being on the side of change."

"I guess I do."

"And you hate me for bringing a thundering roller coaster to Appalachia."

"I don't hate you, Georgia."

"You hate what I'm doing."

"I—"

"If I don't do this design, my company will send someone else."

"I know."

"Everything changes, Ben. We can't stop it."

"I know that too. There's no room in the world for Osceolas."

"Osceola?"

"He was an Indian in Florida who refused to surrender his land."

"What happened to him?" Her voice sounded as if she already knew.

"He came in under a flag of truce and was betrayed by the white soldiers. He died in prison and his head was cut off, for a souvenir. . . . Florida's first, I guess you could say."

They turned from the precipice and moved down the mountain crest toward the trees, where the wind became an audible whistle amid icy branches.

"You know, Ben," Georgia said, "it's possible to look at what we're doing in terms of numbers. Once the park's open more people will see this beautiful view in a single hour than all that came before, including us. That's something."

Ben stared gloomily at the falling snow. He swallowed and forced out the words, making a determined effort to talk about himself. "I got into flying because of my father. I thought it'd be a good way to get to know him, or at least something about his life. He died when I was little—fooling around in an early experimental helicopter. Now, like him, flying's my life. All I have. Still, if everybody had a pilot's license, I don't think I'd want one."

Georgia's smile was full of regret. "What do we do? Climb down the mountain and tell Lexington Arnold his plans offend us?"

Ben knelt and picked up a large stone, glistening with mica, and dropped it back into place. "Arnold will do as he likes. Men like him always do. But at least Mrs. Grandy won't have to leave."

Unslinging her pack, Georgia walked back toward the crest and began laying out the tent gear near the pinnacle rock. "This will make a good windbreak," she called.

"I'll get some wood," he replied, trying to match her bright tone. He slipped off his own pack and, hurrying against the darkening skies, hiked toward the northern woods. Enough deadfall poked through the snow for him to gather a good load quickly. The tent was up and Georgia was tamping in the stakes when he dumped the first armful. He returned to the trees, being more selective than before, and gathered ice-free twigs and branches to use as starter wood.

As he emerged from the thicket with his heavy load, he realized in a heartbeat the simple sight of Georgia kneeling by the tent would live with him for the rest of his life. Diffused light from the invisible setting sun was not enough to cast shadows. Instead there was a muted softness around Georgia, as though the light came not from a fierce source but from the illumination of the air itself. Nestled in a small hollow in the rock and snow the tent was a pastel yellow against winter's white-and-black tones.

Before it he swept a small circle clean of snow and arranged the driest and smallest twigs for an economical fire. It took only a few matches and gentle puffs before flames danced in the wet wind.

"Purists would disapprove," Georgia said as she hunkered down before the fire with a couple of cans, "but I brought wieners and beans."

"Suits me," Ben responded as cheerfully as he could.

It turned out she'd also brought—at Spaulding's insistence—hard rolls, cheese, apples, and a huge Cadbury's chocolate bar, which they shared with black coffee that Ben brewed in a small pot filled with melted snow.

Darkness enveloped them as they ate, reducing their circle of vision to the campfire, blotting out the world beyond and below. A slice of moon slid briefly from the clouds, casting a subtle radiance across the gathering snow.

Georgia caught his eye across the fire.

"In West Virginia it's industrial rigging that dominates almost every natural landmark. Only by stooping, concentrating on a fern or a bud, can you glimpse today what magnificent country it once was. I've seen lilies growing by a tailings pond, and eaten raw mushrooms from openings to abandoned mines—after I brushed the coal dust away. And there's no landscape so obscene as that of forlorn shacks perched beside a mountain of ore. At least that's not happening here."

"Don't mines make money?"

Georgia laughed bitterly. "Sure, and the owners truck it out."

"Like Arnold will do."

"No, Ben," she said with emotion. "There's a huge difference between what he's doing and digging the wealth from the earth, leaving it and its people scarred. Arnold's bringing a gigantic enterprise to an economically barren place."

"You really think the folks who live here will be better off?"

"Because of Arnold, money will flow into the area like a tidal wave."

"Sure, to his golf courses and condos and ski lodges. And of course, the roller coaster. How is that thing going to help the locals?"

Georgia rose. With her hands stuffed deep in her jacket pockets she cut a path through the snow to the edge of the cliff.

"I'm sorry," Ben muttered, coming up beside her.

"Don't be." She touched his cheek. "Don't ever be sorry for sharing your feelings with me. I know it isn't something you do easily. Besides, I can't get around it. You're right. This is not a place to possess. . . . Have you read *Alone* by Admiral Byrd?"

"No."

He took her by the elbow, drawing her to him. The fringes of her parka brushed his face as he leaned over and kissed her. A gust of wind rolled along the lip of the mountain, nudging her harder against him and chilling the exposed skin of their faces.

"Let's get out of the wind," he said and led her toward the tent.

Georgia helped shove the food supplies into their packs, and Ben hiked off to suspend them from a distant tree. He ran back across the tracked snow and hastily pulled off his ice-crusted boots before entering the tent. Inside smelled faintly of spices. As he shed his new jacket, Ben saw that their sleeping bags were zipped together and Georgia was holding open one side for him.

Teeth chattering, he slipped in beside her. Pale moonlight

filtered through the thin tent. Still trembling, he put his arms around her.

"Is it going to be too cold up here for you?" she asked.

"That's not caused by the cold. That's from being next to you."

They kissed again. When he thought his hand was warm enough not to startle her, he slipped it under the loose tail of her flannel shirt and touched her cautiously on the waist. She did not flinch. Instead, her wide eyes, almost lost in darkness, seemed to be studying him as he unbuttoned her shirt and bent to kiss her throat. Her hand stole tenderly into the springy brown hair of his head. The sleeping bag was becoming as cozy as a room with a cedar log fire. His heart racing, Ben slipped lower to nuzzle gently at her warm breasts.

"Let me get out of this shirt," she said after a moment, and shrugged it off. The jeans were not as easy. The two of them had to separate so she could wriggle out of them. Amusement was in her eyes as Ben thrashed about to get out of his own clothes. Afterward he rolled against her, feeling the smoothness of her stomach between them. She had the long flat muscles of an athlete, softened by gentle curves. He held her in his arms, but this time there was no trembling. They were amazingly snug and warm in the closed-up bags.

Ben's lips moved against her hair. "Thanks for asking me to come with you."

"Don't thank me. I just didn't want to climb alone."

When he tensed beside her she laughed. "Can't you tell yet when I'm teasing, Ben Hagen? I've been thinking about coming up here with you all week. It seemed like I was never going to get those damned drawings done—and if I'd let you in my room I probably wouldn't have."

His mouth sought the moist warmth of hers again as she snuggled against him. He began to caress her, his fingers moving gently across her breasts.

"Are you my buddy?" she asked softly.

"Sure am," he replied.

Her hands moved to the small of his back, inviting. He bent to her lips. Her mouth opened, languid, her teeth closing on him. When his heart stopped pounding and Ben knew he was in control of his own desire he rose carefully on top of her, balancing so that she would not be hurt. She put her lips to his neck as they came together. Ben moved upward until he felt himself brushing against her, and felt the heat and dampness. With a gentle push he was all the way inside her.

Her hands tightened on him. Ben felt like laughing with pleasure. "I think it's a fit." He was poised above her, weightless, motionless, savoring the deliciousness of physical passion delayed. She was the first to move, making tiny circles, holding him in her, relishing the sensations. With her knees and body she squeezed him, and the circles she was making became wider and the pressures greater. She was breathing harder now than when climbing the face.

Ben slipped back, just enough to lay his cheek against her breast and listen to the beating of her heart.

"Easy . . . easy," he said softly.

With a deep-throated laugh Georgia rolled him on his back, sleeping bags balling around them until she shoved them down with frantic impatience and straddled him like a horse soldier.

Leaning on one hand over his head, leering into his face, her other hand found and lifted him so that he slid back into her, to settle snug and tight.

She gazed deep in his eyes, looking for . . . what? he wondered. Was that apprehension he saw in hers?

With the rhythm and mounting speed of a merry-go-round she began moving on him. Ben shivered from the joy of it. As the minutes slipped away he again sensed a tension in her. She was trying to make something happen, working too hard at it.

"Georgia," he whispered.

She paused, on her knees, glistening with sweat, the tips of her breasts barely touching him.

"What?" She was panting from her exertions.

"You can't always be on lead." He slipped sideways to give her room. "Lie down."

His arm under her head was the only point of contact between them as they stretched out on their sides. Starting at the soft flesh under her jaw, he traced a delicate trail to her throat and shoulders, under her arms, and in the deep shadowed curves beneath her breasts. Along her ribs and to the rise of her hips he touched her soothingly. The gasping breath, the driving heartbeat slowly waned.

After a while she sank into a sleep so light, so transitory, he knew she wasn't even aware of it. Ben bent to her now cool body and with his mouth caressed one breast gently. Her eyes opened at once, and he felt the stiffening of muscles in her again. Lightly his hands eased across the planes and shadows and curves of her body. She relaxed, able at last to let come what would come at its own time. Their bodies nestled once more, and they moved tenderly together and apart.

Release was awakened in them as a morning glory greets the dawn, imperceptibly, opening delicately and subtly. Once the movement began, each moment carried it, gathering strength, building upon the preceding moment, stretching deliciously, exposing every delicate petal to the pulsating light.

Georgia's hands fluttered at Ben's waist. It washed over her first, but only barely. From where they were joined, tiny spasms swept over Ben like electrified water, tingling and drowning out all other senses.

FOURTEEN

Georgia left the tent first, intending to poke up the fire for breakfast. She didn't get that far.

"Ben, look!"

Tugging on jeans and boots, he struggled out.

The footprints were everywhere. Naked. Human. Crisscrossing their camp. The snowdrift on the side of the tent was heavily trampled. Ben saw in Georgia's eyes that she was remembering that he'd opened that flap for air in the middle of the night.

"We were watched," she gasped.

"Impossible," he said. "It was too dark."

"Who would spy on us? That's despicable."

Ben ducked back into the tent for his jacket.

"Maybe it was somebody's bad idea of a joke," he said when he reappeared. "Nobody goes hiking barefoot."

"Unless they're kooks."

Ben stooped to study the crusty indentations. "All the prints are the same size. Looks like we're dealing with only one kook anyway. Who knew we were camping up here?"

"Spaulding, maybe a couple on the kitchen staff. That's all, but I wasn't trying to keep it a secret." Georgia glanced down the slope toward the trees. "We'd better check our packs."

They found them as Ben had left them, hanging from a tree, but one flap was pulled askew. Georgia hurriedly began to untie the line.

"Give me a second," Ben said and followed the prints into the woods. They faded quickly in the thick undergrowth.

"There's no following him that way," Ben told her when he came back. Georgia was rummaging through their supplies. Her face was drawn tight with tension.

"Nothing's missing besides the empty bean cans." She sounded both relieved and puzzled.

"Strange damn things sure seem to happen on this mountain," Ben said. "I wonder what Dr. Hearst will make of this. Probably say it's Black Dutch."

Color rose to Georgia's cheeks. "This is one mystery I don't want you to discuss with Dr. Hearst, or anyone else for that matter." Her level tone told Ben she meant it.

Their attempts to follow the line of tracks winding around the tent were also futile. Footprints went off in tangents to both the cliff side and the rocky slope to the west. It took only a few minutes for them to dismantle the tent and fold it into one of the packs. All that was left of their camp was a circle of compressed snow, a few stumps of burned wood, and footprints. The sun was invisible in a still gray sky.

They walked down to the tree line and headed west, dropping below the crest to search the backside of the mountain. Tree-covered, rocky, and irregular, it was a landscape in which an army could hide. Far below, Ben spotted a rough circle cleared for a helicopter, and near it a faint indentation in the thin snow where a new ATV trail ran around the mountain's waist.

"You son of a bitch!" Georgia called to the wilderness, skimming a flat stone toward an iced outcropping and hitting it dead center. "Come out."

Ben forced a laugh. "If he's got an ounce of sense, he'll keep away from you. Come on. Let's go down."

They worked their way back to the place where they'd ascended the rock face. Their rigging was still in place.

After testing it, Georgia, now strangely quiet, slipped over the side. Ben followed closely and kept close as she retraced their route. She hesitated briefly where the handholds crossed and then proceeded without a word.

She still didn't speak when they reached the bald. As they retrieved their line Ben found himself in the unfamiliar position of wanting to break a silence. He needed to find a way to tell Georgia that their night on the mountain was too good to mess up this way. But the words didn't seem adequate, so he hiked down the mountain behind her with his mouth shut and his spirits falling.

When they walked through the lodge doors, they stopped short. The great room was redolent with the smell of evergreen and baking turkey. The huge spruce tree sparkled with lights, and from the dining room beyond the bear they heard a happy chatter.

"It's Christmas," Georgia gasped. "I forgot entirely."

"Me too," Ben said. "Merry Christmas."

She turned to him and smiled. "Merry Christmas, Ben. God, that smells good. Let's go see when Spaulding's gonna let us eat."

"He'll probably make us check in first," he teased.

At the archway to the dining room they hesitated once more. The small square tables had been pushed together to form a single long one that stretched nearly the length of the room. It was covered with white cloths and decorated with red bows and sprays of holly. A line was already forming at the buffet table.

"I count four forks by each plate." Ben whispered.

"We don't dare go in looking like this," Georgia whispered back.

"Come on," he urged, and they raced for the stairs.

Within ten minutes they were in line, last, but heartily welcomed by Spaulding just the same.

"Oh, I'm so glad you made it back for this," he said. "Those of us who stayed for the holidays—the lodge staff and the project people—we're all going to eat together. It was Dr. Hearst's idea, and he was very disappointed when I told him you might not be here."

Ben looked around. "Where is he?"

"Oh, he's in the kitchen. Making the dressing. Everyone's pitched in to help. I was even able to recruit Mr. Garrett to churn three gallons of peach ice cream. Can't you hear him singing back there?"

"What can we do?" Georgia asked. "We're kind of late."

"I'm better at washing dishes anyway," Ben said shyly.

Spaulding chuckled. "That will be delightful. You and

Georgia can clean up and I'll give the kitchen staff the rest of the day off."

The Christmas dinner, which started around two, lasted into the night. There were nearly fifty of them, forty or so in the families who staffed the lodge, and the rest workers like Ben and Georgia who hadn't gone home. After a round of toasts and Christmas wishes, there was some serious eating. When that finally began to taper off, more toasts were offered. Spaulding disappeared briefly and came back with a banjo in one hand and a large mouth harp in the other and handed them to two of the cooks. With a little coaxing they played carols while the others sang. Then everyone ate again and settled back for another hour of exchanging stories about past Christmases.

It was nearly ten by the time Georgia and Ben were through in the kitchen.

"You know, I haven't thought much about what happened on the mountain since we got back," she said as they wearily climbed the stairs to their rooms.

"It wasn't all bad," Ben said. "Remember that."

"Bad enough," she replied, adding when she saw his long face, "Well, you're right, some of it was quite nice." She took his arm. "I just realized the only thing wrong with this lodge. It doesn't have a sauna. Come on in. I guess a hot bath will do."

FIFTEEN

The trees on the mountains below seemed to soak up the night, creating a vast black void. No stars were visible in the overcast sky. The only light came from the instrument panel in the noisy cockpit as Ben circled to approach the mountain from the east. Beside him he could sense Hansen straining to see the lights of the airfield. When they popped into view through the mists, Hansen tapped the windshield with relief. This was their last trip of the day to pick up returning workers and supplies, and they were both glad it was over. The weather had been marginal all the way from Asheville.

Landing, the Douglas flashed by a corporate helicopter.

The lodge wasn't exactly bustling when Ben pushed inside, but Arnold's presence was evident. Several of the computers were manned, and Spaulding was busy behind the lodge desk. Ben headed for the stairs.

When he knocked, Georgia cracked the door only an inch.

"We back to that again?" he asked with a small one-sided smile.

"Arnold's returned."

"I know."

"He brought me some new data from his engineers. I've got a lot of work to do."

"All night?"

She sighed, and opened the door. "Come on in. But I'm not promising you a thing."

Ben washed up, took off his shoes, and lay down on the bed to wait for Georgia to finish at her computer. The next thing he knew it was morning, and Georgia was kicking sheets, blankets, and the spread into a pile at the foot.

"Let me see," she said, "I'm going to have two eggs over easy. Make that three. Lots of bacon. Apple juice and coffee and biscuits with marmalade. And maybe grits. Do you like grits? Come on, Ben. Wake up. I'm ravenous."

A weak morning light caught the deep colors in the room, maroon in the paneling, cherry in the bedstead, yellows and blues in the quilt. "Looks awfully early yet." He snuggled up close to her and breathed in the clean smell of her hair.

"It's past eight." She slapped him on the behind. "Come on."

Ben grumbled as Georgia began to peel off her pajamas. He got a brief glimpse of her bare bottom as she scooted into the bathroom. Very awake now, he hurried after her and found the door locked.

"Hey, Georgia. That's not fair. I need to get in there, too."

For answer she turned the water faucet on hard.

Ben stumbled to his own room.

It wasn't long before they met in the hall and, chatting, started down the stairs. Sounds of a loud commotion in the great room below caused them to hesitate.

"What in the . . ." Georgia's voice trailed off as Arnold, buttoning a shirt, burst from his sanctum.

Georgia and Ben hurried down. Workers, milling around after breakfast, parted to let Arnold through, and there in the vortex was Daisy's father shaking a fist in Garrett's face. "I told her she had no business camping out on that mountain with you!"

"I'll find her," Garrett said feebly. Red-eyed and stoop-shouldered, he was anything but the picture of a tough mercenary. His clothes were torn and dirty. His knife scabbard was empty.

"You'll find her? You were supposed to protect her!"

Arnold stepped between them. "Protect who?"

"Daisy," the waiter cried. "She's disappeared. I haven't seen her since yesterday. She went off with him to track the saboteur."

"You took a woman with you on a security patrol?" Arnold's diamond blue eyes were wide with amazement. A murmur ran through the room.

"Look out the window!" O'Sullivan pointed with a shaking hand. "It's foggy. Foggy as I've ever seen it."

"For God's sake," Garrett said nervously, "I tried to talk Daisy into coming to the lodge last night. I swear it. She wouldn't."

"I don't want to hear that!" Arnold boomed. "What happened?"

Garrett bristled, but then retreated. "Let me explain. While Daisy and I were making rounds last night she saw someone sneaking down the old wagon trail toward the construction camps. So we grabbed a couple of blankets and settled in a little hollow off the trail." He stopped, his face turning red.

"And?" Arnold prodded impatiently.

"She needed to slip into the bushes to ah, ah . . ." He stared at Daisy's angry father.

"We know why people slip into the bushes," Arnold rumbled. "Go on."

"When it seemed to be taking a long time I yelled out to her, but she didn't answer. I waited, thinking she might be teasing me . . . but after a few minutes she still didn't come, so I went after her. I looked all night. Hell, I even fell into a ravine."

"But you didn't find her," O'Sullivan shouted. "O Lord, what's happened to her?"

It was the first time Ben had seen anything resembling guilt or regret on Garrett's face. "I was sure she'd come up here," he mumbled.

Spaulding immediately sent the lodge staff scurrying through the halls looking for her.

Arnold signaled to Cal Lorthor. "Have your men search the woods. I want that girl found."

The grim-faced engineer stepped up beside Garrett. "Better show me the hollow."

A throng, including Ben and Georgia, followed as the two men made for the door. At the camp, a half mile below the lodge, Cal sent search teams out like ripples from a dropped pebble. All day the ravines rang with Daisy's name. At dusk the disappointed searchers drifted into the hollow for their second meal of sandwiches and coffee and, after the field kitchen was packed away, went back out in the gathering night fog with flashlights and lanterns.

As they moved farther and farther apart, the forlorn and lonely echo of Daisy's name took up a rhythm, became its own song.

Near midnight Ben and Georgia's turn came to tend the fire at the campsite. After throwing some deadwood on their lonely blaze the two of them settled on blankets and propped up a supply pack for a backrest.

Even with the fire, a damp cold settled on them, and the fog dragged itself through twigs and leaves with a thousand vague rattles. Except for the fire it was dark. The misty hollow in which they sat faced an almost impenetrable evergreen thicket, a blackness shrouded in mists.

"Why does a night wind always sound like it's stealing something from you?" Georgia whispered.

Ben slipped his hands inside his jacket to warm his numb fingers. "I don't know, but this cold's getting to me."

"We were better off searching than sitting."

"Wish we had a tent."

"What for?"

"What for? To keep warm."

"We'd make some watchmen, Ben, snoozing away in a tent."

"What are we watching for? Daisy's not hiding in the woods in this cold. It's my guess she got fed up with Garrett and cut out for town. She could have caught a ride on the highway easy enough."

"Why would she do that when the lodge is so close?"

"Daisy's not overly bright."

"That's cruel."

"She was hanging out with the great soldier of fortune, wasn't she?"

"That doesn't mean you can't show a little kindness."

Ben's reply was mumbled.

"What'd you say?"

"I said we've made such a big deal of her ditching Garrett that she's going to be embarrassed when she does turn up."

Georgia's tone softened. "You could be right."

From far away a lone voice called for Daisy.

The first sound of rustling in the bushes was so slight, Ben wasn't sure he'd heard it, but Georgia's stiffening back confirmed his own alarm.

He listened, straining to catch a sound other than the wind and the crackling of the fire. Yes, it was there, an ever-so-light pushing aside of brittle cedar limbs. Something was stealing through the dark undergrowth toward them.

Ben tried to keep his motions easy and relaxed against the charge of adrenaline coursing through him. His fingers dropped to the cold earth and searched for a rock. There was an ominous pop of a breaking stick. Georgia jumped. As she watched the dark thicket out of the corner of her eye she put her mouth to Ben's ear.

"There's somebody out there."

"I know."

"Maybe it's Daisy."

"A person who's lost doesn't sneak into camp," he replied in low tones. He touched Georgia's arm and pressed her backward from the fire toward a big hickory. "Move back—out of the light."

The kitchen pack clinked across a rock under him. Ben reached for it and, in deeper shadow, unfastened the flap and opened a mess kit. He pressed the flimsy aluminum knife into Georgia's hand. "Run for the lodge. If you're chased, run harder. If you're caught, use the knife—under the ribs."

"I'm not leaving you," she whispered. "Why don't we sit tight and see what happens? It might be a small animal."

"Listen to me," he said tensely. "Whatever's out there is trying to slip around behind us, and it isn't small."

"I'm not going."

"Then stay low. I'll take a look."

"Even better, let's stage a surprise of our own." Georgia rose to a crouch. "You go that way and I'll go this."

"Georgia . . . ," Ben protested, but she'd already started around the perimeter of the fire toward the thicket.

"Damn," he murmured, and scrambled up.

Stealthily they arced away from each other in the darkness. Brambles tugged at Ben's trousers, but he couldn't see or hear

[121]

anything. Minutes passed and with them his apprehension for Georgia grew. Hoping to scare the intruder away, or at least draw his attention, Ben called out. "Georgia—Georgia."

A strangely silent explosion filled his head, and hot blood spurted from his smashed face. Vaguely he was aware his knees were buckling, but he never remembered sinking to the ground.

SIXTEEN

A crowd milled around Lexington Arnold on the lawn of the lodge. He was nervous, every few seconds peering up into the morning sky. At last he pointed to a speck, and they all saw it.

Mac Powell landed the helicopter away from the crowd, and the sheriff eased out the door and ambled toward them.

"Well-l, there's no missin' the injured party here," Rice said. "Howdy, Ben. I hope you got an eye under all that gauze. Are ya really hurt that bad or did the fella who bandaged your head git a little carried away with himself?" He leaned closer. "Your nose 'pears a little more out of plumb, too."

Ben tried to smile as Arnold stepped forward. "Mr. Hagen suffered a deep cut over that eye. I see no reason for levity."

"Levity?" the sheriff repeated. "Well, if you don't see no reason for it, I guess it must be on its way out. Girl still gone?"

"We haven't found a trace of her."

"Then I reckon it's a good thing I brung Toby."

The sheriff raised a hand, and two uniformed deputies lifted out a cage holding a sleepy-eyed bloodhound and lugged it toward him.

"Is one hound and two old guys your idea of a search party?" Garrett asked gruffly.

Rice, his rough homeliness emphasized by a gray corduroy suit and gold tie, cocked his head to get a better measure of the big man. "The governor says I can have our National Guard boys up here on five minutes' notice—if it's called for. You're the one she slipped away from, ain't ya?"

Arnold was the one to respond. "I explained the situation to you on the phone. It is possible the young woman simply wandered off, but after the attack on Ben I thought it best to call. My men are getting uneasy and this is your county, after all."

"If you recognize that, what's this man doin' totin' a pistol?"

"Garrett's in charge of security. That's standard procedure for an enterprise of this magnitude."

"Didya know it's also standard procedure to get security guards deputized when they carry sidearms? Oh . . . that got by ya, did it?"

"I would think you'd be grateful a professional like Garrett's on the scene."

"If he's so professional why don't you keep your road gangs up here where he can watch 'em? That way I won't have my hands full with 'em rollin' in town ever' night lookin' for women and trouble. Come to think of it, some of your women workers come a-lookin', too."

Arnold's eyes were cold with rage. "I called for help to find Daisy O'Sullivan and chase down an intruder on my mountain. Are you ready to do your job or shall *I* call the governor?"

"I know you're a powerful man. You don't need to tell me that. You say jump and the fellows in Raleigh jump. In fact the legislature's passed so many tax exemptions for your fancy playground this county's already hurtin'. It 'pears you're a man who hates taxes with a passion."

"That's ludicrous. Once we're open, a single day's taxes will pay your salary for a decade—providing you stay in office."

The sheriff's long face twisted in a mocking smile. "I'll pass the word along to the folks who're paying my salary now that you're taking up the slack—soon as ya can."

Arnold pointed at the helicopter. "I paid for that thing to bring you up here to search for Daisy, didn't I? Are you going to do anything besides stand here and cry poor mouth?"

"I guess I've made my point. But I'm gonna let Toby sit here until I see what we're up against." Rice turned back to Ben. "I'm ready to look at the spot where you got hit, if you're up to it, son."

His head pounding, Ben started down through the woods, Georgia to one side and the sheriff on the other, his long legs almost mincing as he tried to match Ben's slow pace. They were followed by a tight-lipped Garrett, the deputies, and a number of curious workers, who kept bumping into each other during the slow-motion descent to the campsite. Mac Powell caught up with the group and listened with the others as Ben attempted to tell the sheriff how he was attacked.

Finally he looked to Georgia for help, and she finished the story. "When we heard the noise Ben wanted me to take off for the lodge, but I refused."

The sheriff nodded. "I could understand if you was scared."

"I wasn't scared. I didn't want to leave him alone."

"Oh." He winked at Ben. "Don't the boys ever go out in the woods up here without takin' their gals along?"

"Don't play simpleminded," Georgia said sharply. "I was searching for Daisy, too."

" 'Scuse me. Seems like I'd best let you tell this story in your own way."

Georgia fixed him with a hard look but went on. "When Ben called to me from the bushes, there was a thump, sort of a mushy sound, and a thrashing as if someone was running. But not another word from Ben. I couldn't push through to him so I circled back to the fire and went the other way. I was wandering in the thicket trying to find him, when I stopped cold."

The sheriff's gaze slid sideways. "Do I dare ask you why?"

Beside him Ben groaned. "Georgia, this is ridiculous."

"Better let her talk, son."

Ben's good eye glared at the sheriff.

"It was strange and eerie," Georgia said with defiance.

"What was?" the sheriff prompted.

"Howling."

"Howlin'?"

"That's what I said. A deep, singsong howling."

The sheriff's eyes crinkled in amusement. "Maybe it was the ghost of Vaughn Monroe."

Ben began to laugh, grimaced, and put his hand to his bandages.

"Sheriff," Georgia said, "you aren't nearly as funny as you think you are. And I can't say I appreciate your attitude much either, Ben."

"Sorry, miss. So after this howlin' scared you, did ya run for help?"

Georgia let it pass this time. "I went back to the campfire for a torch. A few minutes later I found Ben—covered with blood. He was so still. When I found a pulse I yelled, and Cal Lorthor and Garrett came."

The sheriff pulled out a small notebook and wrote in it. "Where's this Lorthor now?"

"Back looking for Daisy."

The thicket was visible in the distant hollow, a dark, ragged patch in a muddy slope. The campfire had dwindled to smoldering ashes.

Rice indicated the others should stay back while Ben and Georgia showed him where the attack occurred. A nod sent the deputies scouting around in the thicket. It was a brief search.

"The only thing the ground tells us," one said, returning, "is that a lot of people have been here in the last few hours."

"Guess we can't arrest 'em all." The sheriff strolled over to where Garrett was standing. "Ya didn't do a very creditable job of preservin' the crime scene."

"You try riding herd on dozens of searchers in the middle of the night," Garrett grumbled.

"Too bad ya didn't give me the chance. I would've done just that. Toby's the best hound in these parts, but I doubt even he can pick a trail through this mess."

Garrett sucked in air through his teeth. "You stand here jawing all you want. I'm gonna look for Daisy."

"Hold on." A long bony hand reached out. "First tell me why an old bear like you was foolin' around with that youngun' anyway."

Garrett's red eyes blazed. "I thought you were the sheriff, not the preacher."

"I am the sheriff and I'm askin' you a question. It's possible Daisy could have been wantin' to git away from you to take up with somebody closer to her own age. Or a singin' man like Miss Jones's howler."

Garrett opened his mouth, closed it, and then stalked away.

"Never mind him, sheriff," Georgia said. "You convinced

me. You are a comic. Too bad you're such a piss-poor one. You need to work on your act."

"Could be," he said, motioning for Ben to follow him down the slope.

When they were out of earshot Rice spoke behind his hand. "Could that woman have hit ya, son?"

"You mean Daisy?"

"No, not Daisy—her." His thumb indicated a pair of fierce dark eyes darting their way. "She seems to have a nasty enough temper."

Ben was beginning to wish he'd listened to the new lodge doctor and stayed in bed. "She was with me before it happened, remember?"

"You got any enemies at the project?"

"No."

Rice rubbed his chin thoughtfully. "You one of Daisy's friends? One of her close friends? I'll find out, you know."

"No, that was strictly Garrett's territory."

"Are you sure? Daisy's always liked you scrawny fellas."

The exposed half of Ben's face drew up in a scowl. "I'm sure. Ask anyone. Ask Powell. He'll tell you."

"Powell's already told me what he thinks. Now I guess I'd better get on back to the lodge and deal with her daddy."

They'd nearly retraced their steps to the campsite when a shout rang out. After a couple of minutes Cal Lorthor pushed his way through the underbrush. In his hand was a scuffed sneaker, deeply stained.

The sheriff took it.

His eyes raised to Cal's. "This 'pears to be blood."

"The shoe was found on the old trail to the valley—nearly covered by leaves," Cal said hoarsely. "Look inside."

Rice pulled the laces apart and there in indelible ink on the shoe's tongue a single word was scrawled.

Daisy.

The sheriff signaled to his deputies. "This thing's shapin' up to be ugly. Turn old Toby loose. I'm gonna radio for some more men."

SEVENTEEN

Ben knew after only a few yards that walking down to the campsite with the sheriff had been a mistake. His head hurt more with each uphill step. Everyone except Georgia quickly left him far behind. By the time they reached the lodge he was in no mood to argue with Georgia when she ordered him to bed. She went for the doctor, installed in the lodge after Christmas.

A shot took care of the pain. It also put Ben to sleep. When he awoke it was dark outside and Georgia was packing a suitcase on the couch.

"Did they find her?" he asked.

"Not yet," she answered. "Are you okay?"

"I'm fine," he said. But pain surged through his brain as he said it, and he willed himself back to sleep.

When he awoke again and looked over to the couch, Dr. Hearst was there, reading a book.

"Where's Georgia?" Ben asked in a scratchy voice.

Dr. Hearst peered over his silver glasses. "Gone to Denver."

"Does that mean they've found Daisy?"

"No . . . it doesn't mean that." Dr. Hearst closed his book. "How are you?"

"Better. What's going on, Dr. Hearst?"

"I've been here with you a long time, Ben, but I'll tell you what I know. The sheriff's got his hound and deputies searching along with Arnold's men, but they can't find a trace of that poor girl." He shook his head sadly. "Frankly, Ben, I have a premonition that something terrible has happened to her."

"Because of the bloody shoe?"

"Partly, perhaps."

"What about the sheriff? What does he think?"

"The sheriff is a cautious man. He still believes it's possible that Daisy was running away when she lost her shoe, but he won't speculate beyond that."

"I guess you know what I'm wondering."

"No, what?"

"If Black Dutch has been around."

"After Daisy? Oh, Ben, I hardly think that's possible."

"Why?"

"From everything I've been able to find he shuns human contact."

Ben rolled over on an elbow. "Is he . . . insane?"

The answer was slow in coming. "That's not a scientific word, Ben. What do you mean by it? Irrational? I think it's evident he can reason. To tell you the truth, I've never run into anything like this before. It's very difficult, Ben, when myths develop over decades, to separate truth from fantasy. But one thing I do know, the dweller on this mountain is maligned, whoever he is."

"How so?"

"I have been going over Spaulding's records and scrapbooks. There are letters, and in the early years a trickle of stories which appeared in the county weekly that tells of hunts and traps laid to kill him. More than one hound dog, found with a broken neck, had bits of flesh and dark hair caught in his teeth. But that isn't the worst. A number of mountaineers bragged of shooting him. And traces of blood seemed to verify their claims."

"What did he look like, this guy they were shooting at?"

"Ah, that's the question the myth has attempted to answer. No reliable report ever described his physical appearance, although it must be—unusual—for him to be labeled a monster. Perhaps he's disfigured. Glimpses from afar, like the Grandys', only add to the lore. And all those reports are dated. He's become more elusive. There have been no sightings of a black devil or monster up here for years. Now they hunt the shadow man, the precursor of bad times."

"Why would they hunt him, Dr. Hearst? I don't understand."

"How it started remains a mystery. The stigma of devil was laid on Black Dutch a long time ago. But remember, the harshness of life in these mountains can produce harsh and cruel men. Men with fierce, unfathomable loathings."

"I believe you," Ben said, swinging his feet off the bed. "I met one the other night." His head drooping, he waited for the dizziness to pass.

"How about some supper?" Dr. Hearst suggested.

"Supper? What happened to breakfast, and lunch?"

Dr. Hearst smiled kindly. "You've been sleeping all day."

"I think the doctor gave me a Mickey," Ben groaned, testing his one unbandaged eye on Dr. Hearst. Slowly he came into focus.

"Not today, he hasn't. To my surprise he hasn't even been around, although a maid peeked in a while ago inquiring about the health of *both* of us." The small professor started for the door. "I'll get you a tray."

"A tray? No, wait, I'll get cleaned up and we'll go downstairs."

"Are you sure?"

"Yeah. I can't eat in bed."

At the foot of the stairs they could see the dining room was nearly empty.

"That's strange," Dr. Hearst mused, checking his watch.

Inside, Spaulding was pouring tea into glasses.

"Oh, Ben, Dr. Hearst. Are you all right? Not nauseous, I mean?" he amended, looking at Ben's bandages.

"What's wrong?" Dr. Hearst asked. "Where is everybody?"

"You don't know? It's horrible! Mr. Arnold and at least a quarter of the workers are sick." He paled. "I've thrown out all the food prepared in the last three days."

"You mean it was food poisoning?"

"The doctor doesn't know. He wanted to send Arnold and three others to the hospital this morning, but Hansen's ill and can't fly either."

"How about Garrett, or Powell?" Ben asked.

"They're both sick, too. The doctor's ordered an air ambulance from Asheville for Arnold. This is awful. A disaster. I don't know what I'm going to do if it's my fault."

He motioned to the table. "I'm afraid all we have is cheese, preserves, bread, and pears."

"That's okay," Ben said. "We'll make do."

While they ate, a few others drifted in, tentatively checking out the food.

"Tastes fine," Ben reassured them.

The new doctor, tension on his thin, dark face, appeared at the door. "Spaulding," he called, "I just got off the phone with the town doctor. He's having a hell of a time with this, too. But he thinks he knows what caused the trouble."

"What?" Spaulding asked anxiously.

"Moonshine."

"Moonshine!"

"That's right. A bad batch of home-brew. He's sending some off to the state lab for analysis. I've told Arnold and contacted the hospital to send a couple of nurses on the helicopter to help me up here. They'll need a room."

"I'll have one ready." The innkeeper, smiling nervously with relief, hurried out.

"Since Ben is better," Dr. Hearst said, "permit me to offer my services to these other poor souls."

"I could sure use you," the doctor replied. "I'm setting up a ward on each floor. You can monitor one for me."

By midnight groans were audible throughout the lodge. Unable to sleep, Ben wandered downstairs. The door to the new dispensary, around the corner from Arnold's office, was open, and Ben could hear the doctor on the telephone.

"Antifreeze. How in the hell did that get in the whiskey? . . . Well, it's criminal. We might lose two of the men I sent to Asheville . . . The word I get is he's coming around. Arnold has the constitution of a billy goat . . . I want the sheriff to find that still and . . . He does? . . . On the river? . . . My God, Arnold's going to be furious. If I were the sheriff I'd tear that thing apart and get those men in jail quick . . . Right . . . Well, somebody did it . . . Okay. Thanks for calling."

Ben knocked on the door frame. The harried doctor looked up. "Oh, it's you. Your head still hurting?"

"Not much. I was wondering if I could help."

"Go back to bed, Hagen. A concussion is serious business."

"I'm okay. How's everyone else?"

"Holding on, here anyway. The report on the men I sent to Asheville with Arnold isn't good. And there's a worker in the valley in a coma."

"I gather somebody spiked the local liquor supply with antifreeze?"

The doctor nodded grimly. "Can you imagine?"

"How bad is it?"

"Bad enough. Some of these people may die. Everybody's scared. Thirteen men quit today, and more will leave as soon as they're able. Arnold can't decide if someone was trying to ruin him, or kill him, or both. He's coming back tomorrow, if he can, to stem the exodus."

"*He* was drinking *moonshine!*"

"Afraid so. Hard to picture, isn't it? Apparently he was given a jug of the brew the searchers brought in."

A moan came from the back room, and the young doctor wearily got to his feet. "Go back to bed, Ben. That's an order. I'll be up to see you tomorrow and change that bandage."

"Don't bother about me, Doc."

"I'll be there," he said. "If the men don't pull out of this by morning they're not going to need me. They'll need an undertaker."

The rest of the night passed restlessly for Ben. He spent more time peering out the window than in bed. It was still very unsettling to know that someone lay in wait in the underbrush for the chance to scramble his brains. If the blow had been a half an inch lower he could have lost an eye and been permanently grounded. But as hard as Ben tried he couldn't come up with a reason why anyone would pound on him. It had to be one more random attack on Arnold's project. And despite what Dr. Hearst said earlier, anger was growing in him against Black Dutch.

At dawn he wandered down to the kitchen, had coffee with Spaulding, and volunteered to help with breakfast. Oatmeal and toast were served to the few who could eat. Although no one had died during the night, the lodge was a dismal place.

After the kitchen was clean Ben ventured out on the porch. It was cold but clear and unusually quiet. The road machines were idle. There were no sounds of construction. Without a doubt, when Arnold was released from the hospital he'd be returning to a crippled project.

EIGHTEEN

Firmly, persistently, the thumping continued. Ben, burrowing deeper in the covers, tried to ignore it, but the steady beat went on. Uncovering the top of his head, he looked toward the window. There was no hint of light. The soft glow of his watch told him it was only minutes past five o'clock. The tap came harder. Grumbling, Ben crossed the cold floor to the door.

Georgia stood there, straight as a wooden soldier, one boot lifted, ready to kick again. She was holding a tray with covered plates and a steaming carafe.

"You're knobby-kneed but kind of cute in your BVDs." She swept by him. "Hope you like lots of sugar in your coffee."

He recovered enough to close the door. She smiled broadly at his spiky hair and the dopey expression in his unbandaged eye.

"How's your head?" she asked.

"Fine. How was Denver?"

"The same. But I couldn't wait to get back. It was all over the TV about the poisoning. Have any more died?"

"No, just the one from town who was in the coma. How'd you get back?"

"I got a hop to Larkspur last night, and Powell brought me the rest of the way. He was coming up with supplies for the few guys still looking for Daisy. Arnold's pulled out of the search, hasn't he?"

"He had to, or close down the job. A lot of men still aren't well. A bunch of others quit. Cal's off recruiting now—for more security guards as well as workers."

"Yeah, I talked to Garrett last night. He doesn't know what

to do. He wants to search for Daisy, and Arnold wants him to find out who poisoned that still." Georgia slipped her tray onto the table. "Go dab some water on your face while I set up breakfast."

"When are you gonna tell me why you're up so early?" he asked over his shoulder.

"I wanted to see you before I take off on one of the ATVs."

"Where to?"

"The back side of the mountain. To look for Daisy."

"Why there?" he called from the bathroom. "She disappeared down below."

"That's what Garrett said when I told him last night I was going to have a look. But I've got a hunch, Ben. Nobody's found any other trace of her on the lower slopes. Well, charts show old mining trails run from the back of the mountain on through the gap toward Gatlinburg. We might find something. If not her, at least evidence she went that way."

Ben peeked over a towel as he emerged from the bathroom. A small bandage now capped his injured eye, swollen and circled with a deep bruise, slowly turning yellow. "I'm going with you. The doctor may not want to certify me yet for flying, but I can sure ride one of those things."

Georgia smiled. "What a surprise. Here's your coffee."

The sun was barely up when she led the way down the hall, stopping by her room for packs and a length of line, which she wrapped around one shoulder. When they burst outside Georgia inhaled deeply.

"God, I've missed this clean, cold air."

"Don't those Rockies you keep bragging about have clean, cold air?" Ben asked, keeping to himself just how glad he was to be outdoors, too.

"Denver's not in the Rockies," she responded in rhythm to her feet pounding the trail. "Only in their shadow. On a cloudy winter day we not only smell the pollution, we taste it."

Two ATVs were parked at the edge of the airstrip. Ben mounted one, hit the switches, and felt his usual satisfaction when a machine roars to life. Beside him, Georgia fired up hers.

In the growing light they moved briskly past the planes

and veered off to the northwest, cutting through mists and mountain laurel. Dark slush spat from under the wheels, coating the nearest trees. Beyond the shoulder of the mountain they plunged into shade where the long western slopes bristled with hickory and ash.

Georgia cut turns tightly, roaring at dead-out speed whenever possible. Her knees tight into the ATV's body, she hunched forward, her hair fluttering darkly from beneath a yellow helmet. There was a flash of white teeth as she glanced back to check on Ben. At a spot so narrow that he couldn't get around her, she slowed. Leaving the engine idling she came back, helmet in hand, the bottom of her face gray with grime.

"Did you stop because some blur in the bushes back there might have been Daisy?" he asked.

She laughed. "Okay, I'll ease up. How are you doing?"

"Okay."

She leaned forward and kissed him. The lower edge of his visor pressed into her cheek, but she was undeterred. It was lingering and surprisingly delicate coming from someone who'd been driving like a daredevil.

"I've been thinking about getting under that visor of yours for some time," she said, then walked back to her ATV, straddled it, and roared away.

When the woods thinned, Georgia set course up a small ridge covered with wood sorrel. A trail halfway up the slope struck due south along a suggestion of a shelf. After a mile or so Ben could make out high above them the triangular crag where he and Georgia had spent the night. The trail bent abruptly, running beside a deep chasm, cut by water runoff. Without warning Georgia stopped.

Ben swerved toward the edge to keep from plowing into her.

"Hey," he complained, "how about a signal."

She stood on the machine and pointed. "I think I saw someone way up there on the other side of the ravine."

In the vastness of the forest her voice was like a chime. "Daisy . . . Oh, Daisy!"

There was no answer. Georgia craned her head to trace the rim of the mountain. "We ought to cross this gorge and climb on up there."

Ben surveyed the ravine, a near vertical slope falling off into a dense stand of snow-dusted spruce. Georgia gauged it, too, and slung one of her climbing ropes over her shoulder.

"Daisy didn't go down there," he tried.

"Don't come if you don't feel up to it, but I'm sure I saw somebody. And that's the closest way."

Grabbing a sapling for support, she started over the side of the dark ravine. Ben went after her, moving from tree to tree, jarring his head at every sudden bracing. Briars snagged his trouser legs all the way down. When the slant finally eased, he followed Georgia onto a ledge beside a narrow chute of churning water. The evergreens looming around them limited their visibility to a blue vault of sky. The smell of damp earth was strong. Georgia rock-hopped until she stood over the ruins of an enormous fir angled across the stream below. On the far side sunlight reflected off icy rocks, cracked by the roots of a forest rising at least two thousand feet.

"I'll see if we can use this as a bridge," Georgia said. Ben watched as she lowered herself over the ledge and maneuvered across. Then he made his own way down and negotiated the trunk in a few steps. By grabbing roots they pulled themselves up the steep, slippery bank. Georgia hurried northward along the edge of the ravine to the spot where she'd thought she'd seen someone. There, rock slabs lifted in an angled plane.

"Dai—sy . . . Dai—sy." Only her own voice echoed.

Ben, trailing, found himself staring at a platter-sized crust of snow caught in a hollow twenty feet below. He called Georgia back.

"Footprints," he announced and slid down to them.

Georgia clutched her jacket as though she were suddenly cold. "Are they—"

"—like the ones at our campsite?" Ben finished for her. "Could be."

He worked his way to the end of the lower shelf, opposite the twin yellow ATVs parked on the other side of the ravine.

"No more down here. Tell me again what you saw." His voice had a hollow quality, bouncing off the ravine's walls.

Georgia leaned over the narrow ledge to keep him in sight. "I don't know. It was hardly more than a stirring in the bushes, a big blur."

Ben scanned the horizon. "My guess is whoever it was sprinted ahead of us just far enough to feel safe. He could be nearby. Watching us."

Georgia cupped her mouth. "You're full of good news. If I see him do I wave or shoot him a bird?"

"Your choice," Ben shouted, taking a long step sideways to a stone column. Georgia was a lonely figure at the edge of the ravine.

To get a better view of the little canyon, he slid down the column along the ravine's ancient side. His new jacket scraped on stone as he picked up speed. Realizing it was steeper than he'd thought, Ben reached out to slow his momentum, but there was nothing to grab. All he could do was pedal his feet fast enough to keep up with the rest of his body until he reached the bottom of the column.

"Ben?" Georgia's voice was distant.

He scurried from under the edge of the gnarled stone and waved.

"You need a rope?" Her words bounced between them.

"It would help," he admitted.

"Hold on." She stepped back to uncoil it.

When she disappeared from view Ben felt unbidden stirrings of fear. Georgia was alone, and in a very vulnerable position. He scrutinized the ragged evergreens above, searching for a route. Before he found one she was back.

"Ready?"

"Sure. Hurry, will you?"

She looped an end around herself and a tree, and tossed the other over the lip. It landed lightly at Ben's feet.

Ben quickly tested his weight and stepped into the broken column. Loose rock scattered noisily, but it was silent above and he knew Georgia was waiting patiently. Hand over hand, leaning out, he walked straight up the steep shoulder. When his head pushed past the last obstruction, there was Georgia, pulling away from the tree, one leg straight into the point of support and the other crooked into a brace. The closeness of her, the cocky assurance of her stance, delighted him.

Then he saw that she was not alone.

Behind and above her, his head and shoulders visible, loomed a head grotesque beyond Ben's imagination.

Ben propelled himself upward. "Georgia! Jump! Jump!"

She tensed with alarm but held to the rope.

"Jump!" he screamed again, and instantly knew she was too disciplined a climber to leave her belay with him on a line.

His hands grabbed at nonexistent holds on the rock.

"I'm off!"

With that she plunged feet first down the rocky incline in a controlled fall while Ben's hands tore at the stone for purchase but failed to find it. He dropped backward in a hail of small stones. With his arms and legs out like windmill spokes, he landed at the base of the column on his shoulders and hands, tumbling out of control. His head cracked against a rock before the bruising spin ended against a pine tree.

Up the slope Georgia saw him land and scrambled down.

"For God's sake, Ben, what was it?"

"A wild man . . . with spidery white hair all over his head." He tried to sit up. "Is he still there?"

Georgia peered up the slope. "I don't see anything."

He strained to see for himself.

"Take it easy, Ben. There's nothing there."

She cradled his head in her hands. The bandage was dangling on the side of his face that had been injured before. Georgia gently touched the dark hollow of his eye, caked with gravel and earth. Blood oozed from the stitched seam over it.

Ben painfully rolled from his back to his knees. The bandage swung like a pendulum. He snatched it off in exasperation and craned his neck to stare up once more. The promontory was bare.

Shotgun eyes searched his battered face. "I felt him. I knew something was there, but I didn't dare move."

Her face was so close Ben could see every line and smudge. The concern in her eyes touched him. Georgia settled back, her knees bent, her rump resting on her tennis shoes. Except for a long scratch across her left cheek and ear, she was unhurt.

Ben couldn't keep his eyes away from the still-empty skyline. "I never saw a face like that."

"Scary?"

"I was scared because he was standing right behind you. But with all that hair he was more strange than anything else. It wasn't only on his head, it was all over his face!"

"You mean he had a beard?"

"Yeah, he did, but I think it was growing on his forehead and under his eyes, too, streaming in the wind like ribbons on a battle flag. It's hard to say. The sun was coming up over his shoulder, half blinding me."

"You make him sound like Medusa, or Moses."

"That's what I saw," Ben said. "My God, I just realized! He was wearing my father's leather jacket!"

NINETEEN

Georgia gently wiped a handful of snow across the grime and blood on his brow, folded her silk scarf into a temporary bandage, and tied it over his eye like a pirate's patch. Carefully they climbed out of the ravine and made their way back to the ATVs. Georgia's radio was squawking as they approached, an unnatural sound in what had become for them an unnatural place.

Before Georgia could do more than announce her presence on the line, Hansen's voice came through. "You guys get on back, right away."

"We're looking for Daisy."

"She didn't go that way."

"She's back?" Relief lifted Georgia's voice.

"No. They found her other shoe farther down the mountain near the trail to town."

"Her other shoe?"

"Roger, as bloody as the first one. The governor's got a National Guard unit on standby in case the sheriff wants them. Also, Arnold sent someone up here looking for you, Georgia."

She jammed the radio into its case.

"Take my advice, Ben. Don't let any more women in your room before dawn. Come on. Let's get back."

Georgia stopped by the lodge to talk to Arnold, but Ben went straight to join the reinvigorated search for Daisy. By nightfall it was over.

"No use fightin' this fog," the sheriff said. "I'm thinkin' the second shoe's an old clue anyway. It just took us a long time to be a-findin' it. We've covered the ground down here every which way we can. She's either long gone . . . or we won't find her till spring."

Looking at Ben he added, "Your face isn't improving any as the day goes on. You better git somebody to treat it before you scare someone yourself."

Ben made for the lodge to do just that.

"Read the smallest line you can," the doctor said after cleaning the wound.

Ben rattled off the letters.

"Now the other eye. Backward."

While Ben's examination took place, Georgia stood by the examining table and Spaulding leaned against the doorjamb, his eyes on the great room, the stairs, and the front entrance.

"You've got the eyesight of an owl," the doctor pronounced in mock disgust. "If that chart had a union label on the bottom I suspect you could read it from here better than I could with a magnifying glass."

"He's okay, then?" Georgia asked.

"No new damage to speak of. The hypodermic and salve will take care of any infection. A few cuts are not medically significant."

"Especially on a face like that." Georgia's foot sneaked over to touch Ben in the leg with her toe.

"When can I fly?" Ben asked.

The doctor pressed a fresh bandage on his face. "If Mr. Arnold tells me he needs you to fly, I'll consider it."

Spaulding straightened at his sentinel post at the doorway.

"He may be coming to do just that . . . Good evening, Mr. Arnold."

The doctor glanced up as the entrepreneur stepped into the room. He was wearing a down jacket.

"He's seeing straight? Thinking straight?" Arnold's deep, gravelly voice filled the small space.

"Ben's face will heal and his mind doesn't have to," the doctor replied.

"Ah! That's great. Ben, how about you and I take a walk together." It was not said like a question.

Spaulding's brows rose like startled crows. "You're going out in this fog? You're barely out of bed yourself, sir."

[144]

Arnold glowered at him. "If Ben's up to it I can't imagine what objection you might have, Mr. Spaulding."

"No objections, sir. But I must warn you to be careful. Things seem to—"

"Spaulding, things are difficult enough around here without your spooking everybody. Why don't you tend to the lodge and let me worry about everything else. Ready, Ben?"

"Let me get a jacket," he said and slid off the examining table.

They met at the lodge's front door and went outside. The fog was almost as white as the snow that covered the ground.

"A turn-and-bank indicator might help keep us on our feet, eh, Ben?" Arnold observed as they climbed up the path to the airstrip.

"An artificial horizon would be better, Mr. Arnold. And runway lights."

"Call me Lex. Goddamn, it's a mother of a fog. Wait a second."

He vanished back into the mist, his boots clumping on the lodge steps.

"Garrett!" he yelled at the door. "Call the airfield and have the runway lights turned on."

With only an occasional stumble they reached the first light, its incandescence blurry in the fog. Arnold disappeared as though passing through a wall when Ben hesitated to search out the faint line of lights.

"You keeping up?" Arnold called back.

"Right behind you."

It seemed a peculiar idea to be dragged out in the cold damp for an idle ramble. Arnold's hands were behind his back as he followed the half-buried cable that ran from the diesel generator. Ben found himself thinking of his father's story of a bombing raid he flew over Germany in fog. Only a deeply sensed tingling in his spine had caused him to pull up abruptly, barely missing the turret of a castle.

Another white light floated into view.

Arnold held his hand above it, savoring the heat. "They look so cool. The engineers are having a lot of difficulty making the globes for my tree glow softly like I want but bright enough to be seen for miles."

Ben said nothing.

They passed another light, this one beside a rock ledge that rose near the runway like a bantam rooster's spur. Through an aberration in the shifting mists, the odd outline of the makeshift fuel wagon, sitting atop the mound on automobile tires, came into view.

"What in the hell's that thing?" Arnold rumbled. The tank looked like a movie locomotive about to take a plunge over a cliff.

"Hansen ran that up there for pressure," Ben said. "It takes a lot to lift fuel to the C-47."

"Hope he anchored it well."

"With chocks, I'm sure."

"Tomorrow I'll have Cal stand it in concrete. Wouldn't want the vibration of one of your takeoffs to bring it down." The drift of the fog closed off the view of the wagon. Arnold shook his head. "No goddamn wonder these hill people believe in ghosts. The Flying Dutchman and the Lost Squadron could pass within twenty feet of us and we'd never see a thing."

Walking once more in a northerly direction, he gestured Ben to his side. "I've watched you. You're too damned independent for your own good. Take it from one who knows."

It was a preamble of some kind, Ben realized.

"Ex-military, both of us. I think that's the way it's supposed to be for men. The military part's important. Gives a man a way to measure himself. You in the Rangers, me the Marines. Different eras. Same ideas. The 'ex' part's important, too. Get in, get out, and don't march in any parades you don't have to."

Ben's spine was stiffening. Of all the conversations in the world, he hated military bravado most.

Another white light flared ahead. Arnold was tracking the cable well. Suddenly he turned sharply to face Ben. "Tell me about the trespasser."

"Trespasser?"

"On the mountain. Georgia told me how you screwed your face up again. Don't fuck around with me, Ben. We speak the same language."

"A man older than you. With whiskers and hair floating on the wind. All I saw was his head."

"One ex-grunt to another—he's no devil, right?"

"Right."

"A round between the eyes would have ended his wanderings forever?"

"He didn't do anything but look over the edge of a rock."

"On my mountain."

"Maybe he doesn't know it's your mountain. Maybe it wasn't even Black Dutch. He certainly wasn't black, skin or hair."

They were now at the tie-down area. The cable ran off to the right instead of continuing straight.

"Which way's your plane?" Arnold asked.

Ben took a guess at the angle to the Douglas and pointed. Soon he spotted the landing light on its left wing. A couple of steps to the side and he saw the plane's nose rear aristocratically into the fog.

"Why don't we climb in?" Arnold said. "I flew all over the South Pacific in a C-47."

"Maybe this one," Ben said, unlocking the hatch. The floor rang hollowly as they climbed toward the cockpit. Ben dropped sideways into the left-hand seat. Arnold sat opposite. His hand caressed the copilot's controls.

"A young man's dreams are best. You've got yours here, don't you?"

Ben glanced around the cabin, at the cheap radios, the second-hand gyroscopic compass, the crack in the instrument panel, the blue-and-yellow discoloration where a sandwich of glass was separating on a side window.

"The bank owns more of it than I do."

"That's a bank for you. Always has a piece of what it can't use." Arnold fidgeted with the wheel. "How'd you like to pay this off? Clean up your bills? Not have to haul another parachuter?"

Ben just looked at him.

"When I got hold of you twenty jumpers were kicking the daylights out of the interior of your airplane every weekend. Right?"

Despite himself Ben thought about the prospect Arnold was dangling. A paid-off C-47 would be quite a change. He'd been paying late penalties on notes all his life.

"I take it my suggestion has appeal."

"What do you want from me?"

"I want more of whatever won the trust of that old hill woman, Mrs.—whoever she was."

"Mrs. Grandy."

"Yes, and those people who came to bury her. Dr. Hearst tells me you have a bond with these people that I won't be able to duplicate by spending five hundred million dollars up here and giving them all jobs."

"Jobs helping New Yorkers into cable cars may not fit in with their way of life."

"Bah, Ben. You sound like a TVA hater from the thirties. We're on the way to an economic revolution here."

"These people aren't."

Annoyed, Arnold sat back. "Sure they are. Just like you. You're getting the going rate for hauling cargo up here."

"That's right."

"But I suppose you can see that the roadwork is moving rapidly up to the lodge."

"Yes, I can."

"And that soon your airplane, and you, will no longer be required. Your days up here could be short."

Ben stared out at the fog. "When the job's over, it's over."

"You do this other, and I'll keep you here . . . you and your airplane . . . same rates."

Ben shifted in his seat and faced Arnold. "What's the job?"

"Easy enough. Help neutralize Black Dutch for me, and get the townspeople to accept it."

"Neutralize?"

"Locate is enough, actually. Trace him from where you saw him today. Garrett can do the neutralizing."

"You mean I don't have to shoot him?"

Arnold shook his head. "Oh, no, no. Nothing so violent. I only want him off the mountain. He needs care. He'll be taken to a hospital. Dr. Hearst has finally convinced me that Black Dutch is a personality to be dealt with—and carefully. These mountain people put a great deal of superstitious stock in him.

"Your real challenge is with them. I want the vandalism and sabotage stopped. Some son of a bitch nearly killed me with poison. Whoever did that belongs in prison. But I want the people who live in these mountains to understand that the changes here will benefit them. That's your main job, soothe them, gain their support for what I'm trying to do."

"Sounds like you need a PR man," Ben said. "I'm a pilot."

"What I'm offering you is a chance to keep flying."

"I appreciate that, but you have an exaggerated idea of my relationship to the people here."

"Then you'll do it?" There was a ring of triumph in Arnold's voice. "This'll be the making of you, Ben. I might even find you a bit of stock in the corporation if things turn out well."

"Don't bother to sweeten the pot, Mr. Arnold. Whatever small trust they have in me is based entirely on my honoring Mrs. Grandy's deathbed wish, and I'm not going to betray that for money. Even if I have to leave here tomorrow."

"You're making a big mistake. Think about it."

Ben stood abruptly and started down the slope of the C-47 toward the door. Arnold, after recovering from his surprise, followed him out of the plane. Ben levered the door closed, and relocked it.

The runway markers danced in the mist and dark like St. Elmo's fire. Arnold searched the ground for the cable.

"To your right," Ben said.

Arnold's attitude soured as he trudged in front of Ben. "I don't understand how you can twist a forthright, perfectly legal arrangement into a 'betrayal,' as you call it. You're some businessman."

"I do okay flying. I'm not taking 'bounty' money."

The smell of fuel was in Ben's head. He slowed. From somewhere in the distance, echoing between the hills, he heard tapping—a familiar sound, but he couldn't quite place it. Arnold hurried on, eyes fixed on the cable. Then, off to the left, a lurid orange light flickered briefly through a thinning of the fog and then vanished. Ben's sense of smell, developed by years of exposure to airports, told him with sudden alarm that it was not lingering diesel fumes from the power generator he was breathing.

It was gasoline. And the tapping, louder and more urgent, was coming from the fuel wagon above the path where Arnold was walking.

Ben broke into a blind, stumbling run.

"Arnold!" he yelled. "Arnold. Stop."

The tapping became thundering hammer strokes. A great creaking rent the air, and an enormous orange fireball blossomed high overhead. With a powerful swoosh the whirlwind sucked the fog into it as fire roared out of the top of the fuel wagon.

Lexington Arnold froze. The wagon lurched forward toward the brink of the hill. Gasoline jostled from the open port and fell in a cascade of sizzling fire down the rock. Ben darted toward Arnold and the rain of golden flames that quivered like a great snake. The entrepreneur was paralyzed, staring up at the flames.

With a strength that he didn't know he possessed, Ben dove, grabbed Arnold around his bulky waist, and slung him bodily down the slope at the edge of the runway. Arnold screamed as he and Ben tumbled through brush and pines and flying snow.

Like a seesaw with too much weight at one end, the wagon nosed over toward the vacated path. With a last wrenching shriek of metal its front wheels came down hard on a boulder, throwing the back of the wagon into the air. As it made a slow cartwheel a loud explosion ripped the metal and wood into red-hot fragments, igniting the pine-tree crowns and showering molten pieces like shrapnel.

A poisonous smell was followed by the choking presence of half-burned fuel raging in black, evil, rolling clouds. Heat pounded against flesh like a fist in a white-hot gauntlet. Ben took the back of Arnold's head and shoved his face in a muddy pocket of the hillside, next to his own.

The woods to the north of them were a raging furnace. The base of the fire crept toward the runway's edge. Ben knew if the inferno came down the slope they'd be consumed and it would destroy the lodge and everyone there.

But the wind, as well as the tilt of the land, was against it. After minutes that seemed a lifetime the air began to lose the headiness of gasoline saturation. The canopy above them was gone, burned to falling cinders. Shouts could now be heard from the direction of the lodge.

"We're gonna make it," Ben yelled above the roar of the fire.

Arnold lifted his forehead from the mud and sucked in hot air. "It's just as well you didn't . . . go for the money," he said, coughing. "You'd never have collected." He got to his feet. "I'm gonna turn Garrett loose on that son of a bitch Black Dutch."

TWENTY

Below the airstrip flames leaped from a storage shed filled with lumber and paint. A battery of faces stared at it, the sweat on their foreheads mirroring the flames. Ben raced around the roaring fire to reach a water tap on the building's far side. He discovered it was blocked by a Bobcat trench digger sprawled beetlelike and leaning onto the shed. Through the black smoke Ben saw that the machine's fuel tank was blistered and cracking.

"Get back, for God's sake," Ben shouted to the workers.

They took off as the shed's roof collapsed and a column of sparks shot from the golden-hot core. The Bobcat exploded with a boom and the shock wave knocked Ben off his feet. A yellow-and-black ball of fire blossomed in the sky, casting flickers of light onto the pungent black cloud from the earlier wagon fire. The stench of burned wood, paint, rubber, and fuel filled Ben's lungs as he crawled along the ground. At last the scorching heat eased enough for him to stand and make his way to the line of workers digging a trench around the perimeter of the inferno. He found a place between Dr. Hearst and Daisy's father, who stabbed at the earth with fury.

"Blood and fire!" the waiter cried. "This mountain's cursed and my Daisy's paying the price."

"Nonsense," Dr. Hearst rebuked him. "There's no curse here. This mountain is a place of beauty."

"Beauty? You hear him, Ben Hagen? He's calling this place beautiful. Look about you, man. Is this beauty or the furnaces of hell?"

"What's happened here is the work of man, Mr. O'Sullivan, and will be explained in due time."

"God protect us, it's the work of Black Dutch, I tell you. In my heart I've known that depraved devil took my Daisy when she was but a little girl, and now he's come back for her. He wants to drive us all off this mountain."

"You can't blame these things on Black Dutch," Dr. Hearst insisted. "Are you forgetting when your daughter wandered off all those years ago she was returned home safely?"

"I'm not forgetting anything, including Daisy's two bloody shoes." He threw down his shovel and stalked away.

"I wish I knew how to help him, Ben," Dr. Hearst said as he strained at his shovel, slinging dirt at the burning ground cover.

"Give him some good news about Daisy," a tense voice suggested.

Both men swung around as Georgia picked up the discarded shovel. "Arnold's in a rage," she said. Her eyes shifted from the approaching fire to Ben. "You think someone was really trying to kill him?"

"I do."

"He said you were almost killed yourself." She poked at the frozen ground. "This job's not much fun anymore, is it?"

A blast of heat pounded them as more paint cans in the shed exploded. They covered their eyes and ducked. When the popping ended, they resumed digging the dirt barrier. At last the fire dwindled and was no longer moving in their direction. In the damp forest it metamorphosed from scorching flame to poisonous smoke, and the last of the gasoline was reduced to guttering pools.

With rifle, light, and night scope in hand, Garrett appeared on the slope. "Listen to me, people," he shouted, his green eyes sparkling in the glittering flames. "Once the fire is out I want you inside—and don't come out alone at night anymore. Not until I've got this guy in chains—or in my sights."

There were shouts of encouragement as he disappeared into the night mist.

"He's strutting like Mars Awakened," Georgia observed.

Dr. Hearst paused to wipe perspiration from his eyes. "Blaming this on Black Dutch is a terrible wrong. Remember what Mrs. Grandy said, the dweller on this mountain may be beyond the ordinary but he's not evil."

"This fire looks evil enough," Georgia said.

"That, it does," Dr. Hearst admitted. "And I fear that Black Dutch may become its worse victim. He's on the very cusp of disaster."

Georgia stared at him. "You really mean that, don't you?"

"Without a doubt."

"Well, what if I told you we might know how to find him?"

His eyes opened wide.

"Or at least follow his trail. It's an old one, but it might do the trick."

"His trail? Where?"

"On the face," Georgia said. "Carved in stone."

"The buckets!" Ben nodded with sudden understanding.

"What buckets?" Dr. Hearst asked.

Georgia explained about the chipped-out handholds.

"That route . . ." Dr. Hearst, eyes wide with excitement, hesitated as a tired, raspy-throated Cal approached. He was walking up and down the slope, encouraging those on the fire line to turn over the charred remains and put out any live embers. When he was out of earshot, Dr. Hearst went on, "It must be explored. It might be our one chance to save Black Dutch from harm."

Ben stretched his aching back and glanced at Georgia. "You really want to try it?"

"I've got to admit my reasons for finding Black Dutch are not as noble as Dr. Hearst's, but, sure, I'll go."

Dr. Hearst looked quizzically at Ben. "Reasons?"

Ben shrugged and waited for Georgia to supply an answer. She did, immediately.

"Ever since I set foot on this mountain I've had the feeling someone's watching me," she said sharply, "and I don't like it."

"Watching you?" Dr. Hearst whispered. "That is amazing. Yet, at the same time I'm not surprised you've felt his presence. You are a sensitive young woman."

"Yes, well, he might not think so after I talk to him." Her next words were directed toward Ben. "We'll climb the face until we cross his trail, then we'll follow the buckets to wherever they lead."

"Sounds like an excellent plan," Dr. Hearst said, leaning his shovel against a tree. "I'll go see to the preparations."

"There's nothing for you . . ." Georgia's voice faded away. There was no Dr. Hearst to talk to. He was already hurrying down the fire line. She shook her head. "What have I gotten myself into?"

"I don't know," Ben said, "but he has the right idea. Let's call it quits, too. I need to check on the planes."

Other than a layer of soot on its wide wings, the C-47 was untouched by the fiery explosions and flying debris. As they walked toward the Maule, a Jeep bounced into view, jolting to an abrupt stop by the tie-down area. The sheriff jumped out.

" 'Pears I missed the barbecue."

"Why didn't you get Powell to fly you up?" Ben asked. "We could have used your help a few hours ago."

"Couldn't find him. Probably sleeping one off someplace. They told me at the lodge you might be able to fill me in on how this got started."

Ben told him about the gasoline wagon and the sounds he'd heard in the fog.

"You saying the wagon was let go on purpose?"

"Yes, and Arnold figures it was Black Dutch. He's sent Garrett after him."

"Black Dutch! Now that's a bit of news. What were you and Arnold doing out on such a bad night anyway?"

"Walking. And talking."

"There's your problem." He winked. "Most folks have more sense than to go out in the fog."

"You ever seen him, Sheriff?"

"Who?"

"Black Dutch."

"The legendary Black Dutch? Don't reckon so, and I don't reckon anyone else has either, who's telling the truth. Like the mountain folks, Arnold's choosing to blame all his troubles on the will-o'-the-wisp."

"There's somebody real strange roaming around this mountain."

"Oh, I don't doubt that. These mountains are full of real

strange folk. I suspect some of your city fellas even think I'm strange. But that don't make me no Black Dutch."

"You're not going to call Garrett off?"

To Ben's surprise the sheriff chuckled lowly. "I may tongue-lash him, but frankly, I don't think he's capable of finding a scared skunk holed up under his bed, much less the shadow man. As long as he stays out of my hair I'll let Garrett be. I still got me a missing girl."

"I take it there's nothing new on Daisy," Georgia interjected.

The sheriff scratched the side of his long nose. "Oh, there's a few theories."

"Like what?"

"The one you expect. That old Dutch has 'er. Or that a bear got her. And there's more than a few in the valley who think she's run off with a sweetheart."

"What about the shoes?" Ben asked.

"Well, that brings us to the last theory. The hill folk say the blood on them shoes was a sign—a warning. Lord knows of what."

He peered from under dark bushy brows to gauge their reaction.

"Don't expect me to laugh," Georgia said. "I grew up country. I know superstitions come from hard living and families always being at the mercy of nature."

"Where you from?"

"West Virginia, via Colorado."

"Then I guess you'll understand if I admit to being a bit rattled myself when I looked up this way tonight and saw the fog glowing an eerie red. For a moment I was almost spooked into thinking my old daddy might have been right about a bad spirit being on this mountain."

"No spirit went after Arnold," Ben said. "When that wagon was set loose—by someone—it came close to frying him."

The sheriff reached out with a bony hand and clutched Ben's shoulder. "From the looks of ya, son, I'd say someone might not be too fond of you either. After ya show me where this wagon fell, maybe I better get back to the lodge and talk to the fellas there about what they were doing tonight while you were out ramblin'."

TWENTY-ONE

The grinding of bulldozers on the burned slope above the lodge finally awakened Ben. Even in his room the heavy odors of burnt wood and rubber hung in the air. He dragged himself out of bed and went to wake Georgia. Dr. Hearst, dressed in hiking gear, was waiting for them in the crowded dining room.

"Good morning," he said when they sat down with their laden trays. "Looks like a good day to climb."

Georgia stared at him sleepily over her cup of coffee. "We didn't say we were going up first thing today."

Dr. Hearst leaned toward her. "Oh, but you must," he whispered. "With all these armed men about he's in the most danger of his life."

Georgia sighed wearily. Ben understood her reaction. He, too, was still numbingly tired from yesterday, but he couldn't avoid the anxious eyes behind the silver glasses. "I'll be ready to go as soon as I down a quart of coffee."

"Good, good," Dr. Hearst said excitedly. "We need to get an early start."

Georgia was suddenly very alert. "We? Surely you're not expecting to go with us."

"Of course." Dr. Hearst appeared stunned that she would think otherwise. "The fate of Black Dutch is at stake."

"That doesn't change a thing. I have no intention—and I doubt Ben does either—of taking you on that face."

He spoke hurriedly, and with indignation. "It's because of my size, isn't it?"

"Of course not. It's because you're inexperienced. I can't let you fall to your death to prove a point." Her tone softened at the stricken look on his face. "No one can learn rock climbing in a five-minute lesson. I'm sorry."

There was a tremor to the fork in Dr. Hearst's hand, but his voice was controlled. "I understand. I suppose there's nothing for me to do but express my gratitude that you're willing to go."

Ben lowered his gaze to his plate. When he and Georgia stood to go, he touched Dr. Hearst on the shoulder. "If he can be found, we'll find him."

Once they were outdoors their morning doldrums lifted. The scene of the fire and the noisy machines crawling over it were mostly hidden by morning mists. The temperature lowered almost imperceptibly as they gained altitude, squeezing droplets of water from the saturated air. The clouds overhead and the fog on the ground rolled toward each other, meeting finally without sound or line. As they crossed the bald, Ben pointed at the wooden crates and steel bars stacked along the southern perimeter.

"That stuff for your roller coaster?" he asked.

"No. Cal's getting ready to erect the temporary cable and cage elevator on the face. Wherever Black Dutch is, his days of monkeying around on the mountain are almost over."

Ben thought of his own limited time on the project. "Are you going to be here for the construction of the roller coaster?"

"Oh, sure."

"Then what will you do?"

"Same as you, I guess. Go home."

He watched as she undid the ropes. Finally, he spoke. "When this is over, you think you could come south for a while?"

Her dark eyes raised slowly to his. "There aren't any mountains in Florida, Ben. What would I do?"

"Build a bigger roller coaster?"

"Now that's an idea. Another one for the snowbirds you love so much?"

He smiled. "Maybe."

"And maybe you could come to Colorado, at least to visit."

"I'm sure as hell gonna try."

"How are you at writing letters?"

"Don't know. Never wrote one."

A subdued Georgia fastened the ropes, and they began the climb. Familiarity didn't make them reckless as they moved up the face, but it did speed them along. In less than an hour they were at the narrow ledge that was the junction point for the two routes—theirs and the one hand-chipped. They followed the carved one downward, angling sharply, passing clumps of blueberry bushes rooted in lee pockets of blown soil. The handholds ran all the way to the woods that skirted the northern reaches of what was once the Grandy farm. Massive hemlocks shaded the lichen-covered forest floor from all but the slimmest shafts of light.

"What do you think?" Ben asked, gathering the rope.

"I'd say we made a long pitch for nothing. There's not even a hint of a path."

"Let's give it a look anyway."

They moved stealthily into the semidarkness under the trees until Ben stopped, holding up a warning hand.

"This is a rabbit warren." Inching forward at a slight break in the underbrush, he nudged a twig on the ground and uncovered the remnants of a snare.

"So that's why the stairway led down here," Georgia said, keeping her voice low. "It's his hunting grounds."

"No more," Ben corrected. "Rabbits don't thrive around bulldozers. I'd say neither game nor Black Dutch has been through here for a while. We may as well go back up."

On the return climb, this time with Ben in the lead, Georgia called up, "If this isn't the route he uses, do you suppose he gets to the project by coming over the top, from the back side of the mountain? Maybe that's what he was doing when he spied on us in our tent."

Ben mulled over her words. "I guess it's possible. But that's a lot of climbing to do every day or so."

When they reached the narrow ledge where the routes intersected they pushed on, following the chipped handholds in their angled ascent. Far off there was a hint of thunder. Ben, still leading, came to a shallow, diamond-shaped ledge that sloped upward into the face. Not exactly comfortable, it was a handy spot to wait for Georgia. He undid his canteen and took a long drink.

When she pulled herself up and took her turn at the water,

Ben scanned their surroundings. Below, the tilted ledge narrowed and dropped off into space. Farther up, scraggly weeds swayed among the root masses of a couple of stunted trees. Out of the corner of his eye Ben saw Georgia tug on the chocks he'd put in a narrow crack for their safety line.

His tone was teasing. "I think they're as secure as any you've set on this face."

"Habit," she said and handed him back the canteen. "This is a cozy roost I'd never guess was here."

"Wonder if he's used it." Ben got to his feet.

He worked his way up to a rock column casting a thin vertical shadow. Between it and the face was a narrow, dark gap, invisible from the bald.

"Hey, Georgia, there's a little pocket in the rock." He hitched backward toward it. "A guy could just squeeze in . . . out of sight. This could be where he pulled his disappearing trick on the Grandys."

He levered himself deeper into the notch and felt the ledge under his feet drop away.

"Georgia! Come here!" The thrill of discovery was in his voice.

"Me crawl in there? Forget it! Come on out."

"Give me a second. My eyes need to adjust."

"Your eyes don't need to adjust. Come on out."

"I think I've found something for real!" His voice was now distant, and muffled.

"Damn you, Ben Hagen."

Behind him he could hear Georgia wriggle down the split. A shaft of reflected light formed a halo effect around her head. Ben moved forward again.

"Stop, Ben." Her voice echoed oddly. "We could get trapped in here."

"It opens up," he said. "Come see."

"No. This is far enough. It's pitch black."

Ben hesitated. This didn't sound like Georgia.

He went back to her.

"Relax. Soon as your eyes adjust you'll realize there's plenty of light from that overhead crack."

They waited with their backs to the thin shell of rock. Georgia's anger was palpable, but Ben could not decide who or what it was directed toward. Cool air swept across them toward the opening. It seemed to be exhaled from great silent lungs deep in the earth. The filtered scent of the mountain, clean and vital, filled their nostrils. Georgia twisted to see the rent that ran up the rock over the opening. It widened into a fissure the size of a sapling, providing a long thin shaft of perpetual twilight.

"There aren't any caves in this part of the Appalachians," she whispered.

"This sure looks like a cave."

"You think he knows about it?"

"If I had to guess I'd say he hides here."

A flicker of lightning reflected on the interior wall.

"I'm no spelunker, Ben."

"Me neither. And even if this chamber is as big as Mammoth Cave I'm not going any farther unequipped. It takes special stuff to go cave exploring and we don't have any of it. But at least we can sit out the weather."

"No. I'm going outside."

Ben wrestled with what to say. "I thought you were a mining engineer."

Her eyes never left the slab of dismal light.

"Isn't that what you are?"

"Was. I make roller coasters now. You coming with me?"

"Sure."

It began to sprinkle as they reappeared on the face. Ben scanned first the long crack, and then the sky.

"It's an easy climb the rest of the way," he said. "You want to check for more buckets leading to the summit?"

"I want to go down," Georgia said testily.

TWENTY-TWO

Although the rain was light it gathered in rivulets that ran off the face and turned the raw earth on the newly cleared slope to mud. Georgia trudged through it without uttering a word, and Ben was at a loss to know what to say. Drenched and cold, they descended to the lodge, parting in the hallway.

When he stopped by later, Georgia was in her robe.

"I'm not going to dinner," she said. "What I need is a good night's sleep."

"Wait fifteen minutes and I'll bring you a tray. We've got to talk."

"Thanks, but I'm really tired."

"Make it ten."

"Ben . . ." He was already heading for the stairs.

When he returned she let him in with the warning he couldn't stay long. He'd brought big bowls of chili, covered with grated cheese and onions, a box of crackers, and two big pieces of blackberry cobbler swimming in cream.

"Looks like we're going to have a carbohydrate fix," Georgia said, but her tone was lifeless.

"Spaulding wanted me to bring the veal and asparagus tips. But I'd already smelled the chili. One of the cooks made it for the staff."

They ate at a small table by the window. Wind lashed the rain against the glass.

"Want me to stoke the fire?" Ben asked.

"Don't bother. I'm serious about going to bed."

"Georgia, can we talk about today?"

"What's there to talk about?"

[165]

"Dr. Hearst came to see me as soon as he found out we were back. I told him of our discovery."

The only sound in the room was the rain dancing against the window.

"I'm going back up in the morning to see how big the cave is and to follow the handholds the rest of the way to the top."

Georgia arose and walked about the room before settling on the couch in front of the fireplace.

"I suppose you want me to go with you," she said, her face toward the glowing embers.

"Georgia . . . I don't want you to go at all. I just thought I ought to tell you. I'll do fine climbing alone. We Rangers can bolt our way up anything."

"Maybe. But it'd be safer if I climbed with you."

Taking this as feeble encouragement that she was willing for him to stay awhile and talk, Ben knelt down before the fire and added a log.

"Come along if you like," he said over his shoulder, "and I'll go in the cave by myself."

"You think I'm afraid to go in there, don't you?"

Ben hesitated. The new log began to steam as blue flame licked it. He positioned a burnt remnant with the tip of the poker, then looked back toward Georgia. She was huddled in the far corner of the couch, her dark head propped up in her hand. The light of the golden embers luminesced in her dark, muzzy eyes. "I don't know what to think."

"Not wanting to be closed in doesn't mean I'm afraid."

"I never said it did."

"A lot of people don't like to be cooped up."

"Right. All I meant was if you don't want to go in a cave, that's fine with me."

She met his eyes. "Who am I kidding? I must sound like a fool."

"You don't sound like a fool. And you don't owe me any explanations."

Her words were so low he barely heard them. "I should have known that you of all people would never push me to talk about something I wanted to keep personal."

Ben went to the couch and put his arms around her. Emotions coursed through his body—tender, but inexorable.

"It's no big deal, not wanting to go in a cave. If it weren't for Dr. Hearst, I wouldn't go near the place, either."

Georgia's shoulder nestled under his arm, and her dark fragrant hair rested on his chest. The desire Ben wanted to deny intensified. In spite of his intentions to only hold her, his lips found her cheek, then dropped to the hollow of her neck. Heart pounding, his fingers slipped under the robe, but sudden remorse and guilt flooded him.

"I'm sorry," he said, pulling away. "This isn't the time for that."

She caught his hand and drew it back to her breast. He felt the tender point swell slightly at his touch. It was a signal more intimate than any he'd ever known.

Her robe came off easily for him, and he began to unfasten the buttons of her silky top. When it was off, the firelight was reflected in the delicate oils of her skin. Erotic shadows curved beneath her breasts. Ben wanted to kiss them, but her eyes fixed on his and he could not look away. With one hand Georgia pushed his hair back from his forehead and kissed him on each eye, her lips fluttering his lashes.

Then slowly she lifted her hips so he could pull off the pajama bottoms and drop them to the floor. The shadows deepened as she lay back naked on the couch. His own clothes left his body with less artistry. He brushed against her. This was not a time for lingering caresses. The intensity of his longing was reflected in her eyes.

"Come to me, Ben," she whispered.

He settled full deep inside, and the muscles of her stomach rippled against him. She arched up against him from her chest and knees. Her fingers rested on his shoulders, then on his hips, pressing him, holding him, guarding the point of greatest contact, rocking under him. The magic combination of movement was there again, as wonderful as before, a stretching for joy together. When Ben felt it—a change in her inner muscles that was like an erection over his own erection—it was almost with regret. He didn't want this to end, not ever. But the long, tight ripple swept over him. He pulled against the suction and gave into it deliciously. As Georgia subsided, laughing aloud, he lay his head upon her chest and grinned foolishly, and just a little bit cocky.

Her hand found the back of his neck and caressed it, feeling the spiky dark hairs under her serene fingers.

His hand gently soothed the flat plane of her stomach, finding it smooth and soft, but he remembered the bands of muscles underneath in their spasms of delight.

Georgia shook her head as if she were trying to focus her thoughts after sinking into a dream state.

"I'm going to have to get some sleep if we're going climbing again tomorrow," she said. At her gentle push Ben rolled into the angle of the seat and couch back and let her up.

When Georgia came out of the bathroom she crossed to the big bed. There she glanced back at him still prone on the couch.

"If you promise to behave yourself you can stay."

In the night Ben felt her restless turning.

TWENTY-THREE

It was still dark when Ben slipped from Georgia's room to gather his gear for a solitary return to the cave. Along with a flashlight and rope he packed an old nickel-plated Smith & Wesson .45 he kept in the C-47. Next he dressed in long johns and jeans. His boots were still damp from the downpour, but he put them on anyway. He was tugging on a sweater when Georgia, dressed in climbing gear, appeared at his door.

"Tried to sneak away, huh? Well, I'm going, too, but you got to let me eat breakfast first." There was a touch of the old spark in her voice.

They ate pancakes in the kitchen with the staff while Spaulding hastily packaged them a lunch from leftovers.

Climbing to the face was routine, except that the rocks were still damp. Sounds of a bulldozer floated up in the morning fog that caressed the throat of the cliff like a giant boa. When they came to the hand-hewn route they changed their course to zag up to the cave.

"I suppose there's a chance this cave's not much more than a pockmark in the mountain," Ben said.

"Could be, but what'll we do if he's in there?"

"Try to talk to him . . . if he doesn't run away. Dr. Hearst thinks he's afraid of people."

At the crack Ben inspected both his flashlight and gun.

Georgia eyed him speculatively. "What's that for?"

"A little protection against any surprises."

"Can you handle that thing?"

"I was in the Rangers, remember?"

"Yes, but a cave's a dangerous place to fire a gun. Why don't you leave it behind?"

"There could be snakes or God-knows-what inside." He saw worry clouding her eyes. "Why don't you keep lookout while I scout around inside for a couple of minutes. Then we can climb on to the top."

"No dice," she responded instantly. "We're a team. Together we're a match for anyone. Apart I'm not so sure."

"Okay," Ben said. "But I'm keeping the gun in my belt."

He squeezed sideways and dropped into the damp hollow. Georgia landed beside him gingerly. A cold wet silence enveloped them. Ben flicked on his light, and using it like a night scope, brought up the long muzzle of the pistol. The panning ray caught the glimmer of water standing in pools on the muddy floor. Reddish gray walls curved away from them, and the far side was lost in blackness.

"God, it's huge," Georgia said in a hushed tone.

Ben crept forward a few steps.

"How far are you going?"

"We've stumbled on to something here. We ought to look around a little anyway."

Her sigh diffused in the hollowness. "Okay. But don't get carried away."

"Want to hold the light?"

"I've got my own," she said, and dug it out of her pack.

As they moved across the uneven floor their beams crossed and stabbed here and there. Around the stone corner they poked light at an even larger space with a ceiling that in places stretched up ten to twelve feet. But it was a white mass on the floor that drew their attention.

"Bones!" Georgia gasped. "Millions of them."

"Not so loud," Ben cautioned and knelt beside the sea of ribs, shins, skulls, and spines rippling out before them.

"Sorry," she whispered.

"Looks like small animals, mostly frogs."

"Maybe this is a bobcat's den."

Standing, Ben threw his bright beam in a complete circle, but found no wild, glimmering eyes. Warily he and Georgia crunched and crackled toward the far side of the chamber. There the claylike floor was mostly dry. Clefts and jutting shoulders hid what appeared to be shadowy passages. The concentrated light passed quickly over a narrow ledge and swept back.

"That looks like a bed." Ben, too, forgot to whisper.

On closer examination the shelf showed no signs of recent use. Withered rhododendron leaves crumbled in their hands, releasing a faint sweet smell. But the fragrance was nearly smothered by a heavier odor of burned wood. Both flashlights lowered, the beams uniting on a whiff of smoke rising from a pile of charcoaled stumps. Georgia swung her light to the cave ceiling. Reflecting back was an oily stain of soot.

"Give me a boost."

Ben offered her a knee. Standing almost erect on it, Georgia rubbed a finger along the lip of the crack.

"Caked and dry," she said into his ear as she lowered herself. "Someone's built a lot of fires in here."

"And could be watching us." Ben turned off his light.

Georgia flicked off hers, too, and together they looked back toward the distant natural glow seeping through the long fissure. It cast a deathlike pall over the cave. They strained to detect any sound, but there was only their own breathing and the whisper of faintly moving air.

"Enough of that." Georgia's light came back on, then Ben's, and he pointed it and the big-bore pistol toward dark openings beyond the shelf. Harvestman spiders scurried away from the sudden glow. Several corridors less than shoulder high led off to the south, if Ben's sense of direction was correct. At one of the larger openings farther back there was a distant echo of dripping water.

"I'd like to go in there, at least a little way," Ben said.

"Not without me."

"You sure?"

She laughed nervously. "Don't push it, Ben. Just move."

As he started into the passage, Georgia tugged on his sleeve. "Aren't you going to let out line?"

Ben returned the revolver to his belt and swiftly wrapped his thin climbing rope around a melon-sized stone at his feet.

"There," he said, cinching it tight. "We can go back a hundred and fifty feet."

Paying out the rope a coil at a time, they crept like burglars into the dark shaft. Under their feet the rough, uneven floor narrowed and widened like a rain-swept gully. When all Ben's line was stretched out, Georgia, with a barely audible outflow of breath, tied hers on. Halfway through her rope the vault of the ceiling began to taper and the passage broadened into a wide but very shallow chamber. Georgia's steps faltered.

"Let's call it quits," Ben said. "We've seen enough."

Georgia, struggling with her anxiety, stared into the void beyond him.

"I'll go to the end of my rope," she said, her voice catching. "That's a safe goal. I can do it. But no farther. Not an inch."

Backs and knees bent, they crept forward until they were so stooped their hands nearly touched the floor, then abruptly the cave ceiling began to rise once more. Ben sensed that there was something ahead, around the next turn, but it remained elusive as they came to the end of their line.

"That's it," he said.

"Yes," she agreed with relief. "Time to go back."

Retrieving the rope slowed their movement, but it was good to see it stretching out before them in the darkness. They'd gone so far, passed so many openings, that finding their way out without a guide would have been a risky venture. At the anchor rock Georgia slipped by Ben while he untied his line.

Ben found her in the antechamber, staring at the distant shaft of sunlight coming through the crack. "Shall we pack it in?" he asked.

To his surprise she shook her head. "No, I'm doing okay. This may be the best thing that's happened to me . . . coming in here. Why don't we try another route?"

Ben retied the line to a vertical projection inside a second opening and they started back into it. After a hundred yards or so a ponderous movement of air smelled faintly septic, like a tobacco leaf in an acre of string beans. The passage bent sharply between columns and outcroppings. Small, oblique holes, some the size of sewer pipes, caught their eye as they moved along.

"I'm out of line," Ben announced.

Georgia stopped to uncoil her rope.

"If this was caused by an underground river," he said,

drifting ahead, "it was some . . . oh, damn!" The flashlight slipped from his hand as he flailed out to embrace a column.

Adrenalin rushing, he stood frozen, straddling a pit in the floor. "Oh my God," he murmured.

Georgia eased forward and looked down. The flashlight was a thin star shooting out of sight.

"Just big enough to get stuck in," she said calmly. "I think we'd better be a bit more careful."

"Right," Ben managed, edging forward.

Georgia pulled a reserve flashlight from her pack and stepped over the hole. "Here," she said, "see if you can hold on to this one."

"Caves aren't supposed to go up and down," he muttered.

"That's what Floyd Collins thought," she said, trailing him once more. "This passage smells awful."

"Who's Floyd Collins?"

"A cave explorer in Kentucky, a long time ago. He got stuck in a down shaft and died there while half the state was trying to dig him out."

With every step the musty smell escalated until it became a strong, vile odor barely endurable. Ben drew up. His flashlight beam was reflecting off a dark, oily mess at the base of a short slope. Beyond, the shaft was a straight wide cut through the mountain.

"I don't know what that goo is, but it's food to those things." Ben played his light on a crawling mass of spiders in the pond of putrescence. A steady, steamy mist from above settled onto them.

"Pan up," Georgia told him.

Because of the distance the illumination was faint, and it took a while for Ben to focus on the fuzzy, squealing growth on the high ceiling. An occasional red reflection, only a pinpoint, told him they also were being inspected. "Bats! Thousands of them."

"Revolting looking, aren't they?" Georgia laughed.

"I sure don't like the idea of walking under them."

"You can forget that. We're standing next to a pool of guano that could be ten feet deep. I'd say a retreat is in order."

Backtracking they discovered other passages tucked behind boulders and columns. Ben stuck his head in one of the gloomy interiors. "This cave's an endless maze," he announced, his words echoing back at him.

When they reached the place where their two lines were joined, Georgia slung the coiled one over her shoulder and Ben took over gathering line while she lit the way. They'd moved on at least another hundred feet when Georgia suddenly clicked off her light. In a black world Ben stood motionless waiting to see what she was up to. Her hand found his shoulder and gave a warning squeeze. She took an exaggerated sniff of air.

Fire.

Ben realized he'd smelled it a good while, mixed in with the other strong odor of the passage.

Georgia pressed on him until he dropped into a squat. Then her hand moved to his and, touching the rope, gave a little tug so he'd know what she was going to do.

"Me first," Ben whispered, and edged in front before she could protest.

Stealthily he inched toward the antechamber on his hands and knees. The twitch on the line told him Georgia was close behind. An odd cry, unnatural, rolled through the tunnel. Ben hesitated, then slowly crept foward beyond the end of the rope. Around a boulder gray replaced blackness. A few yards farther dim golden light danced on stone. The eerie sound came again, stronger.

On his stomach Ben dragged himself over sharp pebbles and around the corner to the cave vestibule. Georgia came up beside him. Necks stretched, they peered ahead.

TWENTY-FOUR

It was like a dream picture from the dawn of time. Black Dutch sat by his fire, making unearthly but not unpleasant noises. Smoke wafted upward in a slow, swirling pattern that reached for the cave opening. A soft, gauzy illumination, almost colorless, was cast around the burning orange-and-gold coals. In this eerie scene he was toasting a skinned frog on a stick, like a youngster with a hot dog. The shimmering white hair covering his head and face hung down in silky filaments nearly to his waist, and his eyes glistened brown—or one did. The other was partially masked with a white cast.

Georgia's gasp was barely audible. Ben recognized the infamous mountain dweller at once, although he was still shocked at the appearance of the whole man. He wore, almost jauntily, Ben's flight jacket over a much-frayed pair of overalls. His protruding wrists and legs and bare chest were covered with a coat of hair so thick and shaggy that the dimensions of his body were difficult to judge.

"He looks like a snow-white gibbon," Georgia marveled. "He's gorgeous."

"Maybe," Ben murmured, "but in his youth, if he was as black as Mrs. Grandy said, he must have been an awesome sight."

"Yes," Georgia breathed. "I can see how he could have been forbidding."

The fire drew his attention. Black Dutch sprung to his feet, seized a fat stick from a pile, and snapped it effortlessly. Sparks shot up as he tossed on the pieces of wood. Of medium height, he was apparently wiry under all that hair, and agile.

His teeth shone strong and yellow as he watched the dancing lights rise.

Georgia shifted to one side and loosened the pack from her shoulders.

The throaty noises stopped. Poised over the fire, another stick in his hand, his mouth partially opened, Black Dutch stared into the inner reaches of the cave with his one good eye.

Neither Ben nor Georgia exhaled for more than a minute. The good eye glittered with alarm as it scanned methodically from left to right, searching the darkness. When it got to where they lay, it passed on. Coming back, it stopped. For a long time he stared their way. They remained motionless, barely breathing, knowing he'd sensed them but not knowing what to do. The idea of walking up to this strange, exotic man and introducing themselves no longer seemed reasonable.

Very carefully, as if he were reaching for a rock in a snake's den, Black Dutch picked up a bundle of burning twigs. His eye riveted on their hiding place, he held the torch like a weapon. With a flip of his wrist he sent it spinning toward them. They ducked behind the corner of stone.

"He's got us," Georgia whispered. "What now?"

The face jerked attentively. His gaze still fixed on their spot, he rolled his head to the side to bring an ear to bear. The twigs, a few feet from their heads, crackled and burned down.

Ben pulled the pistol from his belt. He held it in his right hand and sheltered it with his left to keep the barrel from gleaming in the firelight.

"Let him make the next move," he murmured, rising to his haunches ready to spring if an attack came.

"You don't need that," Georgia whispered. "He's only trying to scare us away."

Ben kept the gun at the ready. "Maybe, but too much has happened on this mountain to take the chance."

The gray figure began to back away from the fire until he was against the cave wall as far from them as he could get. There Black Dutch edged to the left until he was out of sight. Ben and Georgia craned around their column and saw him snatch up a burning stick and dart into a small tunnel.

"Damn, he's run away," Georgia said, and scrambled to her feet.

Ben stood, too.

"Listen," he told her hurriedly, "if he comes back—if he attacks and I have to shoot—get out of here."

"For God's sake, don't do that."

A roar that was a perfect imitation of a bear filled the cave, and Black Dutch leaped out of the darkness behind them.

Startled completely, Ben and Georgia stumbled toward the circle of firelight. He sprang after them, thrusting the blazing stick like a circus animal tamer, dancing back and thrusting again, until Georgia raised her head and the woolly man saw her face. Ben brought the gun up, but their attacker didn't move. He stared at Georgia, the torch hanging in his hand.

Ben tucked the pistol back into his belt and grabbed a burning stick of his own. Black Dutch slowly began to retreat.

"Good job, Ben," Georgia said. "Now throw it down."

"What?"

"He's afraid. Throw it down," she repeated.

Understanding, Ben nodded. He waved the stick against Black Dutch's and then tossed it dramatically into the fire.

The cave man grunted. His look of fear was replaced with puzzlement. His own torch moved slowly. With a gesture that suggested the deliberate calculation of a gambler he tossed it into the fire. It landed, Ben noted half-amused, close enough for a second grab if things went awry. They glared at each other. Ben tried a step forward and the caveman jumped back. Ben retreated, and he came forward a half step.

"You're too big for him," Georgia said, moving ever so slightly. Dutch's gaze darted to her.

"I don't like this," Ben said gruffly.

"Talk nice, for goodness' sake." Georgia extended her scratched and grimy hands, palms up, to show they were empty. Black Dutch didn't move. When Georgia got closer, his jaw began to tremble, and a sound, almost like a whine, came from his throat.

"That's close enough," Ben rumbled under his breath.

"Okay. Let's sit down," Georgia said evenly. "We'll appear less threatening."

Deliberately she settled onto a rock in the fire circle, gesturing for Ben to do the same. Mimicking them, Black Dutch sank to a squatting position. Even across the blazing wood they could sense his smell—rich and woodsy and smoky, and not at all unpleasant. The skewered frog lay near Georgia. She nudged it toward their hairy host. He ignored it but not her as he swayed back and forth like a trapped coon in a cage. From time to time he glanced at the gun at Ben's waist.

"You're not going to get very far offering him his own food," Ben observed in an undertone.

"It's at least a friendly gesture," Georgia replied. "He's obviously very frightened of us and trying not to be."

Ben realized with some guilt that the look on his own face must be one of distrust and anger. He tried to smile and forced his voice to a calmer level. "Who are you? What are you doing here?"

The one good eye glittered as it shifted to Ben, then slid back to Georgia.

"Don't you understand English?" she asked.

Black Dutch cocked his ear once more, his mouth dropped open, but no words came out.

"Hablas español?"

"Sprechen sie deutsch?"

"Well, now, Georgia, that's dumb. If he did speak German, you don't, do you?"

"I used to know some Yiddish. I wonder if Dr. Hearst could get him to talk."

"I'm beginning to think this guy doesn't talk—period!"

Across the fire he stared at them and they stared back. He was a sight to behold. His eyes were intriguing, peering out of the white sea of hair, the one dark, lively, and at the moment quizzical, the other with its cast but possibly not completely blind. The bridge of his nose peeked through faintly in the ruddy firelight and the backs of his hands and tops of his feet also seemed to thin out.

"No wonder he's taken for a beast from a distance," Ben said. "I might shoot at him myself if I saw him loping along a ridge."

"He's a man, Ben, just like you, only something happened to him genetically . . . like a throwback. It's happened before. In medieval days they thought it came from mating with wolves, until a prince's son came hairy into the world."

A low guttural noise suggested he knew they were talking

about him and didn't like it. His good eye darted through three points in its ceaseless scan from Georgia to Ben's gun and to the frog.

"Ben . . . this guy's getting to me. His eyes . . . they're kind of like a dog fresh from a whipping."

"Georgia, don't!" But it was too late for warnings. In one smooth gesture she had come to her feet, scooped up the steaming frog, leaned forward in a fencer's thrust, and placed it on a smooth stone before Black Dutch. Already stretched low, she simply brought her back leg up beside the extended one and knelt close to him. Dutch didn't flinch from her nearness. Her eyes searched his hairy face.

One scruffy finger rose to hover for a heartbeat before her cheek. It gently touched the long line of her jawbone, tracing it lightly and then, as if he were startled at his own daring, dropped.

"So you're the wild spirit of the Smokies," Georgia said in a soft tone. "I'm glad we've found you."

What happened next Ben would never forget, although it was meant for Georgia alone. Black Dutch pursed his lips, drew a long breath, and trilled an exact imitation of a mountain sparrow. He went through the entire range of the bird's calls twice and fell silent.

"My God," Georgia murmured, "how beautiful."

The old scraggly creature pursed his lips again and gave out the long, low call of the mourning dove. As the last notes faded he shifted to the rapid sounds of a squirrel announcing its territory, followed by its one-note love song. After that he jumped up, began a deep, gruff noise, and walked on all fours. His shoulders rose and fell in an exaggerated rhythm.

"He's showing us a bear," Ben said.

Their subdued laughter seemed to delight him. He did the bear again and again and again. When at last he could not get more than a chuckle with it, he changed his act. Stretching his arms horizontally, he began to hop around the cave and make a grumbling noise.

"I don't get it," Ben, not thinking, said to him.

They both peered closely, trying to decipher the message. Black Dutch breathed again, louder than before, and rumbled between his lips. He raised on tiptoes, stooped, then raised again.

Ben was astonished. "That's an airplane . . . I think he's doing me!"

As abruptly as it began the game stopped. Black Dutch squatted at his fire, pinched the frog, and tore off both haunches. He offered them to Georgia in his deeply calloused pink palm. Smiling, she accepted his gift.

"Wait a second," Ben said. "We've got lunch right here. Let me try to get it out without spooking him."

He slipped off his pack and poked through it. "Looks like cold tongue sandwiches, deviled eggs, and pickled asparagus."

Georgia wrinkled her nose to the sandwich Ben raised toward her. "Spaulding tries to be so damned European. I'd rather have the frog." And to prove it she tore the tender meat from the bones and ate it. Then she took the sandwich from Ben and handed it to Dutch.

He held it tightly like a prize, smelled it, and glanced at Ben's battered face with mistrust.

Georgia laughed. "I don't think he likes tongue any more than I do. Let's try something else."

Ben handed her one of the egg halves. She passed it on to Dutch, who took a reluctant nibble, then noisily gulped the rest and cast a speculative glance at the open pack. Ben dug down, handed another half egg to Georgia, who handed it to Dutch. He savored it with a grunt. The bucket brigade was repeated, and before Dutch consumed the other half they were handing him whole eggs stuck together by the pasty yellow filling as quickly as they could.

"He must have a throat like an ostrich to get them down that fast," Georgia said, laughing.

"What'll we do now, offer him coffee?"

"I think that's going a little far."

Black Dutch eyed them expectantly. Georgia showed him her empty palms. He sat back.

"Where do we go from here?" Ben asked. "He can't talk and doesn't seem to understand a word we say. All he can do is eat and play charades."

Georgia's gaze slid from Ben to Black Dutch. "That's it! Ben, you're brilliant. I'll follow his lead and try a pantomime."

She stood and arched one hand over her eyes as if she were searching for something afar. Then she gestured with her hands to show how tall Daisy was and outlined a female figure.

"Woman," Georgia tried, tapping herself on the chest.

Rising, Dutch edged forward like a dancer accepting an invitation and reached out toward her breast.

"Hey," Ben growled, touching the Smith & Wesson.

Georgia stepped back. "Relax. He's not trying to hurt me."

Dutch, his hand still outstretched, looked bewildered.

"Let me try something else." Georgia said and knelt by the fire. She picked up a stick and smoothed cold ashes from the edge of the fire into a more-or-less flat plane. "I'm not too good at this," she said, "but I'll give it a shot."

Georgia had barely poked out a rough sketch of a woman's form when a sound, best described as delight, burst from Dutch's throat. He danced from one side of Georgia to the other as she tried to produce a line drawing of Daisy.

Georgia turned to him when she was finished. "Well?"

Dutch stared at the drawing in the ashes and back at Georgia. There was a look of wonder in his eyes.

"He doesn't have the foggiest idea who that is," Ben said.

Georgia tossed her stick into the fire. "Then you think of something."

"How about drawing the fuel wagon?"

"I don't know what it looks like. You draw it."

"I can't draw."

While they talked, Dutch reached down and reworked a few of the lines on Georgia's drawing with his fingernail, reducing the dimensions of the woman's figure almost by half. With a vibrating motion of the hand he bore great dark holes for the eyes and a thin straight line for the mouth.

"Look at what he's doing!" Georgia gasped. Her face was emerging from the ashes as surely as Venus from the ruins of Melos.

Dumbfounded, Ben looked from the bold eyes in the ashes to the almost placid eyes of their creator.

Unsatisfied with their reaction, Black Dutch touched up his drawing. Georgia squeezed his shaggy arm. "It's me, I know."

"Is he a natural-born artist, or . . . what?" Ben asked.

"A savant? What they used to call an idiot savant?" Georgia said. "I doubt it. He's wild and primitive, that's for sure, but I'd bet my life he's not retarded. No man who's lived by his wits on this mountain for God knows how many years could be anything but quick, and smart."

Black Dutch began to gather long branches from the fire into a bundle.

They realized at the same instant that he was forming a torch—a substantial one. The golden glow of it rolled and flickered in his dark eye as he moved toward the rear of the chamber. At the archway to one of the larger passages he looked back at Georgia and grunted.

TWENTY-FIVE

The grunt came again. One hairy hand moved deliberately in a circular motion toward his chest.

"Ben," Georgia exclaimed, "he wants us to follow him."

"Don't worry," he replied. "I have no intention of asking you to trail through this cave after a man out of the Stone Age."

"I did okay before. There's no use disappointing Dr. Hearst. Not when we have our ropes and flashlights."

Ben didn't know what to say. As they drew together before the torch he tried to decide whether she was truly ready to follow this strange recluse into the depths of the cave, or if she was only trying to prove to herself that she could.

What might pass for a smile played on Black Dutch's mouth. When they stepped inside the dark passage behind him a low trill rolled from his throat.

At first he set an easy pace, holding the torch low to light the bottom of the straight shaft, but gradually he jogged faster and faster until Georgia and Ben were racing to keep up. When the tunnel began to twist and climb, Georgia slowed. Ben knew it wasn't because she was tired. Realization was coming to her.

"I don't think we should go any deeper," he whispered.

"Well—" Georgia came to a complete stop.

Dutch trotted back and gestured invitingly once more.

"Oh, Ben, he really wants us to go on." She sounded totally mesmerized.

"So what?" Ben reached for her shoulder. "Come back. He'll follow us out."

As if he understood, Dutch whimpered and stuck a hand

toward Georgia's other shoulder. Ben grabbed for the gun at his belt. Alarm filled Black Dutch's eyes.

"Don't be such a bully," Georgia said and moved toward their insistent guide. "We'll go a little farther."

Ben, the pistol loose in his hand, had the choice of following or being stubborn and turning back. They were nearly out of sight by the time he made up his mind. Muttering to himself, Ben fastened his rope to a column before going on. After a few yards the passage began to narrow. The floor was dry, but a dank smell hinted of an underground stream. Ahead, the pair he was chasing had stopped. As Ben approached, a guttural sound came from Black Dutch. His ivory teeth caught the reflection of the blazing wood held against a splash of yellow on the rock wall. Black curls of smoke roiled upward as he drew the fire-eaten knob through the print. The whites of his eyes gleamed like a leopard's in the darkest shadows of the jungle.

Georgia touched the surface. "It's a primitive painting of some kind."

Straining in the dim light, Ben saw that other blobs of color speckled the area. "You think he did these?"

"I don't know. I suppose they could be Indian pictographs like we saw on the river." She turned to Black Dutch. "Is this what you wanted me to see?"

He darted down the corridor. His torch, fanned by the movement, trailed to points of light, then erupted into a glow of magenta, smoke drifting upward to stain the ceiling. When they didn't move after him, he ran back and began to motion again.

"There must be more," Georgia said, anticipation in her voice. "I see you're paying out line. There's no reason we can't go a little farther."

Again they followed. When Ben's line ran out, he touched Georgia's back, the question unasked.

"Let's go to the end of my rope," she suggested, and handed it to him. He fastened it to his own.

On they plunged until the second line ran out, too.

"Georgia!"

She hesitated. Dutch flourished the torch, showing that

just ahead the tunnel was half-blocked by boulders, dropped eons ago from a monstrous overhead crack.

As if a magnet were drawing her, she moved toward him. "This seems to be someplace special, Ben," she said. Dutch motioned for her to sit on one of the large slabs, then vanished behind a pile of rubble.

Darkness enveloped them.

"Ben?" the cry came instantly.

He turned on his flashlight and made his way to her. "Come on, Georgia. Let's get out of here."

"We can't just leave."

"Oh, yes, we can."

She laughed uneasily. "I'm not going to put up a fight. If he doesn't show up in a hurry we'll start back."

Reluctantly Ben sat down beside her. The blackness pressed around the small beam of light as though the mountain itself were squeezing in. The silence was deep but not total. Air breathed past them and carried with it a faraway, vague melody of water plopping from a great height and somewhere the crackle of a fire.

Georgia jerked upright when she heard other sounds, abrasive ones, of small rocks grinding underfoot. "He's coming."

A glimmer of light grew in the spot where Black Dutch had disappeared. The odor of burning wood followed. They were on their feet when he appeared, exposing the cleft into which he'd vanished. There was a wild eagerness in his eye. Ben, angry now, cocked the hammer on the Smith & Wesson and pointed it at the silver-coated chest. "If you try anything, anything at all," he said coldly, "I'll use this."

"Oh, Ben," Georgia protested as Black Dutch darted behind the cleft, "won't you ever learn?"

After a moment a shaggy head appeared, and then a hand, motioning to Georgia, who, with an angry look at Ben, stood. She walked toward the cleft. Tight-lipped, Ben trailed but, without a rope, consciously studied their route, scanning the walls with the flashlight. The corridor widened abruptly into a room with several openings. Black Dutch raced down one to the left, flames billowing brightly against mica-laced walls. The intensity of the light drew Ben's attention, and he realized with a jolt that it couldn't be the same torch the shaggy man had started with.

"He stockpiles wood," Ben muttered with alarm. "These passages could go on forever."

Ahead, Georgia motioned to him. "Come on," she yelled. "We must be nearly there. He's singing again."

Before he could reach her the walls closed in sharply and the ceiling dropped, forcing Ben into a low crouch. Dutch's burning stick became only a burnished gash in the wall, eerily lighting the way.

"This is getting bad." Georgia's voice took on a strange echo. "I can't go . . ."

A crunching noise was followed by a sharp thump.

"Ben?" Her voice was incredibly distant and weak. "Ben, where are you?"

Ben's heart leaped. Calling her name, he plunged through the narrow space and banged his knuckles on stone. The mournful cry of a meadowlark issued from the squeezeway. Moving back, Ben swept the beam of light over the obstacle, a rounded boulder jammed into the narrow passage. In a panic he shoved on it, put his back to it, even braced his arms against the sides and used the power in his legs. It was wedged in solid. He repeated his efforts, but there was so little room to get a purchase with his feet he slipped hard to his knees. The flashlight bounced away on the uneven floor, leaving Ben in enough shadow to see a speck of light in the slit of space above the barrier.

He scrambled to the spot and placed an eye to it. The glow of the torch flickered away to nothingness around a turn.

He called Georgia's name.

Faintly from a far, far place he thought he heard her call. Or was it an echo?

Cursing himself, he again worked at the cold stone. He managed to rock it using the pistol as a pry-bar. Each slight movement gave him hope, but the dead weight always shifted back.

Five minutes turned into fifteen and then an hour. His hands were slick with blood, his nails torn. At last Ben realized how diminished his visibility had grown. He clicked off the failing flashlight, put it in a pocket, and went back to his frantic task. In darkness he struggled futilely, furious at the stone and Dutch and himself. His sobs and gasps for air failed to pierce his consciousness. Neither did he feel the pain in his hands and lungs. In this overpowering merger of emotion and physical stress an image came to him—his recurring nightmare of a hapless pilot spinning toward death, too frozen with fear to push the stick forward and regain control.

"I can't move it," he shouted despairingly.

He listened one more time at the gap, then in a last, useless gesture jammed the pistol barrel into it like a pick axe. With a cry of anguish he gave up and lay his head against the cold, ungiving boulder. There was nothing to do but go for help.

Leaving Georgia was the most difficult thing he'd ever had to do. If he failed to get out in a hurry, if he compounded his mistakes, she could pay with her life. He took off his jacket and made his way back to the junction of the narrow corridor and the main passage. There he dropped it as a marker.

With enormous relief he found the end of the rope. But that placed him in a new agony. If he left the line where it was and simply followed it toward the cave entrance, he'd have a guide back to Georgia. But he needed rope to get down the mountain face in a hurry.

Cursing Black Dutch bitterly he picked up the end of the rope and began winding it as he walked, scuffing his feet along the floor to mark the trail.

As he worked his way in the dark, he repeatedly called for Georgia. His cries were soaked up by silent stones. Guilt-ridden, Ben searched each corridor he passed for a distant flicker of light. There was none and there was no escaping the certainty of it. Georgia was the prisoner of Black Dutch, and Ben had taken her to him, a gift of flesh for the beast of the mountain. His mind raced from Daisy's bloody shoes to the hammering at the gasoline wagon to the look of terror on the marksman's battered face. Although the cave was cold, beads of sweat ran down his cheeks.

The rope ran out and he slung it over his shoulder. The rest of the way to the surface he was on his own. Saving the weak flashlight for an occasional glimpse, he moved slowly in the dark, sliding his feet ahead, remembering the pit he'd almost fallen into. Was it only hours ago? A number of times he stumbled and fell, wracking his knees and sometimes his face on jutting rocks. Too many minutes passed. Despair enveloped him. His throat was raw from calling Georgia's name and the fear of never getting out ballooned in his brain. With a shaking hand he turned on the light. The cave walls were close, furrowed, and unfamiliar.

"I'll kill you, Black Dutch," he croaked, and was overtaken by spasms of coughing.

The beam of light flickered. He shut it down once more and, bracing one arm against the cave wall, tried to think. Somehow he had to find the way to the mountain's surface, without light, without a guiding rope. But how? He swiped at the sweat stinging his eyes and realized with a start that air was ever so slightly moving over him, cooling his sticky skin. It came to him that this slight current might lead him out, light or no light. He began to move from passage to passage in the direction of the air flow. Although it's impossible to see a mirage in blackness, Ben created one in his mind, seeing the opening to the cave and Georgia, standing there in the misty light. Together they walked over the bones and examined the ledge, and he boosted her up to the ceiling to check the soot.

The soot! He stopped and flicked on the dim light. Yes, there it was, right over his head all the time. A map of Black Dutch's trail. Ben wanted to yell his relief but his vocal cords would no longer oblige him. He followed the black line until the flashlight gave out altogether and no amount of shaking would bring up even a weak glow. He flung it down the corridor and moved ahead, again totally dependent upon the wind behind him. At a couple of passages he guessed wrong, but the absence of flowing air quickly caused him to backtrack and take another route. Time ceased. His concentration on finding the way out was total. If he let his mind wander, the agony he envisioned for Georgia was more than he could bear.

When he smelled smoke Ben cried out with relief.

Stumbling over the piled rock where he and Georgia had lain in silent witness to Black Dutch's singing, he turned a corner. Low firelight greeted him. With bleary eyes he searched every dark alcove of the antechamber. The hope that Black Dutch had returned Georgia here by a different route had been small. Now it was dead. His groan of despair was low, almost inhuman.

Numb with fatique, he put on his backpack and passed through the cave's mouth.

The night sky was a deep navy blue with brittle stars picked out in it like the first buds of icicles. On the precipice he fixed his rope and with a sinking heart leaped into the void.

TWENTY-SIX

Ben, a stubble of beard darkening his lined face, stumbled to Arnold's office, calling for him, beating on the heavy wood with his swollen, cut hands.

"Here, here, what is it?" Spaulding murmured as he slipped out of a room across the way. "It's two A.M." Seeing the exhaustion and anger in Ben's face, the innkeeper hesitated, and then blurted, "Something awful has happened."

"Get Arnold," Ben rasped. "Georgia's in trouble."

Spaulding hurried for the stairs. Trembling, Ben let his eyes close as he leaned against the door.

Lexington Arnold's silk pajamas brushed Ben's arm as he slipped a key in the door lock. "Come in," he said and flipped on the light. "What's this about Georgia?"

"She's been kidnapped," Ben said barely above a hoarse whisper. "Black Dutch has her in a cave."

Arnold looked to Spaulding. "Wake Garrett—hurry."

Ben began to wave his arms. "No, no, forget that. Call the sheriff. We've got to get a team of cave explorers up there."

"That's for me to decide. Where is this cave?"

"On the face, about three-quarters of the way up. Maybe a half mile from Mrs. Grandy's cabin site."

"And he took Georgia in there?" The entrepreneur's eyes were incredulous. "I can't believe anyone could make such a climb carrying a woman."

"No . . . we were exploring it."

"And he attacked you?"

"I wasn't attacked. I was tricked."

"Tricked?" There was an ominous rumble to Arnold's voice.

"He blocked a passageway."

"Was he armed?"

"No, no. I had a gun but he didn't."

"Well, how in the hell did he kidnap her? Did he jump you?"

"No, I told you!" Ben tried to shout, but his voice cracked. "He rolled a boulder into a narrow space between me and Georgia. We were following him."

"And she's still in there?"

Ben nodded in exasperation as Garrett burst in the room.

"What's happened?" he demanded.

"This is no job for us," Ben said to Arnold. "We need the sheriff and trained spelunkers."

"Spelunkers!" Garrett exclaimed. "Why in the hell do you need spelunkers?"

Arnold glared narrowly at Ben. "It would take until tomorrow in this godforsaken hillbilly county to round up spelunkers. Is it your advice that we wait that long?"

Ben swallowed his anger. "We've got to get her out of there now."

"Her?" Garrett intruded. "Have you found Daisy?"

Ben shook his head. "It's Georgia. She's been kidnapped on the mountain."

"In a cave?"

"Yes, goddamnit, in a cave on the face," Arnold grumbled.

"The face? But . . . but this isn't cave country."

Arnold, raising a hand to quiet Garrett, addressed Ben. "Do you think Black Dutch will harm her?"

"He grabbed her, didn't he?"

Arnold's eyes met Garrett's. "And Daisy? Do you think he could have taken her too?"

"I have no idea," Ben said testily. "All I know is we've got to get to Georgia."

"Save your rancor for this monster," Arnold responded bitterly. "If you'd helped me get him off my mountain like I asked, this would never have happened."

"We thought he was harmless . . ."

"Harmless! He almost burned you and me both alive! You

may as well face it, if Georgia has been harmed you bear heavy blame."

Garrett's eyes fell to Ben's waist. "I see you packed a cannon to find this harmless guy."

Ignoring him, Ben met Arnold's angry look with his own. "You do as you like. Send who you like. I'm going to find Georgia."

"Not without Garrett you won't. I don't want this bungled the way you've bungled everything else."

Arnold led the way to the door. In the hall he instructed Garrett, "Take what you need, but don't let Black Dutch escape. Understand?"

"I'll get him."

There was a clatter on the stairs. Dr. Hearst, followed by a rather guilty-looking Spaulding, rushed down toward the three men.

"Wait. Please."

Arnold's eyes narrowed on him. "Go back to your room. I won't have you interfering. And you, Mr. Spaulding," he added, "have overextended yourself in my affairs."

"Your affairs!" The power of Ben's anger forced the words over the pain in his throat. "Georgia's life's at stake. That's all that matters here. Not the project. Not your damned affairs."

Arnold stabbed a finger at Ben's chest. "How dare you say my affairs don't matter. What happens to Georgia reflects on me." The veins in his neck and forehead stood out. "We'll find her, but I'm ending this Black Dutch threat forever. Frankly I hope he's carried off in a box. And you, Ben Hagen, when this is over, are through."

"You can't kill Black Dutch!" Dr. Hearst cried. "This is a unique human being."

"I thought you said he was a spook," Garrett ridiculed, as the kitchen help, most in bed clothes, clustered under the raging bear. Above, more faces, sleepy and curious, appeared on the landing.

"Enough," Arnold commanded. "You all have my orders." He stepped inside his office and slammed the door loudly. Growling for everyone to go back to bed, Garrett headed up the stairs.

Dr. Hearst turned distressed eyes to Ben. "Consider, please, you don't know Black Dutch's intentions."

"I know he's taken Georgia."

"Maybe only to talk to her."

"You're wrong there, Dr. Hearst. He can't talk! And he doesn't seem to understand a thing, except what a gun's for."

"You threatened him?"

"Not enough, evidently."

"Please, Ben, it could be important. Tell me more. What's he like?"

"Oh, for Christ's sake," Ben rasped, "like I told you before, he's old and hairy. It covers both his head and body."

"He lives in that cave?"

"Yes, but not for much longer." Brushing past him, Ben jerked open the lodge door.

"You join forces with Garrett and you're nothing but a lynching party," Dr. Hearst called in a tremulous voice.

Ben hesitated and looked back. "I'm no lyncher."

"You've got the mood of one."

"If Black Dutch's laid a hand on Georgia . . ."

A shudder ran through the professor. "She'll be all right, Ben. I'm sure." His eyes went from the anger in Ben's face to his bloodied hands on the door. "You mustn't kill him."

"All you can think about is Black Dutch. Well, listen to me. Georgia has a phobia about closed-in places. I don't know why, but she does. How do you think she's doing, imprisoned in that cave?"

Ben slammed out and stalked under the icy stars to the radio shack at the airstrip. After digging out a wrecking bar and a fresh flashlight, he washed the grime off his face at the sink. Then he drank handfuls of water, one after the other, as fast as he could swallow.

Back at the lodge Garrett was pacing the porch, scanning the horizon. As Ben had anticipated, the mercenary was overdressed and overarmed to the point of parody. At his waist a long-bladed Ka-Bar, a relic of World War II, replaced the lost commando knife, and he was toting an Uzi on a sling as well as the automatic pistol.

At the bottom of the steps Ben frowned up at him. "We'll need this crowbar more than guns."

Garrett waved him off. "Leave yours behind if you want. I'm gonna get this son of a bitch."

"Then what are we waiting for? Let's get on up there."

"Powell's on his way. He's picking up some equipment and then he'll fly us to the top. From what you said I figure it'll be quicker to rappel down. What's this cave like, Hagen?"

"It's a damn maze."

"How deep does it go?"

"I don't know. There's a big antechamber where he lives and a lot of small tunnels off it. He could have Georgia down any one of them."

"You have any idea why he took her?" The green eyes mocked Ben. "You think he's some kind of sex maniac?"

Ben didn't reply. Fighting both fury and guilt, he sat on the stairs to check his Smith & Wesson with swollen hands throbbing with pain. He wanted to be certain the barrel wasn't clogged or damaged from being used against the boulder.

At the first sound of the approaching aircraft, Garrett made for the strip with Ben trailing. Despite his best efforts he fell farther behind with each step. The brief time he'd rested was just long enough for his tired muscles to stiffen.

Its dim cabin lights made the helicopter appear phantom-like in the rising night mists. Garrett climbed in front, leaving Ben to scramble over piles of ropes and gear in the back.

"The sheriff's coming with the Guard," Powell yelled as he adjusted the earphones on his headpiece. "Wanna wait?"

"Hell, no," Garrett barked. "You can show him where we've gone."

Powell fed power to the rotor. Suddenly Dr. Hearst, breathing hard, grasped the frame of the opened door and looked imploringly at Ben.

"When you find him," he shouted, "for the sake of everything decent have a little pity. It's what Georgia would want."

His mouth set in a hard line, Ben returned Dr. Hearst's gaze grimly.

"Ignore Hearst," Garrett yelled. "Take off."

The heavy helicopter began to lift. Dr. Hearst shielded his eyes and backed away. Snow, gravel, and twigs burst forth from the backwash generated by the whirling rotor. The smell of burning kerosene from the engines filled the air.

Crouched behind the pilot as they lifted off, Ben turned toward the mountain and shouted directions.

"You think this guy took Daisy, too, don't you?" Powell yelled.

"What else is there to think?" Garrett replied as loudly. "Hagen says he's crazy."

Ben bent forward. "I didn't say he was crazy. I said he was living in a cave like an animal."

Powell nodded, his eyes on the tree line. "Whatever he is, it sounds like you're about to skin him. Can't say I'm sorry."

The climb that took hours on foot was completed in minutes. Leaning out, Garrett hunted for the cave as Ben moved the beam of a high-intensity searchlight across the gray stone. He swept it back to a vague ledge.

"There?" Garrett yelled. "Are you sure?"

"That looks like it. The entrance is hidden."

"Up, up," Garrett urged Powell.

The helicopter rose past the lip of the cliff and settled with a flurry toward the mountain. Garrett was out before they touched down. Impatiently he began dragging crates out of the cabin onto the ground. Without a word Ben pitched in, prying the lid from a carton. Garrett waved away the helicopter. Powell lifted the machine with barely a twist of his wrist. It angled over the rim and back toward the airstrip, and the sound of the lonely night wind returned to the mountain.

"No time for that prissy nut-and-jam crack climbing you've been doing with Georgia," Garrett said nastily, pounding a steel stake into a rock crevice.

Bundles of new ropes and slings were spilled from the boxes and attached through large fasteners to eyes in the stakes. Next Garrett pulled out two hard hats with powerful lanterns. He jammed one on his head and handed the other to Ben. Hesitating only long enough to test the anchors, Garrett wrapped himself in the rope.

"Let's go," he said and pushed off the edge.

Ben snapped himself onto a rope, and, swinging out with a hop, rappelled rapidly down the rock face.

As they raced each other in a reckless descent, the mechanical churning of rotors came on the wind again. Ben twisted to search the horizon. A twin-bladed helicopter was beating its way across the valley toward the lodge.

"Fucking sheriff and the weekend soldiers," Garrett called to him.

The huge ungainly aircraft, its interior lit brightly, rode below them like a flying battleship. Through the open cargo doors Ben could see troops and deputies bristling with small arms.

Garrett laughed. "And Dr. Hearst was worried about you and me."

He and Ben were hanging in space, the soles of their boots against the mountainside. The helicopter settled below the tree line, and the sound of the rotors beating the air faded. Garrett resumed his descent. Ben released the braking grip on his own line and fell almost uncontrolled past him. The light on Ben's hard hat slashed wildly across the mountain's face as he searched for the elusive fracture.

"I thought you knew where it was, for Christ's sake," Garrett berated him.

"I do. Everything's changed in the dark."

"You should've left a marker."

Ben's raw throat choked on his answer. "Yeah. I should've." It was one more layer of guilt.

After long minutes he pointed over his head. "It's there."

Garrett, who was ten feet above him, swung skillfully to the exact spot.

"No goddamned hole here."

Ben struggled upward, dragging himself, his gear, and the yard-long steel crowbar with him.

"Get out of the way."

"Hagen, I'm leading this."

"I said get out of the way." Ben's bony shoulder bumped the big man hard.

"Damn you!" Garrett growled as he swung pendulously away from the face.

Ben hugged the wall and worked his way into the cave vestibule. In moments there was the quiet crunch of boots on gravel as Garrett dropped behind him. The cold white light of the torch on Ben's hard hat slashed about the gray walls. Black Dutch's hearth was ashes. Ben's gaze raced from one to another of the archways. He realized with horror he'd also failed to mark the one they'd taken with Dutch.

"Hagen," Garrett said behind him, an ominous softness in his voice, "when we find Black Dutch . . . stay out of the way."

Ben swung around. "Don't get trigger happy. We're here to save Georgia, not play vigilante."

Garrett smiled mirthlessly. "Where'd you lose her? Which one of those holes do we take?"

"This one, I think." Ben lowered his head and brought the light across Garrett's eyes.

"Damn it, Hagen, watch it. You'll mess up my night vision."

Garrett drove another stake into the cave floor and attached an explorer's line. He began playing it out behind Ben. The twisting corridor seemed familiar to Ben at first, but he lost his confidence as it meandered on and on, splitting several places into smaller openings. Anxious and fatigued, he began to guess which way to go, occasionally backtracking to try another passage in the honeycomb.

"This is the third time you've turned around," Garrett grumbled. "Do you or do you not know the way?"

"Damn it . . . I'm trying." The rocks absorbed his words, giving his voice a dead quality.

Ben rounded a corner and his foot encountered a slight slope downward. The scent that reached his nose foretold his mistake, verified soon by a barely detectable squealing. Behind him Garrett jerked his head back, and the light on his cap flashed toward the ceiling.

"Bats!" he said disgustedly. "Don't tell me we have to walk under this."

"No, we've gotta go back."

Garrett glared at him. "I knew it, Hagen. You're nothing but a fuck-up. I could find them quicker by myself."

"Then do it."

"Don't get smart-assed."

With deep frustration, almost more than he could handle in his tired state, Ben followed the line, leaving Garrett to retrieve it behind him. He checked his watch and saw they'd wasted half an hour.

Thumping sounds vibrated down the corridor. Ben plunged

on, sensing that Georgia's rescue was turning into a fiasco. The scene beyond Black Dutch's cold fire alarmed him. Wide-eyed recruits were pouring through the crack, motioned on by dark-faced non-coms with the experience of combat in their eyes. All carried weapons. Ben was about to yell for them not to shoot in the cave when he glanced up and saw the soot. A strange calm overtook him. He knew how to find Georgia.

To one side of the entrance, an ordnance team was working on a rig while the sheriff talked on a field radio. A serpentine collection of light cables coiled around a portable generator balking at efforts to start it.

An ordnance man yelled, "We're taking this front wall out in about two minutes. Everyone hit the deck."

As the recruits dropped to the damp floor, Garrett emerged from the passage. He pushed by Ben and walked boldly amid the prone men toward the sheriff. "No sign of the woman down that one," he said. "Hagen's screwed up. He doesn't know where he lost her."

Seizing the moment, Ben turned off his cap light and slipped along the back wall to a slightly smaller opening, where he stooped and vanished in darkness. It was a disappearing act painfully learned from an expert. For several moments there was silence until Garrett's voice rang out.

"Hagen!"

Ben crept deeper into the mountain as his name echoed down first one and then another of the connected corridors. Moving hand over hand on the wall and sliding his feet along the rocky, uneven floor, he worked his way slowly in darkness. Fading shouts told him that patrols were pushing out in other passages. After several twists and what he estimated was a couple of hundred feet, he could no longer hear them. He switched on his light, and when there was no outcry behind him, left it on. Overhead was the trail of soot. Staying with the darkest stain, ignoring the lighter trails that branched off, Ben rushed ahead. He made an audible sigh of relief when he came to a familiar slide of stones. As he scrambled up the loose underfooting there was a faint tremble to the mountain, barely perceptible but loosing a fine shower of gravel in the passageway. Then came a distant boom. Gone was Black Dutch's secret opening. Soldiers and more guns would pour into the mountain now.

Ben closed his eyes briefly. "God, let me be right."

At the top of the incline the corridor widened into a wedge from which three smaller tunnels ran. Near the entrance of one a small yellow blob on the cave wall caught Ben's eye. His heart pounded. He ran until the tunnel came to the area where they'd sat on the slab. Overhead the soot was burnt-wick black and lifeless. It ran like an octopus in all directions from this one point. Ben followed the thickest tendril. Behind and far away now was the clink of scrambling feet and the occasional sound of voices. But the passage seemed familiar and Ben's confidence was growing. He followed a dusky trail winding about a projection. There were several openings. Inside the nearest was his jacket. Slipping it on, Ben ran down the shaft. He half expected to see Georgia, but there was only another bend in the corridor, and another, until he found himself facing the scarred stone still wedged across the corridor.

With fervor Ben attacked it with the crowbar. He drove the cold steel like a lance into the crevice. Blood oozed from scraped knuckles as he twisted the crowbar for purchase. All he accomplished was to rattle it against stone. Straining, he tried again and again, to no avail. The barrier would not give.

He stopped his useless jabbing. The clamor of the squads following came more clearly. Did he even have time to try a new way? He had no choice, he decided. His light danced on the soot trail above. To his surprise it was so thin that he knew this could not be Black Dutch's usual path. Berating himself for not checking it before, Ben retraced his route to where he'd left his jacket.

And there it was! A heavy cloud of soot led under a rugged arch. As he ran the sounds behind him faded to nothing again. Gradually another factor pricked his senses. Fire. The smell of burning wood in his nostrils was getting strong. Could he also hear it? Or was it his imagination?

There was a light ahead. Light and the crackle of a fire. Ben rounded a last turn and stopped, paralyzed with astonishment. Nothing in his experience prepared him for the scene that opened before his eyes in Black Dutch's hidden world.

It was an enormous domed chamber, filled with columns,

slathered over in runs and gullies. The smooth walls, all the way up to the highest reaches, were painted a myriad of mineral colors giving the effect of a gothic cathedral. By art or by chance the illusion was so overpowering, so much the product of another reality, that it took Ben time to orient himself, to know that he was real and Georgia was real and Black Dutch was real and that everything else was a phantasm, a shaman's work, the elusive memory of an elusive dream.

"Georgia." It came out as a croaked whisper.

Seated, her arms huddled around her updrawn knees, she was silhouetted against a well-stoked and leaping blaze in the middle of the chamber. Black Dutch was crouched on the far side by a pool.

Even from a distance and in the billowing light Ben could see the dark circles under Georgia's hollow eyes as she rasied her head. At the sight of him those eyes kindled with anger. He repeated her name and rushed to her.

"Are you okay? Has he hurt you?"

"Where have you been?" Her voice had a cutting edge and she drew back from his touch. "Why did you leave me?"

"I didn't have any choice, Georgia. I got back as fast as I could."

"You've been forever . . ."

"No. Just hours."

"*Hours?*" The caginess in her eyes showed her disbelief.

"Georgia. Time's distorted underground. You know that."

"I do, do I? Are you playing games with me, Ben?'

"He blocked the path. Didn't you hear me calling you?" His last words were no more than a hoarse whisper.

A softening came to her eyes. "Yes . . . for a while. When he ran back I thought it was to get you, but . . . he blocked the way?"

Ben nodded. "With a boulder." He showed her his bloody hands. "I couldn't move it."

As quickly as that the hard anger left Georgia's eyes. "I thought you'd let me go on alone." She stared at Ben, and then beyond him at the vast, inverted hemisphere, her gaze lingering at each dark hollow that hinted of a passageway.

"He wanted me to see this." Her voice choked.

Ben touched her cheek, then wrapped his arms around her in an embrace of friendship, love, and remorse.

"Do you know how to get out?" she whispered. "He keeps trying to lead me the wrong way."

"I'll take you out, Georgia."

Across the room Black Dutch stirred from his watchful pose and began to creep toward them.

Ben slipped the ancient Smith & Wesson from his belt.

"Don't come over here," he warned. The words were unnecessary. At sight of the gun Black Dutch backed into the shadows.

"Put that away," Georgia said irritably. "He's terrified of guns. Can't you tell?"

"Georgia, he kidnapped you. I'm not going to let him pull anything else."

"Kidnapped me? Ben, look around. Can you imagine how many years it took him to create this? All he wanted was to show it to me . . . to somebody."

Confused, Ben glanced at the giant fresco glittering back at him by the light of the fire. Near the pool an apron of ivory flowstone lapped the base of a column rising bright and rippling to the ceiling. But it was what a lonely man had done, not nature, that dominated. Fierce oranges, reds, and blues covered the gigantic walls.

Around the room, at Dutch's height, Indians and wildlife marched in file on the frieze's border. Stylized animals, both the hunted and the hunters, possessed fierce eyes, strangely magnetic and haunted. In costumes of exotic designs from early centuries, Indians were performing mysterious rituals. Like fork marks around a pie's edge, the drawings ran mansized, intense, full of life and lore but overshadowed by the work above them as cattle in the field are overshadowed by an approaching storm.

A massive painting of a cabin's interior swelled toward the dome. Ben identified it only with effort. It was created by an artist who long ago forgot the purpose and techniques of construction. Branches and leaves grew from the log walls. Furniture, doors, and windows were drawn from the point of view of a person lying on the floor. Or by a child. Shapes loomed large, seeming about to topple, and the vertical lines denied any sense of reality. The artist's attempts at perspective on a round surface failed. Lines converged strangely, causing Ben's senses to reel. The pinnacle was painted a dull yellow in imitation of a lantern's feeble light.

The main figures were overwhelming. On the left was a giant woman reaching down with dark, thin hands crisscrossed with knotted blue veins. There was in her sad dark eyes a look of some knowledge beyond today—or was it only disregard? Ben gaped. Her face, long and gaunt and Indian, was painted a vivid red.

"That has to be Black Dutch's mother," Georgia said, following Ben's gaze. "Her life must have been full of suffering."

The other figure was one of unfathomable menace, awesome and forbidding. It loomed from the opposite wall. A brown-haired man, dressed in faded overalls, peered scornfully down onto the cave room. The large head was narrow, the features sharply drawn, yet there was no power in them, only an undeniable meanness. His rawboned arms thrust upward from a workshirt whose rolled sleeves showed the line where sunburned skin turned pasty white. Clutched in his straining hands—like a weapon—was a shovel, its point reaching up from the wall, crossing the ceiling to hang there poised forever.

Ben struggled to understand. He looked from the walls to Georgia.

"I know, Ben . . . I sat here and stared at that dome until I thought I'd lost my mind. It's tortured and agonizing and brilliant. Dr. Hearst was right. Black Dutch is a messenger. A messenger with the boldness and passion of Rouault. God, it overwhelms me."

Slowly Ben put the gun away and, staring at the heights, edged around the fire. "Georgia," he said in a low tone, "we've got to get him—"

Without warning there were shouts of discovery. Like simians, soldiers came creeping warily into the chamber, their blades of light sweeping through the vast chamber. The beams caught Ben and Georgia briefly, blinding them, and then converged on Black Dutch, backing toward a far tunnel.

Garrett pushed through the soldiers. Instantly his hand

went to his holster. "Don't let him get away." His bass voice filled the dome as he aimed his pistol. "Shoot! He's escaping."

"No!" Georgia screamed. Ben lunged for her.

A thunderous roar set the cave walls reverberating. Black Dutch sagged toward the wall, then sank to his knees.

TWENTY-SEVEN

The hand holding the military automatic lowered to fire a round point-blank into Black Dutch's brain.

In one pulse beat Ben yanked a fiercely blazing pine branch from the fire and sent it whipping through the air like a runaway propeller. Sparkling resin and flaming bits of bark cascaded as the branch caught Garrett on the forehead, showering his hair with glowing cinders. His angry howl was nearly as loud as the roar of the automatic. A patch of painted wall—an Indian's ornamental necklace—was pulverized by the errant bullet.

Down on one knee Garrett waved the gun wildly. His eyes were lost in a mask of ash and blood. "Damn you, Hagen. I'll get you, you bastard."

Ben scrambled around the fire, grabbed at the gun, and brought his knee up to catch Garrett's arm in a painful cross pressure. Another bullet smacked into the dome as they struggled. Garrett's eyes widened in pain and surprise at the ferocity of Ben's grip. The gun clattered to the stone floor. With an oath the big man groped for Ben's throat. Steel fingers closed, and he brought all his heavy muscle to bear, shaking Ben so violently his hard hat flew off and rolled across the rock floor.

"Let him go," a voice rang out and Ben sensed, rather than saw, small hands flailing out. He glimpsed the top of a head and realized it was Dr. Hearst, trying to put his body between him and Garrett.

Another set of hands began to tug at Garrett, distracting him enough that Ben could gasp a breath of air and see that the sheriff, too, was trying to separate them.

"What're you waitin' for?" Rice rumbled loudly. "Get over here and help."

En masse deputies and guardsmen threw themselves on top and like an avalanche shoved the entangled men backward. They fell into a heap. Rice sorted through the arms and legs. "Take it easy, Garrett, or I'll put you in handcuffs."

"The s.o.b. threw a torch at me," Garrett bellowed.

"I'm gonna throw something at you, too, if you shoot another gun off in here. Now get yourself under control." Rice straightened and motioned to a medic. "Take care of this man."

"Where's Black Dutch?" Dr. Hearst asked as he regained his feet.

Garrett raised himself on one elbow and pointed. "Over there," he said with a hint of the old boasting in his voice. "Tell Arnold I got his monster."

The beams of the portable lights went to the area beyond the fire where Garrett was pointing. All eyes were riveted to the spot. The cave became silent.

"What is it?" Garrett demanded.

"He's gone."

"But I hit him. I know I did."

Rice strode over to search the stone. "Blood's splashed here, but there's no trail." He glanced up. Behind the flowstone were several dark openings. "Wish I had old Toby here."

"Forget the damn dog," Garrett yelled, yanking the towel away from the medic and wiping his eyes. "Fan out and get Black Dutch before he kills someone. He's crazy."

The men began to back away, fingering weapons, scanning the openings.

"For God's sake call this off!" Georgia cried, marching up to the sheriff. "Look at these pictures. Can't you see that he's been hunted all his life? Just for being different?"

"Miz Jones," he said, "are you all right?"

Soot and grime covered her face and clothes, but there was fire in her eyes. "I will be if you get Garrett and these soldiers out of here before they do something else stupid."

"In case you forgot, these men came here to save you."

"*Save* me? I'm lucky Garrett didn't shoot me. If it hadn't been for Ben . . ."

The sheriff tipped his hat back with one finger and stared

at her. "I think you might have something there, Miz Jones. But the important thing is you've been found."

"No, the important thing is you don't let these men kill Black Dutch."

"We thought he'd kidnapped you," the sheriff said slowly.

She gestured toward the all-encompassing artwork in vivid greens and reds and yellows that vaulted overhead.

"He thought I was a fellow artist." Her voice quivered. "All he wanted was to show me his work."

The sheriff peered, openmouthed, at the dome. "Well, I'll be. Kinda makes your mind whirl, doesn't it? But I still have to find him. I don't have any choice. But first let's get you out of here and to a doctor."

Georgia shook her head. "I don't want to go."

"You don't? Well . . . If I've learned anything in the last weeks it's been not to tell you what to do. Stay here as long as you like. Just don't get in the way."

She spun around and started over to where Dr. Hearst and Ben were examining the stone stained with Black Dutch's blood.

A National Guard colonel, a walkie-talkie at his ear, hurried into the chamber. "Mr. Arnold is on the way," he called to Rice. "He's heard about the shooting. He wants to see Black Dutch."

"I told you," Garrett's voice filled the dome, "you better get that s.o.b."

"This is a circus," the sheriff mumbled, and pulled the colonel to one side to talk.

Dr. Hearst seized the moment. "Try to find Black Dutch first, Ben. Please, while you have the chance. Get him away from here."

Ben looked toward one of the openings.

"That's not the right one," Georgia said so quietly they barely heard her.

"You know where he went?" Dr. Hearst asked.

"I know which way he went. He tried to get me to follow him, but I wouldn't. I—I couldn't."

"Then tell Rice," Ben said quickly, "before some of these others jokers get to him."

"The sheriff can't control this job. With Garrett egging

them on they'll kill him if they get the chance." She closed her eyes and drew in a deep breath. "You and I have to find him, Ben."

"Just tell me where he went. I'll go."

"You'd never find it." She fixed her eyes on him. "Anyway he's afraid of you. No, I have to go, too."

Garrett was back on his feet and in a rage, arguing with the sheriff as the deputies and guardsmen watched. Rice's voice rose above the others. "As soon as the medic's through with you I want you out of here."

"Hurry," Dr. Hearst urged. "While everyone's distracted."

"Give us your flashlight," Georgia said to him. Dr. Hearst retrieved it from the cave floor and handed it to her. "Stay close, Ben." It was not so much an order as a plea. She ducked into one of the smaller passages.

Grim-faced, Ben followed. He could hardly believe after all Black Dutch had put them through they were going deeper into the bowels of the mountain to save him.

TWENTY-EIGHT

As silently as possible they scuttled into utter darkness. Ben pulled out his flashlight, but the pressure of Georgia's hand on his wrist warned him to leave it unlit. After crawling over a wide rock slab, they were able to stand. Georgia led him by an opening and turned down a tight offshoot. Muffled voices and the click of boots on stone alerted them that their absence had been discovered. Ben inched his way after Georgia. Near exhaustion himself, he knew she was tired, too, tired of the confinement, and the blackness, and the pressing weight. Behind them the sounds faded.

"I bet Dr. Hearst led them down a tunnel away from us," he whispered.

Without replying, Georgia picked her way among the passages, her shoes scraping on the gravelly floor.

"You really up to this?" Ben asked when their space narrowed to barely more than a slit.

"I don't know." Her voice was heavy with fear. After an interval, she added, "Black Dutch led me through here. There's a spot up ahead where I stopped, and for a long time he tried to get me to go on but I couldn't." She flicked on her flashlight. "You'll see why soon."

The bright beam bounced around a small white-and-pink stone chute with lettucelike stone sheets sagging overhead. Georgia stooped, nearly doubled, scanning the lowest rim.

"Here." She sighed. Ben saw resignation and fatigue in her shadowy face. "This is where he went."

Ben squatted and peeked under the rock where Georgia

was directing her light. A thin passage, as confining as a grave, angled down.

"Good God, Georgia, we're not going in there, are we?"

"Look—on the lip."

A dark red blot glistened on the stone.

"He crawled under here a dozen times trying to get me to follow," she said, "but I wouldn't do more than stick my head in."

"Georgia . . ."

"He's in there. I know he is. And if we don't get to him, he doesn't have a chance. He'll run from their guns just like he ran from yours. Just like he's been running from them all his life."

Ben swallowed. The words to stop her, the ones reminding her of a phobia so intense she wouldn't talk about it, were on his lips, but he couldn't say them.

Reflected light off ivory flowstone caught the haunted look in her eyes. With a grimace she lay on her back beside the low rim. "Maybe it's only a short tunnel to another room, or a shortcut out."

"And maybe it divides into a hundred holes."

"If that happens we'll come back, but at least I'll know I tried. He wanted me to follow him so much. I couldn't . . . but now I must. We must."

Georgia writhed under headfirst. "This is the way Black Dutch did it." Her shoulders disappeared, then her body. She was forced to scoot inch by inch because there was not even enough clearance for her knees to bend for leverage. Then she was gone and it was Ben's turn.

The cold of ancient stone penetrated his clothes and settled into his bones as he worked his way into the small cavity. Using his shoulders, buttocks, and heels for purchase, Ben squirmed to catch Georgia, panic at the edges of his mind. He took a deep breath. The big fluorescent dial on his watch cast a cloudy light that dissipated at the gray stone, hanging inches from his nose.

"Are you okay, Georgia?" he asked in a hushed tone.

"This is awful . . . I don't know how far I'll be able to go."

"Any sign of him?"

"No. At first I thought I heard scraping ahead. Now I can't tell with all the noise you're making."

Ben sent his beam into the far reaches and was surprised to learn the low space they were crawling through was wide, endlessly so it seemed. A surge of uncontrolled fear made him shudder and twist frantically for a better view.

"Such a crack isn't structurally possible," he muttered to himself. The flashlight slipped from his clammy hand and rolled down by his ankle. A clumsy move with his foot pushed it farther away.

"Georgia, wait," he called into the menacing stone above his face. "I dropped my flashlight."

The words, deeper than he said them, were thrown back at him. He tried to scoot sideways and couldn't. The ray of light below him bathed the ceiling with an eerie glow.

"Hurry," Georgia's voice seemed to come from far away. "Please."

He swore as he willed his muscles to move backward until his fingers touched the warm metal. He grasped the flashlight firmly and shut it off.

"I've got it," he yelled, pushing frantically toward her. The cold flowed upward from his hips and spine to the thumping core of his chest. On he crawled in absolute blackness, realizing almost abstractly that the wetness in his socks was blood. He'd rubbed his heels raw. Every few yards he reached up to touch the limits of the oppressive weight.

Anxiety, like a hungry wolf, crawled with him. With no signals for his brain other than the lagging fluids of his inner ear and the fading circle of light on his wrist, he had the illusion that he was moving on the sides of the tunnel, even on the ceiling. His watch dial faded. The nightmare dragged on. Ben was unable to tell whether his eyes were open or closed. His hands and knees were also sticky with blood. He battled the fear that it would never end, that they would come to a point where the mountain would squeeze the life out of them. In a spot a bit higher he wrenched himself over in one angry, violent, shoulder-gouging maneuver. Now he crawled like an infantryman with sand grinding its way inside his shirt and rolling down his chest to cut into his skin. With a thump he hit Georgia's boot with his nose.

"Is that you?" she asked shakily.

"I'm right behind you."

"This can't go on much longer." There was a pleading in her voice.

"No, it can't," he soothed her, wishing that he could be sure his words were true.

The sound of Georgia's movements, cloth crunching through gravel, drifted back to him in the dark. He caught both the unadorned subtle scent of her and—was he imagining it?— the earthier smell of Dutch. Instantly another fear gripped Ben.

"You okay?" he rasped.

There was no answer, but the faint chuff, chuff from ahead gave him hope. As long as he heard that steady beat, as long as Georgia could keep crawling, there was sense to this madness.

At last the ceiling rose away from his touch.

The pounding in Ben's chest confirmed his relief, and it was his own cry that he heard when there was a gleam of natural light ahead. Blinking, he made out Georgia scurrying toward it, and he picked up his pace, scraping his torn finger-nails and elbows as he crawled after her into the soft glow emitting from a hatchet-shaped room. The hand laid on his was trembling.

He reached to put his arms around her.

The precious pink light of dawn was streaming through a narrow crack that ran down one side from the room's peak. Through the slit Ben could see that the outside surface of the mountain was many yards away. The only other opening beside the one they'd come in was a dark small hole at the end of the narrow cell. Huddled beside it was a gray mass. As Ben's eyes adjusted he realized it was Black Dutch, squatting, arms clutching his sides.

"I can't move, Ben," Georgia whispered. "I think I'm losing it. Will you see how badly he's hurt?"

Reluctantly Ben bowed to Georgia's wishes and left her side. Fumbling at his belt and inside his jacket, he discovered he'd dropped more than one thing in the cave. The flashlight he'd retrieved was still in his pocket but the old Smith & Wesson was gone, jiggled loose somewhere during their mad-dening crawl. As ready as Georgia was to accept Black Dutch as eternal victim, Ben was still leery of the strange recluse.

Carefully, stiffly, his hands drawn up in fists, he moved forward, alert for an attack. With a groan Black Dutch shrank from him. Guiltily, Ben realized that he was the only one acting like a combatant.

He stooped and gingerly reached out to open his father's flight jacket. It was caked with blood in the lining. Black Dutch sighed like a shot moose.

"Easy, old fellow," Ben crooned, "I'll do what I can for you." He touched the soft white hair at the base of Dutch's throat. Slowly his hand slipped toward the red glistening mat at his side.

"How is he?" Georgia asked in a shaky voice.

"I wouldn't be surprised if his rib's busted, but the wounds are clean, in and out. They're clotting already."

Ben stripped off his own jacket, then his shirt. The sound of shredding cloth brought a flicker of fear to Black Dutch's good eye.

"Easy, Dutch," Ben talked to him. "I'm gonna put my hands around you now and bandage this. That's all."

Dutch stiffened, as if to brace for a blow. As Ben wrapped the strips around him, Dutch's good eye wandered to the pink light and his sadness was so intense Ben felt it as a stab of pain in his own heart. He sat back.

Ben had never seen such vulnerability. It almost paralyzed him.

"Maybe you ought to come over here, Georgia." he managed at last. "To reassure him."

There was no response. Ben turned and looked at her. One cheek was pressed firmly against the gash of light and her face was deathly pale.

"Georgia?"

A stifled noise filled Ben with apprehension. He hurriedly knotted the bandage, put on his jacket, and went back to her. She did not take her face from the knife-slit of a window on the world.

"Everything's going to be okay," he said.

"We can't get out of here."

"Sure we can. We'll go back."

A terror filled her eyes. "No. I can't crawl through there again. I won't. I'd rather sit here and die."

[213]

Her gaze was fixed on the unreachable sky. Powerless, like a revolutionary against the dictator's wall, she trembled next to the heartbreakingly thin passage to freedom.

"There's another way out, Georgia." He tried to pull her to him but failed. "There's a passage over there beyond Black Dutch. We'll try that."

"I can't go on," she whispered. "I told you, I'm losing it."

"You're okay, Georgia. We're okay." He drew an audible intake of air. "Breathe deeply. Can't you smell the pine? We must be near another entrance."

She moaned. "I'm like the worst rookie in the drift—trapped by a hairline crack of light and my own fear."

He tried again to turn her to face him. She brushed him away, but he saw the tears on her cheeks. He spoke tentatively.

"You've been trapped in a cave before, haven't you? A cave, or a mine?"

"Yes," The word was a mixture of meekness and something else—something like a guilty secret, the sort of behavior a battered child might exhibit. She pressed harder to the slit.

There was a stirring behind him, and Ben realized that he'd turned his back on the man he'd been ready to shoot minutes before.

Black Dutch's unhappy gaze was fixed on Georgia.

"We can make it," Ben said to him, to Georgia, to himself.

At the gash Georgia sucked in the fresh air, releasing it in a long sigh. Ben stroked her hair. Her body was trembling.

"Tell me about it, Georgia," he whispered.

"Oh, Ben, it's so awful."

"Tell me."

She lifted her tortured eyes to his. "We were students. Four of us. From the Colorado School of Mines, on a special trip to a German coal mine near München. Only the top students—the four best—got to go . . . Sonny Scott joked we were the four deepest students in the school. Poor Sonny . . ."

"What happened?"

"Methane, they said. Sonny never knew. He was . . ."

"Killed in an explosion?"

"Between us and the main shaft. His head . . ." Her voice was a whisper, barely louder than the mountain wind licking through the crack to which she clung. "He was decapitated . . . poor blond, blue-eyed Sonny."

Ben didn't know whether to encourage her or try to stop her.

"The others from the school were on the far side of the fall. I was with Sonny and Fritz Hochner, a German engineer."

"Were you hurt?"

"A little. Fritz was dying."

Her hands clasped at the vertical lips of the cleft as though she would pull them apart by main force and exit the mountain like Samson.

"How long before they got you out, Georgia?" This was the question he didn't want to ask most of all. He knew whatever the answer, it would not be as long as it had seemed. "Georgia?"

"Sixteen hours before the lights burned out," she murmured. "Forty-nine hours until the rescuers broke through. I've never been able to decide which was worse, being able to see Fritz and Sonny or being in the dark imagining them."

"I'm sorry, Georgia."

She half laughed, half groaned. "You saw through me from the first and I knew it. You saw that climbing the outside of a mountain was something I do—not because I'm brave but because I'm not brave enough to do what I should—go back to the mines." She choked. "I don't have the courage for that."

"That's not true, Georgia. It took a hell of a lot of courage to come in here. And the only thing I ever saw was that you didn't like closed-up places."

Her shoulders shook in Ben's hands.

A gray-haired arm, protruding out of a worn brown sleeve, reached past Ben, and a hairy finger touched the tears glistening on Georgia's cheek. "Yor—yah." The two sounds rumbled from deep in his soul.

She turned, openmouthed, to look into the bushy face. Beside her Ben was equally stunned.

"Yor—yah," it came again almost like a chant.

"You can say my name?" Fresh tears flowed, but the sight of the battered old outcast in ragged overalls and a World War II flight jacket seemed to penetrate to whatever reservoirs of strength remained to her.

[215]

He pointed to the opening at the apex of the room. Ben saw the simple pleading in the mismatched eyes.

"Oh, Dutch," Georgia groaned, "you're tearing my heart out. Am I supposed to follow you through this mountain forever?"

Ben felt his spirits rising. Her words were full of anguish, but they were said with renewed energy.

Dutch seemed to sense the change in her, too. He began to back toward the hole.

"You said yourself, Georgia, that he probably knew another way out of the cave. That has to be it."

She turned, searching Ben's face as if she were trying to judge his words, but she didn't move from the light.

"Come on," he encouraged her. "It's almost over."

She peered through glassy eyes. "How do we know he doesn't want to take us deeper into the mountain?"

Ben made his way over to the low tunnel and lit up the first twenty feet of it.

"Come see for yourself, Georgia," he said excitedly. "It gets bigger as it goes. I think this is it."

"Do you mean it?" Georgia asked, sounding like a child.

"Yeah, I do. Inside it's at least four feet high."

She wiped her eyes on her sleeve and started over. It was what Black Dutch had been waiting for. He bent into the tunnel.

Trembling, Georgia stooped and entered the gritty space after him. Ben brought up the rear once again. As they moved forward hunched-over and in single file, Georgia was quiet and Ben knew she was drawing on all her resources. He started talking as he'd never talked before in his life. He told her about flying, about the dinner Spaulding would fix for them when they got back, about his rock climbing for the Rangers, about anything to keep Georgia from thinking about being trapped under a trillion pounds of mountain.

In cross section the tunnel was like an inverted canoe, deep in the sides and arching at the ceiling. Ahead, Dutch scuffled through the grit. After what Ben guessed was a quarter mile there came a perceptible change in the pitch of the floor. Instead of a flat run, the gravel gave way to a downward slope. The angle of descent kept increasing until Ben was walking sideways to keep his balance. Gravel broke loose under his feet and he slid stiff-armed into Georgia. There was a muffled, scrambling sound as they tumbled down the dark channel and crashed into Black Dutch. The three of them landed in a tangle at the base of the gravel fall. Groaning, Dutch crawled away, and Georgia sat up.

"Where are we?" she asked. "It's awfully dark."

Ben felt a stabbing pain in his hip, realized it was his flashlight, and shifted to pick it up. The light bounced against a wall a few feet in front of them.

"Oh no," Georgia said, "it can't be. We're at a dead end."

Ben sat there in disappointed silence and stared at the gray rock. Beside him Georgia curled up in a ball, hiding her face. Anger began to well in Ben, and an enormous sense of desperation. How was he ever going to get her to crawl back through the mountain? The sound of falling pebbles caused him to look up. Black Dutch was hoisting himself painfully over a ledge nine or ten feet above the floor.

"Yor-Yah." The low plea echoed.

"Up there, Georgia," Ben said.

She raised her head. "Oh, God, another crack."

Ben climbed several feet and felt something warm brush his hair. He twisted his head and saw Dutch's hairy hand. Ben grabbed it and pulled his shoulders up over the ledge. Dutch was stretched out beside him. In the dark Ben made out an overhanging rock within hand's reach. There was not even a passageway.

"Jesus Christ," he muttered and closed his eyes.

Beside him Dutch shifted his weight and dropped his legs over the far side of the wall. Ben blinked his tired eyes. And blinked again. Low, on the other side of the ledge, where Dutch's legs were hanging, was a line of creamy light. Ben dangled over the ledge. The line became broader.

"Georgia!" he cried. "Light, there's light!" Pushing himself back, he half fell down the wall beside her.

"What?" Georgia asked, brightening instantly.

"I saw light—real light—daylight. On the other side. Come on. We're going to get out of here."

He pulled her to her feet.

"Climb, Georgia. Climb. See for yourself."

She started up and saw Dutch's hand stretching for her. She reached for it. When she was leaning over the ledge Ben called, "Look over and down. It's an overhang. See? See!"

TWENTY-NINE

Its dimensions were lost in shadows but the core of the chamber was bathed in ghostly light drifting down from a gash high in a roof fracture. Glistening white stalagmites and crystal water falling into terraces of naturally formed stone saucers made the broad cave chamber look like a garden in a Roman temple. Laughing joyfully, Georgia hurried to the pool and brushed handfuls of water over her face. Black Dutch, imitating her, threw it in an arc over his head. The light caught the drops as they fell glinting to the stone around his feet. Relishing the moment, Ben still stood by the overhanging ledge that hid their route through the mountain.

From her perch by the pool Georgia leaned back and stared straight up into the milky light. Then, satisfied, she looked around the sparkling white chamber, her inspection stopping at boulders behind the terraced waterfall.

"Look, Ben. We can climb out!"

A big grin spread over his face. "I don't think I've ever seen a more welcome sight in my life."

His boots stirred up ashes from old fires as he eased around the cave's edge toward her. Pinpoints of light in the shadows caught his eye. Curious, Ben lifted a fist-sized chip and examined it in his flashlight.

His whistle was low. "Georgia, you're not going to believe this."

She left the water and came to his side. Her cool, wet hand slid under his.

"Is that what I think it is?" he asked.

A crystal as thick as Ben's wrist glittered in reflected light. Packed in crevices were traces of soft dull metalwork.

She gasped. "I don't believe it! Gold in a quartz matrix. Just like Spaulding's."

Ben played his light on the sparkling ceiling. "There must be a fortune in here."

As if on signal they both turned toward Black Dutch, now dabbing water on himself, not unlike a sparrow, dipping and splashing and shivering.

"Whose gold is this—Arnold's or his?"

"Interesting question, Ben. I don't know."

"Yeah, well, it won't matter to Dutch anyway if we can't get him away from here."

"And to a doctor. But I'll be damned if I know how we're going to handle it. The mountain is covered with men ready to shoot him on sight."

There was no sound in the cave for a long moment except the splash of water.

"I suppose I could stay here with him while you go for the sheriff," Ben said. "He's the only one I can think of who'll keep a cool head. But for God's sake make him come alone."

She smiled wanly. "Dutch isn't going to like it if I leave."

"I know, but you're the better climber."

"And besides, you want me out of here, right?"

"I left you once in this mountain. I'm not going to do it again."

Georgia handed the crystal to him. Kneeling, she spoke to Black Dutch in low, even tones.

"I'm going for help, Dutch." She motioned toward the opening overhead. "I'll come back. I promise."

Confusion spread behind the tangled whiskers. When Georgia began to climb the boulders near the pool, Black Dutch grunted and moved his hands in that familiar circling motion before his chest.

Georgia hesitated. "I don't know what to do."

"Just go," Ben urged.

She started up again, but Black Dutch, protesting louder, leaped to his feet. Bent toward his wounded side, he disappeared in the darkness beyond the shaft of light. After a

[220]

moment he reappeared, repeated his act, and once more ducked under a shoulder of the cave.

"Ben, he wants me to follow him again."

"Just get the sheriff," Ben said, waving her on. "I'll go after Dutch."

Sweeping the darkness with his flashlight, Ben also ducked under the rock shoulder. The bright arc penetrated the shadowy recess before him and picked up the gray form bending over a terrace of flowstone. Black Dutch was rocking back and forth. As Ben worked his way toward him a mournful keening began.

"Georgia . . ." The name echoed through the chamber. "You better come back, after all."

She dropped to the cave floor and bent to slip into the oysterlike rim of the cave. "Oh, no." Her hands came up to her mouth. "It can't be."

Dutch was on his knees beside a white sheet of stone—like a bier.

Upon it was the lifeless body of Daisy O'Sullivan.

She was laid out in ceremonial fashion. A hammered metal disk glowed on her forehead and around the body quartz crystals were placed forming a long oval. Her clothes were spread straight and neat, and her long brown hair, framing her face, flowed down her sides. One shoulder rose strangely, as though propped up by a stiff pillow. All these details meant nothing to Georgia as she approached and peered into that once cheerful, plump face.

It was not a trick of the light.

Daisy's face was painted bright red. And in her hand was a wooden carving, a replica of her face, also painted red.

Georgia's voice throbbed with anguish. "Oh, Daisy! Oh, Black Dutch!"

His heart sinking, Ben tried to shake off his own shock. Was this awful violence the result of all the years Black Dutch was forced to live as an outcast? Was he crazy after all?

Squatting at Daisy's head, Black Dutch fingered a curl reverently.

"Maybe it was an accident," Georgia agonized. "Maybe she fell and he found her."

"You don't believe that," Ben said. "I'm afraid he's a madman, just like Arnold thought."

"What are we going to do?" she asked.

"You've still got to go for the sheriff," he said, looking from Dutch back to the body. For the first time his eyes fixed on the strangely positioned shoulder. Brushing her hair aside, he grasped her arms. Daisy was cold, the temperature of the cave that had become her sarcophagus.

"What are you doing?" Georgia asked, sounding as if she thought Ben had gone mad, too.

Not answering, he carefully rolled the stiff body to one side. The dislodged disk clinked to the damp stone floor with a tinny reverberation. Grunting his disapproval, Dutch got to his feet.

"Be careful," Georgia warned. "You're upseting him."

Ben grimaced. "It's all right," he said, swallowing hard. "Black Dutch is not the monster on this mountain."

Georgia drew nearer. Ben's light, hard edged so close up, was focused below Daisy's shoulder blades. Protruding from her lower spine, its blade angling up toward her heart, was the ebony handle of a commando knife with a serrated knuckle guard.

"That's . . . that's—" Georgia was stunned.

"—Garrett's," Ben finished for her.

Sounds of distress came from Black Dutch. He brushed at Ben's hand to make him return Daisy to her position of rest.

As Ben reached to shift the body, Georgia spoke sharply, almost angrily. "Take it out."

"What?"

"Take it out."

"I can't touch the knife. You know that."

"Get it out of her. I can't stand the idea of that thing being in her. It's horrible."

Her request was irrational, but Ben understood the emotion behind it. The knife was grotesque, slicing through the pink thermal jacket. From a gritty pocket he fished out his handkerchief and wrapped it around the handle. Both Georgia and Dutch watched intently as he tried to ease it out.

"It's imbedded in her spine," he said.

"Try," Georgia pleaded. "We can't leave her like this."

Ben braced one hand against Daisy's cold back and pulled with the other. At that instant a metallic snap echoed through the cave. Ben froze. He knew the sound. He whipped around as a small canister bounced once on the lip of the pool and rolled in their direction.

"Grenade!" he shouted.

There was a tremendous concussion, throwing Ben and Georgia together against a column like the muzzle blast of a cannon. As Ben struggled to stay conscious a hailstorm of rock and quartz pounded them. Ears ringing, he rolled off Georgia, who flinched and clutched at her leg.

The first thing Ben was able to hear was the labored breathing of Black Dutch, caught in a wedge of rock on the other side of Daisy's bier. The second riveted his attention to the heart of the cave. Grating sounds told him that someone was scrambling down from the slit in the ceiling. Through the dust cloud and glittering flakes of crystal he was unable to see who it was, but he heard the heavy thump as boots hit the gravel-covered floor. Next a powerful light stabbed through the roiling atmosphere in erratic circles.

Ben ordered his legs to move, knowing that whatever chance he and Georgia and Black Dutch had to survive depended upon his acting before the air cleared. His foot scraped across a stone as he raised to a crouch.

The light swept back through the haze, and the cold echo of Jim Garrett's voice filled the cave. "So you're alive. Too bad for you, old man. Dying by a grenade would have been easier."

Pebbles crunched as Garrett came steadily forward. In the maelstrom Ben saw the stubby outline of the Uzi.

"I'm grateful to you for making this so easy," Garrett said in a flat voice. "Daisy would be, too. She never liked being alone."

A rock crashed noisily into a flowstone column by his head. Cursing, Garrett fired blindly into the murky reaches. Black Dutch unloaded another missile. The Uzi hummed like a stirred-up hornet's nest. Ben felt the sting of a metal fragment on his ear and flattened himself on the damp cave floor. Bullets ricocheted around the chamber, causing crystalline quartz to filter like snow through the vapor. A dislodged boulder shattered on the rim of the pool, sending up water and another cloud of dust.

When the shooting stopped, the cave was filled with an unearthly silence, intensified by the grainy sound of raining particles. The odor of burnt gunpowder was like pepper in the air. Waiting, every muscle tensed, Ben wished for his lost Smith & Wesson. Not until he raised the back of his hand to wipe his eyes did he realize the commando knife, black with Daisy's dried blood, was in his hand.

At the snap of a bolt he sprang, skidding across the slick stone floor. He more crashed into Garrett than attacked him. The big man swiped at his head with the squat submachine gun, missed, and came down hard on his knees. Ben leaped on his back and locked one arm around his thick neck.

Garrett twisted violently, pounding Ben in the side with the gun. The knife in Ben's hand was in a Ranger position, butt to thumb like an ice pick but flat against Garrett's chest because Ben was not yet ready to go to the last extremity of battle. Their struggle edged them into the pale illumination by the flowstone pool. Digging his boots into the floor, Garrett rolled Ben off balance against the ragged teeth of quartz. Caught between unyielding rock and a body larger and more powerful than his own, Ben groaned in agony. His head banged against stone. The same darkness that overcame him at the campfire during the search for Daisy was descending once more.

It was almost a respite when his attacker switched tactics, shoving him downward, gouging one cheek against the biting quartz. With a flick of his wrist Ben brought the razor-sharp blade across the biceps of Garrett's knotted arm.

"Ah!" Garrett cried lustily. It was neither a renewed challenge nor an acknowledgment of the pain. It was a cry of fierce delight that his foe was better than he'd thought. The little machine gun clattered to the floor, and Garrett whirled to take Ben on face-to-face.

Neither of them saw Georgia limp from the shadows, grab the weapon, and retreat. Garrett pulled his knife from its sheath and circled Ben. Almost as long as a sword, it gave the big mercenary a two-foot reach over Ben, who still held the shorter commando knife upside down, the blade lying along the inside of his thin arm. Behind him, Georgia sidestepped to get a clear shot as Garrett's knife flashed across at nose height, a vicious cut Ben was barely able to dodge. When he lunged again Ben blocked him on the forearm with his own weapon, leaving a blood stripe like a chevron across his attacker's right sleeve.

Undaunted, Garrett stepped forward to pin Ben against the wall. The Ka-Bar mowed hair and a patch of scalp from Ben's head. With a cry Ben joined his hands and thrust upward. The butt of the commando knife snapped Garrett's jaw with the sound of a firecracker. As he stumbled backward, the bloody blade, still held against Ben's arm, raked Garrett's chest. His startled eyes showed he knew well the next step of the drill. Desperately he moved to ward off the blow with his weakened arm, but the point of the sweeping knife snagged on a rib, and bit into the mercenary's side.

"Oh, shit," he groaned and sagged to the floor. The knife that he'd used on Daisy protruded from his right side like a gearshift. Spreading blood turned his jacket dark as he struggled to sit up against a quartz-veined ledge, sparkling in the filmy circle of light.

Ben stumbled toward Georgia, knelt, and ripped open the soaked leg of her pants. Blood ran down her shin from a shrapnel wound below one knee.

"Hold still," he said and tore off a piece of the ragged material to tie over the wound.

"Is he still alive?" she asked.

"I don't know."

When Georgia's leg was wrapped Ben returned to the downed man and placed a hand over his chest. The heartbeat was erratic. "He's alive, but we've got to get him help in a hurry."

Garrett's eyes opened partway as Ben tried to lay him down in an easier position. He gave Ben a contemptuous smile.

"Don't fuck this up with a phony display of remorse. I don't need it." His voice, despite its clear defiance, was weak.

"We'll get a doctor. Hold on."

"Hold on. To what?" Garrett started to laugh, but stopped abruptly at the pain. "You were a little low for a classic thrust, but it'll do."

Georgia touched Ben on the shoulder. "I'll go."

Garrett shook his head. "Why bother? I'll die anyway—for Daisy's murder." The ragged canine tooth bit into his lower lip. "It would have been a lot easier to kill the lot of you than her." A bubble of blood formed on his lips. "I liked that fat little gal."

"But you liked the gold better," Georgia said bitterly.

"It was my ticket out of this shitty business. She was with me when I followed the old man here. What choice did I have? She was climbing out, chatting about how happy she was going to make her father." Ben stared at him in contempt. "Said she'd found the rock candy room of her childhood. She figured Arnold would give us all a reward."

Garrett's eyes went to the bier where Daisy lay.

"I couldn't trust her to be quiet . . . and I thought it was going to be so easy to shut up the old man. I almost got him in that Sistine Chapel of his."

"Shut him up?" Georgia repeated. "You fool. Black Dutch doesn't know how to talk."

Surprise and chagrin registered in Garrett's eyes, then his chin dropped to his chest. Georgia leaned in front of his face, forcing him to look at her.

"You hit Ben that night we were searching for Daisy, didn't you? And you planted her shoes down the mountain so we'd stop looking up here."

Garrett stared at her contemptuously. "You figure it out. I'm not going to help you."

"I think I already have," Georgia said. "It was you who poisoned the workers and let loose the tanker. To kill Arnold. You were trying to halt the project, weren't you?"

A pathetic smirk drove the pain momentarily away from Garrett's face. "Don't leave Ben out of the equation. I'd have loved to see him cook." Dust began to settle on his half-closed eyes. He pointed painfully to Black Dutch. "If I'd gotten that old fucker I'd have made it, too. Didn't know he had a second cave. When he disappeared after I shot him in the other one, I figured they had to be connected."

Georgia stood up suddenly, her eyes darting about the shadows.

"Black Dutch? Where is he?"

Ben moved toward the flowstone.

Through the dim light he saw Black Dutch restoring Daisy's bier. He was cut on his forehead, but that seemed to be the worst of the new damage he'd absorbed. Georgia hobbled to his side and helped him arrange the crystals around her body. When they were finished Dutch gently replaced the carving and stepped back. He seemed satisfied.

"Georgia," Ben said, "I can't leave you down here, and I can't leave these two. Can you walk well enough to go for the sheriff?"

She nodded.

Black Dutch watched as she slowly climbed the rock to the thin gash in the cave ceiling. At the opening she paused, suspended halfway in the underground and halfway in the light.

"What do you see?" Ben called.

"Give me a second. The river! A long way down. We're on a wooded cliff."

She hoisted herself up over the lip. When she disappeared from sight Black Dutch crossed agonizingly to the rocks and started up after her.

"Hey, stay here," Ben shouted.

Without glancing back, Black Dutch made the painful climb and hefted himself through the opening.

"Damn," Ben said.

He checked Garrett's ebbing signs of life. The older man's eyes were closed and his breathing was shallow. Ben grabbed up the submachine gun and made his own way up the rock staircase. His exit was a clumsy roll over the lip.

The fresh air was like a jolt of smelling salts. He stood. The sun was low in the eastern sky. Several yards beneath him, in a clump of scraggly cedars, he saw the gray head of Black Dutch and, beside him, Georgia's dark hair. Far below them was the river.

"Wait, Georgia," he called. "We've got to get Black Dutch to stay here."

"Come look, Ben. It's beautiful."

A notch in the rocks beside him made an easy climb down.

Georgia was standing on the edge of the precipice. Beside her Black Dutch, in Ben's blood-caked jacket, hugged his arms over his wound and watched her happily with his good eye. A hundred feet below, the narrow flashing river plunged through its deep channel. To the west a shallow slope led far down to the back of the mountain. Snow was in the hollows.

"Up and over's the only way," Georgia said. "But now I guess you'll have to go. I'll stay with Dutch."

"I don't know, Georgia."

"It's the only way. He'd follow me and get himself killed . . . after all of this."

"Maybe we can brace him between us and walk out to—"

A pebble bounced down the slope behind them.

They all three twisted around.

Garrett, the stubby black knife handle still protruding from his side, was staggering to his feet at the cave opening.

"You haven't beat me yet, fuckers," he cried, and jumped.

Ben braced to meet him, but Black Dutch pushed both him and Georgia away and took the full force of Garrett's body on his own shoulders. He cried out and fell toward the edge, unable to stand up against the enormous weight. His eyes sought out Georgia frantically.

"Your-Yah," he gasped. He stretched out his hand to her.

"Dutch," Georgia cried. She clutched for him, but all she got was a fist full of silky gray hair.

The two men tilted on the verge of space. Garrett grabbed a blueberry bush to save himself, but the roots tore loose from the rocky soil. Ben made a desperate attempt to snag a hairy foot but missed. There was fear in Dutch's face as he fell away, struggling to free himself from Garrett. Georgia gasped in horror.

It was an eternity before twin plumes of water shot up and a split second later they heard the smack of the impact.

"Oh my God. Oh my God." Georgia wept.

Ben retreated into silence.

THIRTY

Opening day at Mystic Mountain was pushed back six months, then a year, but at last it came, on a June day of brilliant sunshine and a hint of a breeze. The front walks and tram rides through the park were jammed. It was only midmorning and already the count was more than one hundred thousand visitors. And that didn't include the hundreds of newspaper and television reporters headquartered at the new hotel on the bald.

Ben's first glimpse of Georgia was through the crowd on the roller coaster platform. Tanned and slender, she was wearing a red sleeveless jumpsuit and what looked like white patent leather climbing boots. Her hair was held back from her face by a shiny white band. She was laughing, exchanging banter with a flushed, exhilarated Arnold. He'd arranged for her to be on the first official ride of the Death Spiral with him, paying her expenses all the way from Peru, where she was working on a mining railroad. The fame of her roller coaster design had opened new doors for her.

Ben stood alone, watching from the shadow of the big lucite tree that stretched above him nearly a hundred feet. He was present at the grand opening because Spaulding, on his own, entered his name on the computerized guest list. Ben had flown tourist class from Florida to Asheville, where Mac Powell gave him a lift in his helicopter for the last leg.

As a brass band played a loud fanfare, the Death Spiral cars started up the incline. Grinning, Arnold settled back, lifted both his arms in a wave, and whispered to Georgia. Instantly she raised her arms, too. When the car plunged through the first series of loops Ben turned and walked away.

After the ride, Georgia pushed a path through the crowds to the spot where she was to meet him and Spaulding. She greeted them both with hugs, but the one for Ben was a good bit longer.

Spaulding, decked out in a white suit, complete with vest and white tie, led the way to the staff entrance for the cave ride. As they descended into the mountain, Ben glanced toward Georgia. If being underground bothered her anymore, she was doing a fine job of hiding it. Her face was radiant. She winked at him.

At a guard station Spaulding showed his ID. "Good morning, Roy. Have you seen Dr. Hearst?"

The uniformed man pointed down the long tunnel. Spaulding nodded and they hurried on. It took Ben several moments to realize that the guard was Mrs. Grandy's son.

"Eventually this corridor will also service the chamber of gold," Spaulding chatted.

"How's Arnold developing that?" Georgia asked.

"It's a ride . . . but an unusual one. Visitors will go through it in sealed cars. Sort of like taking street people on a tour of Tiffany's, Mr. Arnold says."

Ben thought about Black Dutch and said nothing. Beside him, Georgia was also quiet.

"I need to prepare you for what's happened to the cave paintings," Spaulding said apologetically, as if he were responsible.

"It's that bad?" Ben asked.

Georgia sighed. "I still want to see them. Sometimes I feel that everything that happened up here is unreal. And this . . . this . . ." Her arm arched out in an encompassing gesture. "I'm struggling to even remember what the mountain was."

Down the tunnel a red glow appeared, accompanied by the snap of a heavy electrical circuit opening and closing. As Ben and Georgia drew near they saw that a round viewing room was rising smoothly toward the cave roof like a carousel on an elevator shaft. It plugged a hole in the rock ceiling as precisely as a stopper in a drain. The air throbbed with whirring sounds.

In the shadowy tunnel Dr. Hearst was seated beyond the

glare of a couple of naked bulbs dangling from the platform's bottom. Georgia embraced him awkwardly, then he turned to Ben. Grimly they shook hands.

A loud click signaled another descent of the platform. The four of them watched wordlessly. Colored lights flashed as the platform settled on a collar around the steel stalk, ten feet above the floor. One small portion of Dutch's painting was illuminated. A recorded voice addressed the passengers, seated in a theaterlike arrangement, all facing the same way. The voice was only a murmur to the four observers in the tunnel, but they could easily hear the audience's hearty laughter. With a rising tide of music the machine rotated to a new position. Spotlights blazed into full power to reveal the tortured eyes of Dutch's father raising that shovel over his head. A scattering of gasps came from the platform's occupants, and then more laughter.

Spaulding glanced over to see the expressions on Ben's and Georgia's faces as a dark form on a long rod began to rise in an arc from the cave floor, like a pendulum of a clock mounted upside down. The voice inside the theater rose dramatically as the form flashed across the viewing area. Twelve feet tall, shaggy and hideous of feature, the mechanized mannequin clung to an artificial tree trunk.

The grin on his hairy face was fiendish.

Screams came from the steel-and-glass dome. Muted laughter followed.

The lights went off. Dutch's stand-in rode his tree backward in the semidarkness to be ready for the next show, and the platform began to rise slowly. When it reached the top the machine executed a small segment of its circle so the visitors could disembark.

Spaulding coughed, breaking the terrible silence in the tunnel. "Don't hate the machine too much. Mr. Arnold says he chose it to protect the paintings."

Ben, his fists jammed in his pockets, turned away and stared into the darkness.

"This is a travesty," Georgia exclaimed angrily. "It's demeaning and dishonest."

Dr. Hearst shook his head sadly. "Yes, it is. I wanted to resign my job here the day Arnold approved the plan for it, but

I couldn't. Once I leave, all the research on Dutch's work will end."

"I'm going to talk to Arnold," Georgia said. "He's turned Dutch into a sideshow."

Spaulding winched. "Maybe so, but the tourists love it. At all of the previews this spring it was the favorite attraction. It even drew more riders than your roller coaster."

Georgia joined in Ben's indignant silence.

"Please, understand. I haven't abandoned Black Dutch," Dr. Hearst said defensively. "At my behest art historians from around the world are coming to see these paintings. They may have some influence on Arnold."

"Art hardly lays down a withering fire of protest in America," Georgia said. "What makes you think Arnold will listen to them?"

"They will not be alone in their quest. I am in touch with experts in a half dozen scientific fields, including anthropology and archeology, about Black Dutch. They are as perplexed as I am as to how a primitive, nonverbal man could draw figures and objects never seen by modern man except in museums."

"Surely the paintings are a product of his imagination," Spaulding suggested.

"That's the most intriguing part of all. There are historical elements that cannot be explained as the result of imagination, or of memory. At least not memory as we know the term. Arnold is allowing me to photograph and catalog each design for further study."

His voice quivered with emotion. "Somehow Black Dutch had a taproot that reached the heart of the Native American experience. When my work is ready, I intend to take it to the Cherokees. Look here."

He led them to a low portion of the painting's border, lost in shadows even when the ride was turned directly toward it. Ghost figures, Indians in battle display, were gathered around a central figure.

"Lore masters," Dr. Hearst explained. "They are giving instructions in the ancient way of the Cherokee spirits . . . to him."

He indicated a naked boy, attending raptly to their message. The gaunt figure was painted boldly black, speckled with what appeared to be blood. His eyes were large, and lonely. Ben stared at him long and hard, then gazed once more at the gigantic melancholic dome painting with its incredible sense of impending doom. "What can the Cherokees do?" he asked.

"It is my hope they will claim him as one of their own," Dr. Hearst replied, "and ask the federal courts to put this cave back the way it was, as a sacred site."

Spaulding allowed himself a fraction of a smile. "Even Mr. Arnold may find it difficult to resist that kind of persuasion."

"Let's hope so," Georgia said.

"I guess what you're trying to do is a good thing," Ben said, with a contemptuous glance at the glittering mechanism overhead, "but I don't want to ever come back here again."

Silently they followed Spaulding toward a metal stairway, which led to an exit on top of the face. On the other side of the door a brightly lighted pavilion was inundated with a delicious aroma coming from an old-fashioned popcorn wagon, stationed to one side. Spread out behind it was a doll shop with a hundred faces of a hairy, fierce Black Dutch in its windows. In the distance, the pastel globes of the silver tree twinkled. They took the tiered escalators down to the bald, where the Bavarian village of shops and arcades was overflowing with tourists. A line snaked back and forth before the elevators to the roller coaster. From above came piercing shrieks.

As they neared the cablecar station, Georgia and Ben lagged behind.

"How does it sound?" she asked anxiously. "You keep writing you want to see me. Well, here's your chance."

"I can't, Georgia."

"Why? I'll get you a contract. Ferrying gear, just like you did here. Only it's years of work. This railroad's a challenge and a nightmare. Your old plane's just the ticket."

"That's my problem. The sheriff's impounded it for the bank. I've hired into a Bahamas freight run out of Miami to save up enough to get it back. Right now I'm flat broke."

"Do you still have the carvings?"

"I can't sell those, Georgia. I may let Dr. Hearst put them on display in a museum somewhere, but I won't give them up."

"I know. It was ridiculous for me to even mention them. It's just been so . . ." Her voice trailed off.

"Could you come back to Miami with me for a few days?" Ben asked. "Or we could fly to Asheville."

"Anywhere but here?" Georgia smiled sadly. "I wish I could, but I have to go back tonight." She peered up at the rock face, half hidden by steel and concrete. "It was so brief, our time. And yet it still means so much. All of it." She stopped walking. "I just had a thought. Maybe I could get you a big enough advance to get your plane back. They're eager to keep me on this job. That is if you're willing to leave Florida."

He wanted very much to take her in his arms and kiss her. Instead he looked sadly into those shotgun eyes. "Florida doesn't have much hold on me anymore."

"Then, by God, we'll make something work." She took his arm. They started to walk again. "I wish we'd had enough sense not to go back into Dutch's cave," Georgia said after a while. "I keep seeing that hideous thing going back and forth."

Ben spoke so low she was barely able to hear him over the crowd noises. "He'd still be alive if I'd been more careful."

"Oh, Ben, don't blame yourself. I'm the one who called you out on the cliff."

Down the sidewalk Dr. Hearst waited, his gaze darting from Ben's to Georgia's face. He fell into step beside them. "Forgive me for intruding, but it is difficult to see you so sad. I want you both to know that although he is gone from here, I do not accept that anything so pure of spirit as Black Dutch truly dies. And who knows? Perhaps even his human form survived. His body was never found."

"You didn't see him fall," Ben said.

"Or see the terror in his eyes," Georgia added.

"No, I didn't," Dr. Hearst conceded with equal emotion, "but I did see him that one, brief moment in his home inside the mountain. And I felt his influence from the first day that we arrived here, as did you . . . as you still do."

He stopped, and they stopped, too, to peer with him over Arnold's Mystic Mountain to the endlessly merging slopes on a blue-tinged horizon. "Listen to me, Ben and Georgia, the presence may be gone from this place, but it is not gone from this world. In the silences it will be heard. In the mists it will be seen."

Back, back into the forest he plunged, staying with the mountain sides, alert for signs of anyone following, fearing a horde.

No one came.

The woods closed over his head. He foraged a lot and hunted a little. His body, as in the past, healed itself. Spring rains cleansed his wounds and soothed his aching head.

As he wandered a feeling possessed him, a feeling that he'd never know before in his long, lonely life. It tormented him by day and at night invaded his dreams until he moaned aloud with agony.

Always he wandered. Spring faded. Summer burned away. Still he wandered. It was not until the trees were bare and stark against the horizon that he saw a dark slash in the side of a V-shaped precipice and felt a sudden longing.

He climbed.

It was only a hollow under a huge rock slab, but it was deep enough for him to get out of the wind, high enough that he felt safe from predators and far from the eyes of man.

Below, a gurgling creek ran through the twisted ravine. Its sandy bottom sparkled with shards of rock and darting fish. At sunset he heard the frogs. Here he would stay.

The cleft he narrowed with rocks, shutting out all but a shaft of light. Boughs of evergreens formed his bed. The jacket he'd awakened in beside the tumbling water became his pillow.

Across the precipice at dawn he saw a reflection of water. A stone saucer was nearly hidden in a place of green shadows, crowded with ferns and flowers of a tender whiteness scattered like stars in the morning shade.

His gaze traveled slowly upward. A stone knob wider than he could reach across hung like a great egg, channeling water, drop by drop, into the depression below.

He looked at the oval stone. Breezes filtered through his shaggy hair, now a luminous white. Slipping from his haven, he descended to the bottom of the ravine, then climbed the other side.

A broad ledge beside the stone jutted out into space. He stood on it and ran his hand across the cracks and ridges and pockmarks.

That night dinner was a raw fish, caught by hand in the stream. As the moon came up, he stared at the stone. For weeks he stared at the stone and tried to fathom both the feeling and his elusive memories.

One cold sunset from his cleft he saw smoke and crept down to a campfire. Five hunters were skinning a deer. A mist rose from the still-warm flesh. He watched, the cold digging into his bones.

All he could see of the hunters, bent to their work, were the tops of their heads, thickly covered with long black hair stirring in the biting wind. Finally the solemn men went to sleep around the crackling fire. Ever so quietly he approached and ever so slowly lifted a glowing limb from the ashes.

Winter passed. In the spring with the budding of new life the feeling tortured him most severely. He sat for long hours at his little hearth, doing nothing, wanting to do nothing. At night his visions were blurred under the tiny hooves of deer and the padding steps of foxes.

That summer, when hemlock and sourwood bowed and trembled in the mountain air, he climbed to the stone again, carrying loads of splintered rock quarried from the stream and shaped in his sanctuary at night.

His hands gently brushed the surface of the protruding stone knob. Heart pounding, he selected a chisel of rock. With another held in his palm like a hammer, he struck the egg-shaped stone.

A small patch of weathered rock broke away. Far below he could hear the gravel and bits of stone pattering on the leaves.

He took a great breath.

Through autumn and into winter when the ice storms swept through the ravine he worked at the stone, he worked each day until his fingers were too numb and stiff to hold a tool.

Then he crawled back into his cleft and dreamed of the one image that consumed him while the winds howled through the trees.

By the time the earth began to thaw deep in the hump-backed eternity of the Smokies, in a ravine choked with misty green life, the face of Georgia Jones was emerging, coaxed from stone by a man driven by love.

If you have enjoyed this book and would like to receive details on other Walker Thriller and Adventure titles, please write to:

Thriller and Adventure Editor
Walker and Company
720 Fifth Avenue
New York, NY 10019